Sue Haasler lives in London with her husband and small daughter. She has written one previous novel, also published by Orion.

Praise for Sue Haasler's first novel, *Two's Company*:

'A delightful debut' *Daily Express*
'A funny and touching novel about motherhood, romance and responsibility' *Woman's Own*
'. . . a fresh and funny take on the chicklit novel' *Hello!*

Time after Time

SUE HAASLER

ORION

An Orion Paperback
First published in Great Britain in 2002 by Orion
An imprint of Orion Books Ltd
Orion House, 5 Upper St Martin's Lane,
London WC2H 9EA

ISBN 0 75283 837 7

A CIP catalogue record for this book
is available from the British Library

Typeset by Deltatype Ltd,
Birkenhead, Merseyside

Printed in Great Britain
by Clays Ltd, St Ives plc

For Heiko and Mika again
and for Karen

Acknowledgements

Big thank-yous to all my family and friends, and especially to Heiko for designing the website; to all at A. M. Heath and Orion; to Rachel Leyshon; to the RNA; to Jonathan Lingard and Bryn Hughes for help with the surfing details; and to Carratu International, who would *never* employ Derek or condone his methods.

Visit my website: www.suehaasler.com

A Night To Remember

'He's not worth it, Shaz. Don't give him the satisfaction of crying about him, the bastard.'

'I'm going to kill that Julie.'

'Don't give her the satisfaction, Shaz.'

'I'll never know what he sees in her anyway.'

'Well, she's a slag, isn't she?'

'He's welcome to her. I never fucking liked him anyway.'

'Course you didn't, Shaz, you're worth fifteen of him. And that Julie.'

'You're worth a hundred of that Julie.'

'How could he do this to me? I want to die!'

'No, you don't, Shaz. Dry your eyes. You're going to go out there, hold your head high, rise above it. That's what you're going to do.'

'I'm gonna rise – burp – above it. After I've given that Julie a good twatting.'

I ducked my head to check my makeup in one of the slightly-too-low mirrors. There was a familiar smell of Jeyes Fluid and pine disinfectant, with a hint of cigarette smoke that, frankly, had no right to be there. The door swung open and the sound of 'Fade to Grey' by Visage surged louder.

'Cass! There you are,' Heather said. 'I've been looking all over the place for you. Alison and Pete Bog have just arrived.'

'This is weird, isn't it?' I said. Heather was studying her hair from every angle, bent at the knees like a downhill skier so she could see in the mirror. 'Everything seems smaller. Even the toilets and the washbasins.'

'*We* were smaller last time we were here. I know my thighs were.'

'I was just thinking about the way there always used to be someone crying in the toilets at the end of a night out.'

'It was usually me,' Heather said.

I laughed. 'I can't remember a single time when it was you in tears.' She'd always been one of those golden, charmed people. If we'd been brought up in America, Heather would have been the prom queen, class president and chief cheer-leader.

'There's a first time for everything. Anyway, come on.' She checked her hair one last time. 'Alison has brought a load of photographs, and there's a hilarious one of you and Punky Harker in full Love-Will-Tear-Us-Apart mode.'

I followed her out into the long corridor that smelt of floor-polish and a whiff of tea-towels from the domestic-science room towards the sound of Duran Duran singing 'Wild Boys'.

The reunion was warming up. A dozen or so people were even trying to dance in a disjointed fashion, looking like their dads. We rejoined the group we'd been sitting with earlier, a disorderly queue of Heather's admirers past and present waiting for their turn in her spotlight.

A small, brown-eyed woman detached herself from the gaggle and smiled at me. 'Hi, Cass.'

'Alison!' We hugged each other – she was a rounder, softer version of her former tiny self – and Heather hovered nearby, ready to hug both of us all over again. When we'd finished hugging, Alison introduced me to her husband Pete, a man who was handsome yet strangely inert. I saw Heather mouthing the word 'Bog' at me over his shoulder and tried not to laugh. Then Pete was promptly, and all too easily, ignored while Alison, Heather and I huddled in a corner and had a good gossip about old times.

'Show her those photos,' Heather prompted, and Alison

took out a brown envelope full of over- or under-exposed snapshots of various combinations of us with assorted but invariably horrible hairstyles: Alison, Heather and myself at a fancy-dress party as Bananarama, complete with little skirts, big earrings and bandannas; at the Pleasure Beach on a day trip to Blackpool; on a school trip to Chester Zoo; in various dingy places I could no longer remember.

'Look at this one, Cass – you'll die!'

I took the picture from her. There I was in my seventeen-year-old glory, thinner and a lot more sulky-looking, with short, fluffed-up, dragged-through-a-hedge-backwards hair. I was dressed entirely in black: a tiny flared skirt over black leggings, Dr Marten's boots and a baggy, oversized T-shirt that bore the washed-out legend 'Oh Bondage Up Yours'. And standing next to me in the picture, with his arm draped across my shoulder, was Gideon Harker. Six feet four, as thin as a rake, his hair a mixture of black and growing-out bleached blond, his gorgeous green eyes circled with eyeliner. I suddenly felt all emotional.

'That was his T-shirt,' I said, remembering the soft, washed-thin feel of it.

'Oh, bless them, they even wore each other's clothes! It must have been true love!' Heather laughed.

'I wonder if he's coming? Has anyone seen him?' Alison asked.

I'd been looking around for him ever since we arrived – really he was the only reason I was there at all.

Ghosts

It had all started with a letter that arrived on a freezing spring morning. I'd done the usual sprint down to the front door, trailing my dressing-gown behind me, grabbed the pile of letters and quickly retreated back up the stairs to my flat. It was the only part of Coltsfoot Hall that was warm that February morning, and I made a mental note that I really ought to get dressed before I ventured forth in future – a dressing-gown and slippers were really not protection enough against the building's ancient cold.

A small, dapper man who claimed to have psychic powers had visited the Hall soon after I started working there. He cited the icy chill of the main hall as proof positive of the presence of ghosts. 'It's a cold spot,' he'd shuddered, clasping his pudgy hands together in haunted rapture.

I didn't have the heart to tell him that the entire building was a cold spot, and it wasn't caused as much by spooks as by the huge gaps around the doors and windows. Coltsfoot Hall had been built by the seventeenth century's version of a team of cowboy builders. I could picture them bent over a pile of bricks, a gap between doublet and hose revealing a generous expanse of ye olde builders' bumme, stopping for frequent malmsey-breaks (or whatever the drink of the day was) and to yell the occasional, 'Zounds, behold yonder comely wench,' at passing fair maidens. It was obvious that they hadn't had their minds on the job, anyway.

I sat down at the kitchen table, and glanced at the clock. It was after eight thirty, and there was no sign of Greg getting up yet. I couldn't remember what he was supposed to be doing today, and whether or not I ought to be waking him,

4

but after all, he was a grown man and if he was late for anything it was his problem.

I turned my attention to the post, separating it into three piles: business, personal and junk. The first letter went unopened on to the junk pile.

'OPEN NOW!' red letters screamed on the envelope. 'YOU MAY HAVE WON £50,000!' I was almost tempted to open it but I'm not so gullible that I don't know you don't get the £50,000 until you've got your subscription to *Reader's Digest*, and in all probability not even then.

The rest of the post, as usual, was mainly bills: Coltsfoot Hall cost a fortune to run, and these bills would shortly be joining the depressingly large pile in the tray on my desk marked 'It's in the post – honest'. As well as the bills, there was something from English Heritage and a letter from Carmen Dykes, the secretary of the Wyoming War Poets Society, a regular correspondent. In other words, the usual sort of thing.

That morning there was only one letter for the personal pile. I didn't recognise the large, loopy handwriting, but the northern postmark intrigued me: it was very close to the town where I'd grown up. I hadn't been up that way since my grandfather died twelve years earlier. He was my last family tie with the area, and since his death I suppose I'd practically started to think of myself as a Londoner, so much so that I felt a little bit surprised when people still detected the remnants of a northern accent.

The letter was from someone called Alison Stoker. The name didn't ring any bells, until I noticed that under her signature she'd written 'Alison Stoker *née* Mutch'.

Alison *Mutch*? Mutch Ado About Alison? Like a snatch of a long-ago song lyric, thinking of her name transported me back to the school playground, some time right at the beginning of the 1980s. Alison Mutch, Trudy Boswell, Annette Gillingham and me sitting huddled on the cold, damp concrete, duffel coats pulled tightly around us, talking about periods.

'It's *horrible* when you cough,' Trudy Boswell informed us. She and Annette had started their periods; Alison and I had not, and we were paying rapt attention.

'Yeah,' Annette agreed, nodding vigorously. 'When you cough, you splurt!' She coughed dramatically, and we watched her face carefully. Then she shrieked, 'Ooh! There! I splurted!' and Trudy nodded in a fellow-sufferer way. It sounded disgusting, but at the same time I was deeply envious. I was already wearing a 'training' bra, but the onset of menstruation was the real badge of womanhood. When I was thirteen, even the *word* 'menstruation' sounded exotic (and it still always seems to me to have a consonant missing somewhere). The big advantage of being 'on' was that you could get out of having a shower after PE, and if you had really bad cramps you were allowed to go to the sick room and lie down. Trudy had perfected her timing of this, and managed to miss double maths at least once a month.

Annette rummaged in her cavernous bag, on which she'd carefully stencilled the name 'Gary Numan'.

'I don't know what you see in that ugly little freak,' Trudy remarked.

Annette looked appalled. 'He is not ugly.'

'He is,' scoffed Trudy. 'Ugly *and* sad. He's just a little, fat, pasty-faced bloke.'

From the bag Annette produced a crocheted scarf and wound it round her neck several times. 'It's brass monkeys out here,' she complained, obviously having decided to rise above Trudy's criticisms of her hero. It *was* cold, but she was saying this partly for effect: she and Trudy insisted that you felt the cold a lot more when it was your 'time of the month', and thought that girls with periods shouldn't have to go outside at break time if they didn't want to. I personally felt that this was taking things a bit too far, and would result in some kind of dreadfully embarrassing puberty apartheid.

Middleton Road Comprehensive already had its own branch of apartheid, in that the playground was divided into two by a knee-high wall that ran at a right angle from the main school building: boys and girls were required to occupy different sides of the wall. Sitting on it was strictly not permitted (the legend was that a girl could get pregnant just by doing so). At the end of the wall the concreted yard gave way to a large sports field, but even there the divisive wall seemed to continue, a thing of the imagination, the boys religiously keeping to 'their' side and the girls to the other. The wall was known, for obvious reasons, as 'the Berlin Wall'. This cold-war architectural theme was an echo of the school building itself, which was of an attractive eastern bloc style, built of concrete the colour of baby poo.

Annette had noticed Alison gazing in a rapt sort of way over the Berlin Wall, towards the boys' side.

Trudy had noticed too. 'I bet I know who you're looking at, Al,' she said, digging Alison hard in the ribs with a duffel-coated elbow.

Alison blushed a pretty pink and muttered, through closed teeth like a ventriloquist, 'Is he looking?' She watched as the three of us all tried to peer across the playground without looking as if we were looking; it must have been as obvious as hell. Opinions were divided. Annette thought he *was* looking, Trudy and I thought not, but when I saw the disappointment in Alison's face I changed my mind.

'He *is* looking,' I said. 'Him and Kevin Davis are both looking.'

'Kevin Davis fancies you, Cass,' Trudy said.

'Oh, piss *off*!' I was appalled at the very idea. Kevin Davis was quite possibly the ugliest boy in the school. He looked like he had a permanent cold: there was something about his face that suggested snot even when, mercifully, no actual snot was apparent. It was far less embarrassing to be fancied by no one than to be fancied by Kevin Davis.

'He does fancy you, anyway,' Trudy insisted. 'But they've gone back in now, so you can stop sticking your tits out, Alison.' Alison glanced around to check that the object of her affection, a prefect called Jimmy Oldroyd, had indeed vanished.

The bell rang for afternoon lessons, which in my case meant the dreaded double maths. As I gathered up my stuff, I suddenly had this horrible feeling like my insides had turned to cold dough. Oh . . . my . . . God . . . I hadn't done my maths homework.

'Have any of you done that maths for Okey-dokey?' I asked desperately. The response was a trio of blank faces.

'I don't have to do mine till Friday: I was hoping I could copy yours,' Alison said. The other three were lucky enough to have maths with a different teacher from me, but none of them had done this particular homework.

'You're usually such a swot, Cass,' Trudy moaned. 'We *always* copy from you.'

I ignored the insult. I was too worried. 'Okey-dokey is going to go *mental*,' I fretted. 'It's the third time this term I've not done my homework. I just can't work out how to do it. I'm completely lost with equations.'

'You could pretend to be "on",' Trudy suggested helpfully. 'Always works for me.' I considered this for about a nanosecond, but it would have been far too embarrassing. No, there was no option but to face the music.

I experienced a cold feeling of dread settling in my stomach as I sat at the kitchen table with Alison Mutch's letter in my hand. Even all those years later it was still quite common for me to have nightmares that I hadn't finished my maths homework, and I was due in a lesson with Okey-dokey.

8

Usually in the dream I couldn't remember which room the lesson was supposed to be in, either, and ran up and down corridors, peering through glass-panelled doors at classrooms that were sometimes full of complete strangers or, even worse, those scary-looking children in the Boomtown Rats' 'I Don't Like Mondays' video. I always woke up in a cold sweat.

I can't remember Okey-dokey's real name now, only that he got his nickname because whenever he'd finished explaining a new concept to us he would finish with the rhetorical question – you guessed it – 'Okey-dokey?' The correct response to this was a vigorous nod and a mumbled, 'Yes, sir,' as any display of confusion or incomprehension was likely to result in a clonk on the side of the skull with a textbook. The shortage of maths textbooks in the 1980s was, in my opinion, largely because Okey-dokey spent the decade wrecking large quantities of them against people's heads. He also had a savage line in sarcasm, and humiliating pre-pubescent teenagers was his favourite fun.

Maths lessons were the purest form of torture to me, and I dreaded them like nothing else on the planet, even on days when my homework was all present and correct. However, things were about to change: the double-maths lesson on that cold afternoon in 1981 was destined to be something I would never forget. It was the day I fell in love.

I settled down for a full-scale reminiscence about that lovely day, but the sound of Greg finally surfacing from the bedroom and plodding across the landing to the bathroom brought me back to reality. I'd never met anyone as heavy-footed as Greg in my life. The next sound, as inevitable as the seagull following the fishing boat, was Greg cursing the ancient and unreliable plumbing. When Coltsfoot Hall had been equipped with a flat for the use of its staff, every convenience had been planned, but the plumbing simply refused to be coaxed into the modern world and always took a while to get going in the mornings; in this it was rather like me. It invariably annoyed Greg, who only left himself five minutes at most to prepare for the day ahead, and never took my advice that the way to deal with the shower was to avoid it altogether and take a bath. Shrugging to myself, I turned my attention back to the letter, which was really nothing more than a note:

Dear Cass

I bet you didn't expect to be hearing from me after all this time!

The reason I'm writing is that I had a call from Judith Bardsley, who used to go to Middleton Road. She's had this idea to organise a reunion of everybody who was in the sixth form in 1985 – it's fifteen years, and the millennium, so it seems like a good time to do it. I'm enclosing an invitation, and I really hope you'll be able to come. Judith was going to write to you herself, but I persuaded her to let me do it – I knew you wouldn't come unless I forced you under threat of hideous retribution. Seriously, you *have* to come; everybody else is, it'll be such a laugh.

Look forward to seeing you there!

Best wishes

Alison Stoker (*née* Mutch)

RSVP Judith Bardsley

Greg appeared in the doorway, wearing only jeans, with a pale blue towel hanging over his shoulders and his dark blond hair still curly and damp from the shower. 'Any coffee?' he asked. 'I haven't got any time for breakfast now, thanks to your antique shower. I have to get down to Stamford Bridge for a press conference.' He grabbed my coffee cup out of my hand, took a long slurp, then handed it back. He gave me a quick kiss on the cheek, and was already on his way out of the room again, presumably in search of clothing.

'I'll call you later, Cass!' he yelled, a few minutes later, and I heard him galloping down the stairs. My coffee cup was now more or less empty, so I plonked it into the sink, and went to get ready for work.

It Ain't What You Do It's The Way That You Do It

I'd come to Coltsfoot Hall almost by accident. An English Literature degree fitting me for nothing particularly useful in the world, I had ignored the advice of a depressed-looking careers' tutor ('Have you thought of joining the RAF? I certainly wish *I* had') and followed my degree with a part-time business-studies course, during which I embarked on a series of temping jobs. Having no particular life-plan mapped out, I was wary of committing myself to any one thing.

Yet at the same time I knew that, during what I've come to call my 'wandering' phase, I was searching for something. For want of a better word, I was looking for something or somewhere I could call home.

My last proper home had been with my grandfather. When he died during the time I was at university I felt completely adrift, with no roots any more. My mother, on a brief visit from the United States for the funeral, suggested that I come and live over there for a while. The thought of living in America might sound exciting, but I wasn't tempted even for a second. I'd spent time and energy getting to know London and making friends, and I couldn't bear the thought of yet another upheaval, particularly as my mother's social circle involved a lot of people who either thought Elvis was still alive or made a living from pretending to *be* the late great crooner.

So I became a professional temp. I worked variously as an usherette in a theatre, which I loved but the pay was awful; then as a filing clerk in a travel agency, which I hated and ditto the pay. After that I did lots of things too short-term to bother describing, then a longer spell helping to run the clubhouse of a large, prosperous golf club, and it was there that I met Eleanor Yarr.

'One Below Par Yarr', as she was known at the golf club, looked like Princess Anne on a bad-hair day and had an attitude to match. Her business, Eleanor Yarr Associates, was an interior design company, specialising in 'beautiful interior solutions' for people who lived in the kind of enclaves of London that used to be described as 'gentrified'. Eleanor seemed to regard the golf club as her own private office, and many a deal was struck at the bar.

For some reason she took a liking to me, and eventually offered me a job. With a pretty shrewd idea of what my pay must have been, she offered enough of a rise for it to be an incentive without any risk of over-generosity.

I wasn't one of the Associates, of course: I was very much a junior, and as such my usual task was to trail behind Eleanor or the Associates, Pam and Victor, holding tape measures and swatches of fabric.

The thought of helping to make homes more elegant and beautiful, and of helping to spend other people's money while doing so, appealed to the artistic side of my nature, but it turned out to be hideously uncreative: clients either wanted matt-black-and-chrome eighties styling or pseudo-Regency leather and damask like you could buy wholesale anyway at Laura Ashley. Victor referred to it as 'satin and tat, with the emphasis firmly on tat'.

Occasionally I would attempt to step outside my swatch-holding role and suggest something a bit more daring. I'd been good at art at school, and fancied I had a bit of an eye for a colour scheme; in my *naïveté*, I thought Eleanor had spotted a latent talent in me when she'd plucked me from the golf club. However, any even vaguely original idea was always promptly squashed by one of the Associates.

I only started to make sense of this when I overheard Pam and Victor discussing a commission.

'That place is just screaming out for a sort of art-deco look,' Pam was saying.

'Don't dare say that to the client,' Victor said. '*She*'ll go mad.'

I assumed 'she' was Eleanor. I was incredibly curious, so I wandered into the room as casually as possible. 'Why will Eleanor go mad?' I asked innocently. Pam looked annoyed, and sucked hard on a cigarette: always a sign that she was tense.

Victor heaved a huge sigh and said, 'She may as well know.'

It turned out that Eleanor had put a considerable effort into cultivating a regular set of suppliers from whom she bought at a knock-down (or possibly knock-off) rate. Needless to say, this saving was not passed on to the customer, hence Eleanor made a bigger profit. The downside was that the only two styles really catered for under this arrangement were either mock-Regency or eighties matt-black-and-chrome: any other style might have required making purchases from outlets where she wouldn't end up with such a healthy profit margin.

Maybe I could have coped with working under such a corrupt system – I could hardly feel sorry for the customers, who clearly had more money than sense to consider employing the Associates in the first place – but it was the *feng shui* that finally finished me off. Since we were already well into the 1990s, the eighties matt-black-and-chrome look was already past its sell-by date, and the Associates went through a lean period before Eleanor spotted a newly formed gap in the market and introduced *feng shui* to the Eleanor Yarr repertoire. Pam and Victor bitched about this non-stop: it had been tricky enough having to work around conventional considerations, like ceiling height and location of windows and doors, without having to accommodate a pressing need to include wood and moving water in the eastern corner to strengthen family life, but that was what they were now required to do *Feng shui* might well be a great school of eastern wisdom, but Eleanor had gleaned her total knowledge of it from a book called *Feng Shui Your Life in Five Easy Steps* that she'd picked up at a service station on the M3.

Thus it was that one day I was in the home of a client, and was forced to sit and wait while Victor conducted a thorough *feng shui* audit. I was not officially one of Eleanor Yarr Associates *feng shui* masters and my tape measure and swatches were not needed for this operation. While the proper positioning of crystals and mirrors was being warmly debated, I flicked through a copy of the *Lady*, which had been left on the table.

'No, no, no, Mrs Spencer-Chester,' I could hear Victor saying. 'Toilet seat down at all times! You don't want to lose all that *chi*.'

I tried to look covertly at the situations-vacant pages: I had definitely had enough of the world of interior design, and was thinking about contacting my old temping agency to see if there was anything interesting around.

My attention was caught by a photograph of a beautiful house, the kind of house a Jane Austen character would live in, and Jane herself would have described as handsome and elegantly proportioned. The kind of house you could love. It was being run as a museum and needed a caretaker-administrator. The pay was peanuts, even less than I'd been paid at the golf club, but the carrot was that the job was live-in. As soon as I saw the photograph, I wanted desperately to live in that house. If I'd believed in reincarnation I would almost have believed I'd lived there in a former life: it looked like home.

Welcome To The Pleasure Dome

This feeling was confirmed the first time I stood outside the place. Coltsfoot Hall glowed in the morning sunshine with its warm, chestnut-red brickwork and gleaming windows. The house was almost symmetrical, with the main entrance in the centre and windows arranged evenly at either side of it. All the paintwork was white, and the roof was tiled and steep, with three tall chimney-stacks, and the house was surrounded by gently rustling chestnut trees. Inside it was oak-panelled, elegant, and on that late summer morning blissfully cool; the winter implications of this wouldn't become obvious until I'd been resident for several months.

I was greeted by a young man in jeans and T-shirt, which instantly made me feel horribly overdressed in my 'interview outfit' of calf-length dress and matching cardigan. Then I noticed that, although he was wearing trainers, they were spotlessly clean, and he was rather pristine generally. He shook my hand amiably and introduced himself, with a warm Australian accent, as Zak.

'The Ancients are assembled in the drawing room, ready for you,' he said. 'They're just waiting for Lady Eugenie. She's powdering her euphemistic nose.' He invited me to sit down, and I perched on an overstuffed *chaise longue*.

'Not there!' he yelled, and I jumped back up, startled. He dragged a chair from behind the reception desk. 'That's an English recamier made in 1875.'

'Sorry,' I said, feeling very stupid and thinking I'd probably blown it before the interview had even started.

'No worries,' he said, smiling apologetically. 'I get a bit protective about the exhibits sometimes.'

'What do you do here?' I asked him.

'I'm an archivist, officially,' he said, 'which means at the moment I do just about everything apart from the cleaning, which is done by a woman called Sheryl, who can, frankly, be a bit heavy-handed with the Mr Sheen. She needs watching. I can't wait till you start work. You don't have to give much notice at your current job, do you?'

'Well, no, always assuming I get this one,' I said.

He grinned again. 'You will,' he said. 'I reckon Lady Eugenie is going to take a proper shine to you.' For some reason, rather than being cheered on by his confidence, I experienced another wave of paranoia about my outfit: perhaps I should have gone for a more businesslike jacket and trousers. Maybe I looked more like an exhibit than a prospective employee.

The huge oak door behind us creaked, and a tiny figure forced her way through the gap. 'Ah! Visitors!' she exclaimed, as she saw me. This turned out to be the aforementioned Lady Eugenie Thick, doughty daughter of an earl and dowager head of the Thick polyresin dynasty: the former owner of Coltsfoot Hall, no less. The 1990s had not been good years for Thick polyresins, I learned later. Too much competition from imported Asian plastics and the strong pound had forced the family to scale back somewhat on the lifestyle they had previously enjoyed, and the major expense was their ancestral home, which in fact they hadn't occupied for many years. Facing bankruptcy, they had been only too glad to sell up to the local authority, who had

16

stepped in at the right moment with an offer and a promise to keep the Hall as a resource for the benefit of the local community.

Lady Eugenie's late husband, Sir Sheldon Thick, had served in the First World War alongside the poet Siegfried Sassoon, and possessed several letters and a couple of lines of poetry scrawled on a train ticket. These artefacts formed part of the eccentric collection of the Hall.

Lady Eugenie tottered towards us, at a rate of apparently half a mile a century. She was dressed in the kind of sensible pale blue mac with which old ladies seem to be issued along with their bus pass. Her gnarled legs were ably supported by stockings so thick they might have been from the same batch that had once warmed the legs of Sassoon himself, in the trenches of the Somme. 'You the new girl?' she asked me, peering with intent blue eyes.

'I'm here for an interview,' I said.

'You're the new girl.' She nodded, and tottered towards the door of the drawing room.

It seemed, as Zak had predicted, that Lady Eugenie had indeed taken a shine to me, and his clairvoyant skills produced a further piece of advice: 'Don't let Robertson freak you out,' he said, as the door through which Lady Eugenie had disappeared was opened again by a tall man of about fifty who looked like he'd been carved out of two blocks of not very friendly stone, one for his body and one for his head. I'd never seen anyone with such a rectangular head.

'Please walk this way, Ms Thomson,' he said, and an Australian voice behind me muttered, 'If you walked that way you'd be in need of medical attention.'

I followed the man into the interview, where I was faced with Lady Eugenie, another elderly lady and an elderly man, all enthusiastically tucking into a pot of tea. I was offered tea, and there was much clattering of cups and complicated-looking business involving tea strainers before everything settled down. It was such an eccentric scene I expected to see a dormouse in the teapot and the Mad Hatter to appear at any moment, but since the room in which I was now sitting was yet another gorgeously oak-panelled extravagance and I already loved the house passionately, I concentrated my mind on getting the job.

The block-headed man introduced himself as Randall Robertson, the local authority's representative, and I took an instant dislike to him. His manner was both contemptuous and patronising, and he gave the impression that he felt he was lowering himself by being there at all. Lady Eugenie sat sucking her teeth and glaring at him in a way that indicated she shared my opinion.

The interview was a breeze. Randall Robertson asked all the proper questions, Lady Eugenie undermined him with an agenda all her own and the other two dozed.

'What changes would you implement to enhance Coltsfoot Hall as a community resource?' Robertson asked.

'We don't want changes,' Lady Eugenie insisted. 'It's been like this since I was a girl. No need for changes.'

I attempted to negotiate the middle ground between a 'proper' interview answer and something that Lady Eugenie would be able to approve.

'I think I would concentrate on marketing the Hall to the local community. Let them know what an asset they have right on their doorstep,' I said. This seemed to go over well, so I used the same approach with the next couple of questions.

'Are you married?' Lady Eugenie enquired suddenly, and my heart sank. I wondered if someone of her generation and background might be better disposed towards me if I *was* married, and how best to reply: should I tell a white lie and elevate Greg's status to 'fiancé'?

'Lady Eugenie, equal opportunities—' Robertson started to

say, but she waved her hand impatiently. Evidently a response was called for.

'I don't mind answering,' I said. 'I'm not married.'

'Boyfriend?'

'Erm, yes.'

'It's really only a one-person flat,' Robertson pointed out tersely. So much for equal opportunities.

'Oh, he won't be living with me,' I assured them. 'Just visiting.'

'Blood and sand, man,' Lady Eugenie turned to the local authority's representative, 'have you forgotten already what it's like to be young?' Then she turned to me and beamed widely. 'Move in whenever you like, dear,' she said. 'And tell your young man he's welcome any time.'

'Lady Eug—' She silenced him with a look that might not have carried the weight of the local authority but which certainly had the confidence of generations of Thicks.

So that was how I'd ended up being the administrator of this odd little museum in London. Technically it's only *just* inside the outer boundary of one of the outermost London boroughs, and with the vagaries of electoral expediency it might easily one day find itself in one or another of the Home Counties. I always thought it sounded much more impressive at a party to tell people my job was running a museum in London and, without offering any additional detail, wander off to the kitchen or the loo and leave them with envy-inducing mental images of my high-powered life at the V and A.

Coltsfoot Hall couldn't have been further removed from the V and A. For a start, it boasted a paid staff team of only two: me and Sheryl, the cleaner. Zak, the archivist who'd greeted me on the day of the interview, explained cheerfully afterwards that he wasn't allowed to earn any money because he was in England on a tourist visa but he was hoping to stay and marry his girlfriend. In the meantime he wanted something local to keep himself occupied while she was out at work, so Coltsfoot Hall had been lucky enough to get his expertise for free.

There was also a posse of ageing volunteer guides, who would station themselves on small wooden ladderback chairs at the information desk and glare at the general public, whom they outnumbered more often than not. The lack of visitors was partly explained by the Hall's unpromising location, which could best be described as the middle of nowhere, and partly by the lack of anything exhibit-wise that people would really be interested in seeing.

Apart from the small selection of Sassoon memorabilia, the building was furnished with pieces that ranged in age from Jacobean to 1950s kitsch: whatever had appealed to the incumbents of the day, who evidently hadn't been thinking about posterity. There was a permanent exhibition devoted to the history of the polyresin industry and the Thick family's role in same. Some of the rooms were so sparsely furnished as to feature only a couple of chairs (Zak had tied string across the arms of these so they couldn't be sat on) and a glass cabinet, and there was one room, so small that it had probably been originally intended as a broom cupboard, devoted to 'The Modern Age'. The centrepiece of this was a photograph of the Beatles, autographed by Paul McCartney's brother Mike, who'd visited the Hall in the late 1960s when he stopped to ask for directions on his way to George Harrison's house.

The Hall had a beautiful conservatory, which had recently been turned into a coffee-shop, and this was turning out to be successful. The area wasn't short of ladies who lunch, although the problem was that once lunch was over they usually hastened off to play golf or bridge, rather than linger to admire the exhibits.

Trying to turn the museum into a going concern was going to be a bigger nightmare than maths lessons with Okey-dokey, but on the day when I took the job I looked out of the window of my new flat at the municipal park, which had once been part of the Hall's grounds, the trees beginning to turn to autumnal gold, and thought that I'd never lived anywhere as beautiful in my life.

Tell Her About It

I usually started my working day by having a cup of coffee with Jackie, who ran the coffee-shop. She was always at work hours before me, and I was often woken up by the delicious smell of bread and cakes baking: the aroma as I walked in that morning was particularly gorgeous. Jackie was busy filling little pots with freesias to put on the tables. She was around my age, small and pretty, with incredible curly red hair that she pinned up into a bunch when she was working. She always seemed to have loads of energy, even first thing in the morning when I was typically feeling more worn and antiquated than most of the exhibits in my charge.

'Morning,' she said, smiling, and handed me two of the little pots of sweet-smelling flowers. I placed them dutifully on tables. 'Do you want the good news or the bad news?'

'I'm not sure I'm ready for any news at all,' I said, 'but try the bad news first.'

'I'm glad you said that,' she said, finishing the flowers and picking up the steaming coffee jug to pour us each a cup, 'because there isn't actually any good news. The bad news is that Randall Robertson just phoned, and he's on his way over for a meeting.'

'Oh, marvellous. Did he say why?'

Jackie shook her head. 'The usual, probably.'

I nodded, taking the cup she offered me. We sat down at one of the tables. Jackie had been right when she described the phone call as bad news. A visit from the local authority's representative on earth was exactly what I didn't need on a Monday morning. Randall Robertson's position as (more or less literally) the holder of the Hall's purse-strings meant that I had to be at least superficially pleasant to him, and since every meeting with him had confirmed my initial impression that he was one of the most irritating people on the planet, this was always an effort.

Jackie and I sat in a companionable but gloomy silence for a while, sipping the delicious coffee.

'Greg was out early this morning,' she said.

I treated her to one of the special mirthless laughs I'd perfected on the subject of Greg. 'I've hardly seen him all weekend,' I grumbled. 'That's one of the drawbacks of going out with a sports reporter: he's always reporting sport. Now that there's football on nearly every day of the week, I hardly see him at all.'

'You could go with him.'

'That's an appealing idea,' I said. 'Sitting in some freezing cold press box, not being allowed to talk in case he misses something vital, being entertained by the so-called wit of the other hacks at half-time.'

Jackie sipped at her coffee. 'Well, I would go. He's really cute, your Greg,' she said.

That much I had to concede, remembering how he'd looked that morning with the blue towel hanging over his bare shoulders. But cute was about as far as it went. The truth was, Greg and I were not the romance of the century. We never had been: it was not even as if we'd started out that way and mellowed into cosy coupledom. It had been cosy coupledom from the kick-off. Greg was like a comfy bathrobe: nice to come home to, lovely to cuddle up with, but not worth putting your best earrings on for. Or maybe I was feeling particularly harsh towards him that morning because Alison Mutch's letter had reminded me of my schooldays and how I'd felt the first time I was head-over-heels in love.

'I got something interesting in the post this morning,' I told Jackie, and showed her Alison's letter, which for some reason I was carrying around in my pocket.

Jackie skimmed her eyes over it. 'Could be fun,' she said. 'Are you going to go?'

'I don't know,' I said. 'I haven't seen any of the people from school for so many years. It might be kind of embarrassing.'

'Why embarrassing? You can show off to the old school-chums about your exciting career.' I raised my eyebrows at her over my coffee cup and she grinned. 'And your scrumptious journalist boyfriend. They're probably all working in building societies and married and all that boring stuff.'

'Maybe that's what worries me. There are some people I would just rather remember how they were.' Without realising it, I'd been silently decapitating a freesia. Jackie removed it gently from my hand and moved the pot to her side of the table. She ducked her head down until I was forced to meet her gaze. Her face was curious and amused.

'You'd rather remember *some people* how they were?' she said. 'I'm guessing from the state of that freesia that you're not talking about the girls in the netball team. Is there an old flame in the picture, by any chance?' Now I wished I hadn't shown her the letter, but I reckon your subconscious does stuff for a reason, and the reason in this case was that I needed to say his name out loud, to experiment with the idea that soon I might be seeing him again.

Love Plus One

I told Jackie about that afternoon in 1981, when I hadn't done my maths homework.

After afternoon registration, we all rummaged through the desks in the form room to get what we needed (apart from nerves of steel) for double maths – textbooks, exercise books, pens and pencils, geometry sets, log tables, calculators. The bell rang and everybody trooped off down the corridor, to Okey-dokey's lair.

As we entered the room, he was busily chalking up impenetrable-looking equations on the blackboard and studiously ignoring us. We all sat down quietly, without any of the usual chattering and fool-playing: it was speculated that Okey-dokey was either psychic or, more plausibly, that he could see everything going on behind him reflected in his glasses, because it wasn't uncommon for him to whirl round suddenly and whang the blackboard duster at someone's head with deadly accuracy. Since the said blackboard duster was made of a block of wood with a thin strip of felt attached to one side, to be on the receiving end was to be avoided at all costs, so we all kept nervously quiet while he finished his chalkings.

A slippery ball of fear had taken up residence in the pit of my stomach and sat there getting larger by the second. When the word 'homework' was mentioned, the ball of fear bounced sickeningly. Okey-dokey was walking up and down the aisles between the rows of desks, collecting the exercise books into a pile. He paused by my desk. 'Miss Thomson?' he said, as I failed to hand him my book. 'Homework?'

The ball of fear was trying to force its way up into my

throat, and I swallowed it down hard. 'Sorry, sir, I—' Wham! He slammed the pile of exercise books down on my desk, making papers fly and pens roll off on to the floor. I saw out of the corner of my eye one of the other girls looking at me smugly: *you're in for it now!*

'I sincerely hope you're not going to tell me you haven't done your homework,' he sneered. I nodded, and thought I was probably going to cry and desperately didn't want to humiliate myself any more than I already had done. 'Is there any particular reason for this?' Okey said, and added, without a trace of humour, 'Perhaps you've recently lost a beloved grandparent or household pet?' He paused dramatically. 'Maybe war has been declared and, for some inexplicable reason, I haven't heard about it?' I shook my head. He shook his too, eyes huge and unblinking behind his glasses, partly mimicking me, partly doing that fake-regretful teacher thing.

He opened his mouth again and I cringed waiting for the inevitable verbal assault that would be far worse than a blackboard duster across my ear, but before he could speak a boy's voice behind me said, 'I had some trouble with that homework too, sir.'

Okey-dokey didn't even glance up: the only indication that he'd heard anything was a twitching muscle on the side of his face. 'Shut it, Harker,' he muttered.

But the speaker appeared not to hear him. 'I couldn't work out how to do question seven,' he persisted, his voice clear and unintimidated. 'Struggled with it for hours. I even wondered if they'd printed it wrong.'

Finally Okey-dokey tore his accusing gaze away from me, and shot a menacing look around the room in general. A couple of people had started to giggle, but they were instantly silent. Then he turned his glare on the person who'd been doing the talking and snapped, 'In this room, Harker, there's only room for one smart-arse, and that's me. If you as much

25

as *breathe* audibly during the rest of this lesson, you will be out of here so fast you'll leave skidmarks.'

He turned back to me, but the interruption had been enough to put him off the flow of his tirade, and he simply muttered, 'Tomorrow, Miss Thomson.' Meaning, I guessed, that I had another day to complete the homework. This was unheard-of leniency, and people were staring at me open-mouthed. He gathered up the pile of exercise books and proceeded to the front of the room again. While he was doing this, I glanced quickly behind me.

My fourteen-year-old saviour grinned at me and winked.

Gideon Harker: a name straight out of Thomas Hardy and a face made by the angels. I fell in love on the spot.

When You're Young And In Love

When I got home from school later that afternoon, I made myself some toast and marmalade and a mug of instant coffee. My mum was putting her face on, prior to meeting her friends from the bakery where she worked for a drink.

'Mum . . . how old were you when you fell in love with Dad?' I asked her.

'Old enough to know that there wasn't realistically much point in hanging around waiting for Paul McCartney to get bored with Jane Asher.' She flicked her cigarette ash into the empty marmalade jar, and I tried not to wince.

'But how did you *know* you were in love with Dad?'

I searched her face, waiting for that misty-eyed look women in the movies got when talking about their one true love, but she just shrugged and smoked. 'How do you expect me to remember that far back?' she said. 'There's been a lot of water under the bridge since then. Anyway,' she said, zipping up her makeup bag and getting up from the table, 'I'm off to watch *Crossroads* before I go out: David Hunter's personal life's in turmoil yet again. I suppose you've got homework to do.'

'Yeah. Maths,' I said.

She pulled a face. 'Well, I can't help you with that. I'm useless with figures, just ask Edna at the bakery.'

'It's okay,' I said. 'A boy at school explained to me how to do it. He's promised to help if I get stuck.'

My mum narrowed her eyes against the smoke from her cigarette and studied me for a second or two. 'Be careful, Cassie,' she said. 'You don't want to go getting into anything at your age. I remember when you were mooning about Timmy Travers all the time.'

'Mum! I was *six*.'

'So now you should know better. Just don't make a man your whole world.' And with that obscure, or maybe prescient, remark she went off to the living room and a few seconds later I heard the *Crossroads* theme tune.

I went to my room, the smell of cigarette smoke trailing me up the stairs. I automatically switched on Radio 1 and took out my homework, spreading the books across the bed. As I picked up my maths book I felt a warm glow, recalling how I'd been standing so close to Gideon Harker in the corridor outside the form room that the sleeve of his blazer had thrillingly touched my wrist. He really was lovely: clear, green, amused eyes, almost-black hair and perfectly straight nose. Even nicer-looking than Adam Ant.

I finished the maths fairly quickly, and picked up my English literature homework, which was so wonderful it couldn't be called work at all: *Far from the Madding Crowd*, by Thomas Hardy. I was deeply, devotedly in love with Gabriel Oak – he was my ideal man, even though I did rather wish that he'd been played by Terence Stamp rather than the less physically attractive Alan Bates in the film (although it's true that Terence Stamp might not have looked as relaxed as Alan Bates assisting sheep suffering from 'the blasts'). His name was so perfect: Gabriel because he was Bathsheba's guardian angel, always watching over her and looking out for her welfare to the best of his mortal ability, and Oak because he was solid, faithful and steadfast.

And that evening the story had an even deeper resonance than usual: because that day I had found *my* Gabriel Oak.

Even if he wasn't much more than an acorn at the time.

Under Pressure

Of course, I gave Jackie the heavily edited version of all this. I'd merely wanted to say something about Gideon, to test my reaction to saying his name out loud. And now I'd come over all warm and wistful.

'So, does Greg know about your little childhood sweetheart?' she asked.

'There's nothing to know,' I said. 'It's not like I'm hiding fifteen of his illegitimate children somewhere. I was thirteen, for heaven's sake.'

Jackie rolled her eyes. 'Sorry,' she muttered, under her breath. 'Touchy.'

To my intense relief – and I never thought I'd use that expression regarding Randall Robertson – at that moment there was a peremptory knock on the door, and Jackie sprang up to let in the grants officer. I was struck anew by the observation that he had an almost completely shoebox-shaped head, which had recently been accentuated by a pseudo-trendy hairstyle involving a teensy little Julius Caesar-style fringe. I suspect Randall thought it made him look like George Clooney in *ER*.

Skipping the pleasantries (I'm not sure he *did* pleasantries) he said, 'Where do you want to do it? Here or the office?' Jackie and I caught each other's eye, and tried not to giggle. It was a juvenile running joke with us that the grant officer's speech, whether wittingly or not, seemed to be peppered with sexual innuendo.

'I need to stay here to keep an eye on my Bath buns,' Jackie said, waving her oven glove. Randall, whose generous opinion of his own abilities was only matched by his warm sense of self-importance, sighed and slumped down at one of the tables, as if it was the greatest burden on earth to him. He shoved aside the pot of freesias to make room for his briefcase and took out a blue cardboard folder with 'C'FOOT HALL' printed on it in marker pen. Jackie brought the coffee over and sat down with us. Although the coffee-shop was run separately from the museum and therefore didn't strictly come within Randall's orbit, I always liked to involve her in these meetings. After all, the two businesses were directly related. It was also far preferable to having to deal with Randall Robertson on my own.

Irritation was his standard-issue facial expression. He usually reserved his super-irritated look for when he had to deal with the board of trustees, but he was wearing a fair approximation of it now.

'The budget you submitted to us last week, Ms Thomson,' he said. 'Am I right in assuming that maths wasn't your best subject at school?'

For one second I thought he'd heard me telling Jackie about Okey-dokey and felt ready to die of embarrassment, but when he didn't elaborate I realised he couldn't have done. And besides: 'There wasn't anything wrong with that budget,' I said. I was a lot more confident about maths these days.

'Except for the deficit.'

'But you know about that,' I pointed out. 'It's not a deficit, it's the amount of subsidy we get from the council to keep going.'

Randall sniffed wetly. 'It hasn't escaped our notice,' he continued, 'that despite Ms Harrison's best efforts with the food concession,' he nodded at Jackie, 'Coltsfoot Hall is still losing money hand over fist.'

Randall sat twiddling with his sad little Julius Caesar fringe for a moment, then fixed me with a stare that was almost as scary as that of Okey-dokey himself, although now I wasn't thirteen any more and I stared right back.

'Council finances are tight. There are cutbacks in every department and, frankly, this place is heading for the top of the list when it comes to my big chopper.'

Jackie choked on her coffee. Randall ignored her. 'So, the bottom line is, you need to start showing a healthier financial position or we pull out,' he said. 'Any ideas how you're going to do that?'

I was completely thrown. 'Well . . .' I said. 'It's only February. Things won't really get going until at least Easter, and I've got some Easter things arranged for the schoolkids.'

'Such as?'

'An Easter egg hunt, for one. The Easter Bunny will be—'

'The Easter-bloody-Bunny?' he spluttered. 'That's the best you can do? It's going to take a lot more than some twat in a rabbit costume to turn this place round!'

I ignored the interruption. 'I've got someone from the Wyoming War Poets Society writing a piece on the Sassoon letters for the Society magazine.'

Randall sighed. 'It's hardly a master plan,' he said. 'The members' – meaning the local borough councillors, but again Jackie grinned like a first-former at the *double entendre* – 'are losing patience with this place. I've been instructed to inform you, and I shall be writing to the trustees to the effect, that unless Coltsfoot Hall is paying for itself by the end of the next quarter, we will have no option but to put this place on the market. I have to tell you that we've already had expressions of interest from several potential buyers, and with all the cutbacks the council is having to make, we'd be mad to pass them up.'

I couldn't believe what I was hearing, and looked at Jackie for support, but she was still grinning about the members and trying to get over her coughing fit.

'Hang on,' I said. 'It was my impression that the council had an obligation to subsidise the Hall as part of the agreement of the sale. Why wasn't any of this mentioned at my interview? I've only been here for five months, so it must have been something you were aware of before that.' Randall attempted to look hard done by, and failed so miserably that I realised I was right. 'There's no way we can make the Hall pay for itself by *June*,' I said. 'If we had more time we could apply for other funding, and I've been looking into getting us accredited as a venue for weddings and holding art exhibitions and so on, but there's nothing I can do by June, short of charging an admission fee of about five hundred pounds a person.'

'Ah, that facility with figures again,' Randall said.

I glared at him, sitting there smugly with his stupid hair and his stupid briefcase and his total lack of interest in anything except money. 'You've got no intention of keeping this place open, have you?' I said, trying hard not to let anger make me sound hysterical. Finally Jackie had stopped grinning and was looking as serious as I felt.

'Like I said,' Randall tugged at his fringe, 'if you're showing a surplus by the end of next quarter, there isn't going to be a problem.'

'Showing a surplus? It would take a miracle,' I said. 'Places like this just don't make money. Even the V and A has had a massive fall in attendance recently.'

'Exactly the members' point,' Randall said. 'Which is why, in their infinite bloody wisdom, they've paid for you to go to this.' He reached into his briefcase and pulled out a leaflet, flicking it on to the table in front of me. It was neon-coloured and bore the title 'Hands-On History: The Future of the Past'.

'What's this?'

'This,' he said, 'is your last chance, though it looks like a bit of a lost cause to me. It seems that the members feel that this place needs a kick into the twenty-first century. Interactivity is the buzzword these days, the Internet, "e-initiatives" and all that crap. People don't just want to wander passively around a load of antiques marvelling at how old it all is. Well,' he conceded, 'maybe Americans do. But your more sophisticated consumer wants a hands-on, participative, educational experience. This workshop will enlighten you as to how to achieve that,' Randall explained. 'It's in Plymouth next month, and you're already enrolled, thanks to the generosity of your borough council. We're bending over backwards for you on this one.' This time Jackie didn't laugh at all. If she had, I might well have hit her.

'But our visitors are mainly older people,' I objected. 'They'd be horrified if we filled the Hall with flashy gimmicks. They'd consider it very disrespectful.'

Randall ignored this. 'Take it or leave it,' he said, 'but I strongly suggest you take it. We want to see the ideas you pick up at this event put into practice by the end of the next quarter, or this place will find itself turning into something more profitable, like a home for old dodderers, or a drug-rehabilitation clinic.' He snapped his briefcase shut. 'And don't think for a moment we wouldn't do it. Have fun, won't you?' He pushed his chair back and was out of the door before I could think of anything else to say.

'That's it,' Jackie said. 'You're stuffed. And if *you*'re stuffed, *I*'m stuffed, as Randy Robertson would say.'

'*You* aren't, necessarily,' I pointed out. 'If they turn it into a drug-rehab clinic they'll still need catering. Once people are off their appetite suppressant of choice I bet they go mad for Bath buns.'

'Shit! The Bath buns!' Jackie dashed back to her kitchen where it smelt as if the Bath buns were, as Randall Robertson might indeed put it, reaching a climax. 'I'd better get ready for the ladies who brunch,' she said, reappearing in her oven gloves, 'while I still can. Seriously, Cass, you've got to do something about this.' Her face was worried. 'I've got a lot of money tied up in this place.' She disappeared into the kitchen, and I went to open the front door to the museum, hopefully to admit some paying customers.

I didn't know whether to be worried or angry. It seemed to me that I'd been set up: given a home and a job in a place with no future. The suggestion of turning the fortunes of the museum around with interactivity was ludicrous, and the short period we'd been given would effectively ensure that there wasn't anything we could do sufficiently quickly anyway. It felt like a stitch-up.

I looked around the hall, at the gleaming wood and brass, buffed to a rich shine by Sheryl, who might also be redundant soon if I didn't do something to improve the museum's finances. I thought about the *Reader's Digest* letter that had arrived that morning. 'OPEN NOW! YOU MAY HAVE WON £50,000!' If only life was that simple, and that kind of money really did arrive in the mail.

An old man was standing on the steps outside, shivering in the February cold. Of his face, only his watery blue eyes were visible between his scarf and his deerstalker.

'Stan!' I said. 'Why didn't you come round to the coffee-shop door? You must be freezing.' Stan followed me inside. At eighty-two he was the oldest of the ageing volunteer guides, but he was probably the most energetic and hard-working of the lot. He'd lived in the area all his life. For many years he had worked in the polyresin factory, and thought of

33

himself as something of an ancient retainer to the Thick family.

'I saw that council idiot's car outside,' he said, wiping his feet with exaggerated care on the doormat. 'I wasn't going to come in till he was well out of the way. It's too early in the day and too late in my life to start being patronised by that fool.' He followed me through to the small office. I sat down at my desk, which was covered in photocopied flyers on yellow paper advertising the Easter egg hunt, while Stan took off his gloves, overcoat, scarf and tweed hat. Underneath he was wearing impeccably ironed dark-blue trousers and a matching V-neck pullover, over a white shirt and blue tie. This was his invariable uniform, whatever the weather. Stan had left the army in 1964, but the army had never left him. 'Have you seen his car?' he asked me, still on the subject of Randall Robertson. 'One of those four-wheel-drive monstrosities, looks like a big, chewed-up toffee. Charges around in it like he owns the place.'

The problem was, Randall Robertson, or at least those he represented, *did* own the place.

Work For Love

Sheryl cornered me just before she left work for the morning. 'I'm right out of Mr Sheen.'

'You do seem to get through it rather quickly,' I said. The Hall's budget could hardly cope with Sheryl's over-zealous application of cleaning products, and Zak felt that the exhibits were suffering under her ministrations and had asked me to 'have a word'. The problem was that Sheryl was fiercely proud of her work and would brook no criticism.

'Can't do a proper job without the right equipment,' she

pointed out, automatically running her chubby forefinger along my desk to check for dust.

'Maybe a supermarket's own brand might be a little cheaper?' I suggested, but she fixed me with a look that meant only Mr Sheen would comply with her professional pride.

'I wouldn't mind some of those high-tech dusters, while we're at it,' she said. 'Attract dust like a magnet, they do.'

I wasn't convinced. 'Would you be able to cut down on the Mr Sheen if you had them?'

'Oh, definitely.'

'It's a deal,' I said, unlocking the petty-cash box. 'And don't forget to bring back receipts.'

A small party of schoolkids turned up at about ten thirty. Stan followed them from room to room, making sure no one touched anything. Interactivity may have been the 'buzz-word', as Randall had insisted, but I was pretty sure that Stan wouldn't allow any interactivity on *his* watch. Most men of Stan's age have been in the army, but I think Stan was *born* with a military bearing. Even the most boisterous schoolkids jumped to attention. Towards lunchtime I was summoned to assist a woman in reassuring her tearful child that the spooky wax-faced dolls in the 1900s dolls' house didn't in fact come alive and bite people's legs as soon as darkness fell. This I did with a conviction I didn't entirely feel: I'd always thought those dolls were pretty damn creepy myself.

Soon after that Zak turned up, appearing in the office in a state as flustered as his usual laid-back antipodean demeanour could accommodate.

'Sorry I'm late,' he said, though since his position was voluntary and unpaid, his hours of work were really up to him. 'Just had an almighty bust-up with Flora you would not believe. She is being so unreasonable, I told her I might as well go back to Melbourne.'

'What was it about this time?' I asked him, wondering if it was going to be one of those nights when he'd end up sleeping on the sofa-bed in my sitting room. Zak and Flora's relationship was somewhat volatile.

'Would you believe, she said I was an anal retentive?' he said. I muttered something vaguely consoling. 'I'll give her a ring,' he said. 'She might be seeing reason by now.' He gazed around the office. 'Shit, Cass, look at the state of your desk. How can you work in that mess? This lot needs a bloody good tidy-up!'

I could only feel sorry for poor Flora. 'The state of my desk's the last thing on my mind, frankly,' I said. 'We've had a visit from Randall Robertson, and I'm afraid your day is about to get even worse.'

Zak didn't share my opinion that the council had ear-marked the Hall for closure even before I'd started work there. 'I would have heard something about it,' he said. 'It's just Robertson. He's one of those power-crazy guys. I guess he just thinks this place'll roll over and die, he gets to make a big saving in his budget and there's no repercussions.'

'Well, if it isn't going to roll over and die we're going to have to do something soon.'

'What about all those grants you've applied for?'

'Wouldn't come through in time,' I said. 'Plus most of them are dependent on the other funding still being in place. They won't fund us if the council are pulling the plug.'

'We could get a petition up.'

I sighed. 'We could do that, in fact I think we ought to do it whatever else happens, and contact the local papers and so on, but it's hardly going to have a huge impact. We're lucky if we get ten people in here a day.'

I told him about the proposed trip to Plymouth to discover how to make Coltsfoot Hall more 'interactive'.

Zak curled his lip. 'That sounds like a crock of shit to me,' he said. 'All that stuff costs money to install, which we don't have, and takes extra maintenance. Then there's no guarantee it'll pull in the punters.'

'Seems like I don't have any choice,' I said. 'Apparently if we're not on the road to user-participation in a few months, that's it. Plymouth or bust.'

'Where the hell *is* Plymouth, anyway?' Zak asked, the geography of Britain not being his speciality. He wandered off to make sure Sheryl hadn't left any of the paintings hanging skewed after dusting, and I spent what was left of the morning pondering the hideous state of the museum's finances and feeling increasingly depressed.

Favourite Shirts (Boy Meets Girl)

When I finally locked up the museum and climbed the stairs to my flat I was tired and stressed, and in need of some tender loving care. For once, amazingly, Greg had the evening off: there were no football matches on in the whole of London that evening. No Premiership manager had resigned, no expensive foreign player was signing for any London team. There was nothing to report.

I bunged a supermarket lasagne into the oven, and he opened a bottle of wine.

'You'll never guess who I was talking to today,' Greg said, as we were sitting down to eat.

I ran through a list in my head. It was bound to be someone to do with football. 'Gary Lineker?' I suggested.

He looked disappointed. 'How did you guess? He was up at Chelsea recording a piece for *Match of the Day*. I told him my girlfriend was mad on him.'

'You did *not*!' I said, mortified.

'I did. He thought it was really sweet and he sends his love.'

'Greg! That's really embarrassing.'

It's ironic that I get so mad with Greg for spending all his time at football matches, because it was at a football match that I'd met him. A few years earlier I'd shared a flat with a friend called Nadia. She and her brother had had season tickets for Tottenham Hotspur since they were children. When her brother went to work abroad for a year, Nadia persuaded me to come to a match with her on his ticket, and I ended up going to almost every home game for a whole season. When I told people how I spent my Saturdays they always looked at me a bit sideways. Maybe it didn't seem to fit with working for an interior-design company and being devoted to the Brontës, but if you've ever been to White Hart Lane on a freezing February night you'll know it's not that far removed from *Wuthering Heights* in terms of climate, and it almost has the edge in terms of high drama.

Unfortunately Gary Lineker's days as a player at White Hart Lane were long gone by the time I went there. The big star at that time was David Ginola, he of the lush French tresses, and Nadia always insisted we were in our seats early so she could watch his warming-up routine. The bit she enjoyed most was when he placed his hands on his hips and swivelled his pelvis; no doubt he was trying to avoid muscle strain in these delicate areas but the way Nadia reacted he might as well have been a lap dancer.

So I blame David Ginola. If it wasn't for him Nadia and I would have been keeping warm in a nearby pub, or still making our way to the ground at two thirty on that frosty Saturday afternoon, or we would have been gossiping about the people she worked with in her flashy City job, and I wouldn't even have noticed Greg.

It was a bitterly cold day and the roofing over the stand provided no shelter whatsoever from a whipping northerly wind. I was wearing so many layers of clothes, including several sets of thermal underwear, that I could hardly move (even if it had been possible to move on those tiny plastic seats): my arms stuck out from my body at a forty-five-degree angle. Most people were sensibly staying somewhere warmer until the last minute, so the area around us was practically empty. Just Nadia, me and two people we always referred to as 'the lad and his dad' were occupying our particular subsection.

While Nadia gazed enraptured at David Ginola, I was looking around – at the seagulls wheeling overhead, the people looking enviably cosy and warm in shirtsleeves in the executive boxes opposite, the sprinkling of away supporters at the Park Lane end who were attempting to sing. After a while I noticed a rather pleasant-looking bloke making his way between the rows of seats, dispensing drinks from a contraption on his back that looked like the Proton Packs worn by the Ghostbusters.

He stopped next to me. 'Drink?'

'No, thanks.' Instead of moving on, he waved his hand to attract Nadia's attention. She turned round, annoyed that something was obstructing her view of the pitch, but when she saw Greg (for, yes, it was he), she smiled widely.

'Drink?'

'Well, I'm free after the match,' she purred.

Greg looked confused. 'I mean, do you want a drink *now*?'

Nadia, belatedly realising that he was selling rather than buying, shook her head impatiently and returned her attention to the pitch.

'Business doesn't seem to be very brisk,' I said.

Greg sighed and shifted the weight of the ghostbusting equipment on his shoulders. 'It'll pick up when people start coming in,' he said, then sat down beside me. 'That's better.' He sighed. 'This thing is bloody heavy.' I mumbled sympathy. 'Gets me into the matches for free, though,' he continued, and pointed across at the press box. 'One day I'll be in there,' he said.

'Selling coffee?'

He laughed. 'This isn't the extent of my ambitions, you know,' he said. 'I'm going to be a football journalist. I've already had a few pieces published in fanzines.'

David Ginola had gone indoors for a rub-down, or whatever they did after warming up, and Nadia reclaimed my attention.

Greg stood up. 'Best get back to work,' he said. 'Don't want to get the sack just when I'm starting to enjoy the job.'

For a few weeks after that Greg would always happen to appear at about the same time as David Ginola sprinted out on to the pitch, even though we sat in a very under-populated section of seating where customers were scarce.

Nadia got very irritated that my attention was being distracted from the French footballing hunk. 'You've become an Acquisition Target,' she observed to me once, because she worked in the City and said stuff like that all the time. I didn't know if she was right, but I hoped she was.

Then one Saturday Nadia was away on a course and Greg ended up sitting with me for most of the match. He'd been going to Tottenham since he was a little boy, and knew everything there was to know about the club. Perhaps warning bells should have sounded at that point: the topic of conversation was almost exclusively football, but we were at a football match after all.

After the game was over we walked back down Tottenham High Road together with the crowds, to Seven Sisters tube station. I expected to wave goodbye to him at the station; he'd told me he lived in Walthamstow and I was going towards Finsbury Park. But he jumped on my train and sat down next to me.

'Aren't you going the wrong way?' I said.

He smiled his confident, open smile and said, 'I can't let you go into the heart of Gooner territory on your own, can I?'

'I've lived round here for years,' I said. 'I think I can cope.'

'You never know,' he said, pulling up the collar of his coat. The train was pulling into Finsbury Park station. Greg jumped up from his seat as the doors opened and stood in the doorway, FBI-style, his back pressed against the wall. He peered out. 'All clear,' he hissed, and beckoned me to join him as he jumped out on to the platform. He rushed me through the tunnels, stopping at every corner to check round it. He was the Sweeney, a one-man SWAT team, my own personal bodyguard against an imaginary horde of menacing Arsenal fans. 'No Gooners,' he confirmed.

'There's not likely to be.' I laughed. 'They're away at Coventry today.'

'Best place for them,' he said, 'but you can't be too careful.'

Greg walked me home, and when we got back to my flat, equipped with fish and chips and several cans of beer, it didn't take long for the mood to get romantic. Or what passed for romantic in Greg's world.

'I think you're probably the most gorgeous season-ticket holder in the whole of the Premiership,' was his declaration of intent.

And, as easily as that, we became a couple.

The following lunchtime, he had to leave for a match at Selhurst Park. When he returned later that evening, he arrived with a gift for me: a radio-alarm clock.

'I noticed you only have one of those wind-up clocks,' he said, 'and there's no way I can get up in the morning without hearing the news.'

And that was how it was. The clock took up residence on my bedside table, Greg took up residence in my life, rather like an endearing kitten who follows you home and before you know it you're buying cat litter and flea collars.

'But honestly, Greg! Telling Gary Lineker your girlfriend fancies him! You make me sound like I'm thirteen years old.' I stabbed my fork sulkily into my lasagne, but secretly I was

41

rather impressed that Greg had actually spoken to the great man.

'Aren't you going to eat that?' He swiped the last piece of garlic bread from the plate and devoured it. 'Anyway,' he said, 'how was your day?'

I pulled a face, and told him about the visit from Randall Robertson.

'What is that guy's problem?' Greg wanted to know.

'Well . . . there's an ever-increasing budget deficit for a start . . .'

'No, I mean why is he always sniffing around Coltsfoot Hall? I reckon he's lusting after Jackie.'

'Why can't he be lusting after me?' I said indignantly.

'Would you want him to?'

'Ugh, no!'

'Well, just be grateful.' This wasn't exactly the support that I'd been looking for.

'There's a good possibility this place might be shut down,' I said, trying again. Greg had got up from the table and was rummaging in the kitchen cupboards.

'Any more wine in this place?' I shook my head. Greg sighed. 'Well, look on the bright side. You're in the middle of nowhere out here. If you have to leave, you can look for somewhere more convenient.'

'As in within range of an off-licence?'

'Well, it would be handy.' He slumped back on to the sofa and started toying with the TV remote.

Changing tack, I told him about the conference in Plymouth. 'It's going to be a complete waste of time,' I said. 'Can you imagine this place all full of computerised gadgets and flashing neon thingamabobs? It would completely ruin it, even if we could afford it.'

'But Robertson's right, in a way. No one wants to wander round a load of mouldy old junk, without even a gift shop or a McDonald's at the end of it.'

I thought of that afternoon, when a woman who'd been visiting the Hall since she was a little girl (the Thicks had occasionally opened the house to the public while they were off on their annual grouse-shoot) had brought her own daughter to show her all the treasures that Mummy used to love. I thought of how the house had stood for so many centuries, the biggest and proudest house in the area, and I thought of Zak and Stan, Sheryl and Jackie.

'I just don't think turning it into a theme park is the only way,' I said stubbornly. 'And I don't want to go to Plymouth. It's going to be really boring staying in a hotel by myself.' Then I had an idea. 'You could come with me,' I suggested. 'I'm sure I won't be conferencing the whole time. It's by the seaside, I think.'

Greg yawned and stretched. 'It might be by the seaside, my love,' he said, 'but it's many miles from any decent football. If it was in a couple of months' time I'd say yes, but I can't just wander off into the wilds of Division Three so near the end of the season.'

'Oh, fine, then,' I said, aggrieved as usual that, as far as Greg was concerned, I was never going to be much competition for football. With a lot of men football's their hobby, their obsession, even, but with Greg it was those things plus it was his job, a twenty-four-hours-a-day, seven-days-a-week deal. Rival claims on his time didn't come close. 'So, I take it that you wouldn't be interested in coming up north with me for a weekend?'

He laughed when I told him I'd been invited to a school reunion. The whole idea was a bit of an alien concept to Greg: he'd gone to school only a couple of miles away from where he presently lived (when he wasn't staying with me), and saw most of his ex-schoolfriends regularly in the pub.

'You're not going to go, are you?' he asked.

I shrugged. 'Why wouldn't I?'

'Well . . .' he said, leaning back in his chair, 'For one thing,

43

you haven't seen any of those people since you left school, as far as I know. So you've managed to get by all your adult life without having anything to do with them. Why bother now?'

He had a point. He was a very logical person. 'But it might be fun,' I said, 'seeing how everybody's changed.'

'Depressing, more like. Once everybody's asked each other if they're married, have they any kids, what do they do, there'll be nothing else left to say. You may as well get them to fill in a questionnaire.' He snuggled up closer to me on the sofa. 'Wouldn't you rather be coming to the world-famous home of the Spurs with me?'

'No, to be honest,' I said.

Greg looked a bit miffed. 'You never go to a match these days,' he said huffily. 'I'm beginning to think you and Nadia only ever went to the Lane to see David Ginola's legs, after all.'

'Not just his legs,' I said. 'Don't forget his bottom and his gorgeous hair.' Greg didn't look amused. 'But honestly,' I said, 'it's football overkill round here. It's your job, and I'm glad you love it, but don't ask me to love it as well. It was just something I used to do, a phase of my life I'm over now, like Spandau Ballet and the Style Council.'

'You shouldn't even talk about those things in the same breath as football,' he said. 'Like Bill Shankly said—'

'"Football isn't life or death, it's much more important than that."'

'Exactly. Wise words.'

'It's rubbish,' I said. 'Football's only a game, and there are bigger things to worry about, like whether I'm going to have a place to live or work in a couple of months' time, or if Randall Robertson is going to turn this place into a home for detoxing supermodels.'

Greg ignored the blasphemy, and merely responded that he felt he could cope with a Coltsfoot Hall full of elegantly wasted waifs. But wherever Greg laid his hat and his radio-alarm was his home, and the only things he could get sentimental about were the Tottenham Hotspur golden days of Danny Blanchflower and Jimmy Greaves and the time he watched Spurs beat Arsenal 3–1 in the FA Cup semi-final at Wembley.

I couldn't fault his logic regarding the reunion. But, as we well know, women are capable of the most logical, rational thought on earth, and we are equally capable of throwing all logic out of the window if we feel like it. And I felt like it.

'I think I'm going to go anyway,' I said stubbornly. Greg shrugged and aimed the remote control at the television set. A football match flickered into life.

Walking On Sunshine

Nineteen eighty-three was the year my friends and I took up under-age drinking – after all, there was little else to do where we lived. At the time it seemed like the pinnacle of excitement to be sitting in a smoky pub with a gang of your mates from school. The girls would be posing in Boots 17 makeup, slash-neck tops, legwarmers and hairstyles that were more hair-spray than hair. Some of the boys attempted to look cool with their jacket sleeves pushed up to the elbows like Don Johnson in *Miami Vice*. At least they were making an effort: the majority of my male peers stuck to their tried-and-tested distressed denim jeans, though in the early 1980s even jeans were worn nicely pressed.

We took our under-age drinking seriously. What you chose as 'your' drink was a make-or-break decision, image-wise. I used to feel very sophisticated asking for Bacardi and Coke, though Alison said it made my breath smell like Zip firelighters. It was also damn expensive if you were living, as I was at the time, on pocket money from my parents and a couple of quid from a Saturday job at the baker's shop where my mum worked. Most of the time I made do with half a lager shandy or soft drinks; not exactly a life of debauchery but it seemed thrilling at the time.

Our hostelry of choice was the Duke of York, because they not only turned a blind eye to but seemed positively to encourage under-age drinkers. Like banks try to tempt toddlers to open accounts in the hope of securing a lifetime of loyalty, the management of the Duke of York fondly nurtured their next generation of customers. No matter how fresh-faced or pimply you were, you would never be refused a drink in that pub. On Friday nights it resembled a youth club.

This moral slackness extended only as far as allowing the consumption of alcohol. 'Lewd' behaviour was another thing entirely, and one thing they would not tolerate was 'necking': anyone seen to be indulging in this pastime was ejected immediately from the premises. My peer group fell into two categories, depending on whether you would view such an ejection as a triumph or a tragedy. For me, it would have been a bit of both – I would've been mortified if I'd been thrown out of anywhere for any reason, though it would have given me some kind of satisfaction to be notorious for 'necking'. The problem was, who to neck with? Not many options presented themselves. A couple of boys had made it clear they fancied me (by dribbling in my hair during the last slow dance at youth-club discos), and I tried my best to get interested in them, but it didn't work. There were only two men I was interested in 'in that way'. One was Tony Hadley, the singer from Spandau Ballet with the unfeasibly deep voice, but even in my wildest fantasies I had to admit that the chances of being thrown out of the Duke of York for necking with Tony Hadley were remote.

Even more remote was the chance of anything along those lines ever happening with Gideon Harker. Ever since the incident in the maths lesson two years earlier I'd been unerringly, faithfully besotted with him, but I'd always kept my feelings for him to myself. This must have been unique in my circle of friends: that's what your mates were for, after all, to share your crushes and lusts with – Alison and I had spent enough time discussing the sexual allure of Adam Ant and certain members of Spandau Ballet, and Bryan Ferry before that, and I'd been party to every eventless nuance of her unrequited crush on Jimmy Oldroyd. But this was different. For one thing, Gideon Harker was only the same age as us, and it was unheard-of to fancy somebody in the same year. The object of your desire had at least to be in the fifth form, or even better a prefect like Jimmy Oldroyd, because as the magazines were always telling us, girls mature earlier than boys, and a fourteen-year-old boy was neither use nor ornament to a self-respecting, hormone-packed girl. I couldn't possibly admit I fancied Gideon Harker who, as well as being in our year and having a peculiar name, had a reputation for being a 'brainbox'.

So it was still the love that dared not speak its name. Even though my best friend, Heather Alderman, was going out with *his* best friend, Ian Kane (by the fifth form, boys were deemed to be developmentally catching up with the girls), and Gideon occasionally came to the pub with us, even though as a result I spent entire evenings literally with my knees pressed against his under a small pub table made out of an old-fashioned treadle sewing-machine, even though I talked to him every day at school, there was still a part of me that continued to worship him from afar, dying inside whenever I saw him talking to another girl.

Until one evening, in the autumn of 1983, I was in the Duke of York with Alison and Heather. Thin Lizzy were on the jukebox. We sat in our usual seats in the corner where we could keep an eye on who was coming in or going out, drinking lime and soda because none of us had any money.

Heather was expecting to see Ian, and my insides were in their usual state of turmoil: if Ian was coming, there'd be a chance Gideon would come with him. I couldn't concentrate on the conversation the other two were having, probably about last night's television, or homework, or most likely men of some description or other: we were fairly obsessed by that subject in those days. I was sitting with my back to the door and relying on Heather's face as a barometer of when anyone of importance arrived.

I felt a blast of cold air as the door opened and noticed a look of absolute horror cross Heather's face. 'Oh, my God,' she said, 'what's that?'

'He's gone New Romantic,' Alison said.

'That's not New Romantic,' Heather replied, 'that's a bloody Replicant.'

I turned round to look. Gideon Harker, all six feet four of him, wearing a battered, full-length leather coat, all worn like the cover of an ancient Bible or an old, much rolled-up map, skin-tight black jeans, pointy boots, black eyeliner and his dark hair bleached a startling white blond. Heather was right: he looked like Rutger Hauer in *Blade Runner*, though obviously younger, better-looking and with thicker hair.

I completed the final stages of puberty in about 2.5 seconds. 'He looks beautiful,' I said.

Alison and Heather almost choked on their lime and soda. Although Heather was my best friend, she could be very sarcastic and would certainly have said something cutting at that point, had she not noticed that Gideon Harker wasn't alone. Hovering uncertainly behind him was her boyfriend, Ian Kane, with a bleached strip in his hair that made him look like a nervous skunk.

'Oh, no,' I heard Heather mutter. 'He is *dead*!'

Gideon and Ian came over to our table, watched, I think, by most of the pub. Eccentric modes of dress were not encouraged in that establishment, or in the town generally, which had remained relatively untouched by the sartorial excesses of Punk Rock, New Wave and New Romantic. It was the kind of place where Boy George would have been run out of town without a by-your-leave. The bar staff were looking from our table to the landlord and back again, apparently waiting for an official directive as to how they were supposed to treat this dangerous phenomenon.

Gideon was grinning broadly, enjoying the entrance he'd made. It was the same grin that had won my heart two years earlier and kept me in secret thrall for all that time. 'Anyone for a pint?' he asked.

Ian nodded, trying not to look at Heather who was giving him daggers. I nodded, too, not trusting myself to speak, sensing that this wasn't the moment to be drinking Bacardi and Coke and ending up with breath like a firelighter.

'Vodka and Britvic orange,' Alison said. 'For Heather as well,' she added, as Heather and Ian were occupied in a non-verbal face-off.

Gideon swung himself out of his seat and swaggered – that really is the only word for how someone in a full-length leather trenchcoat and spiky, bleached hair walks – over to the bar. The bar staff decided that clearing tables was the most pressing task in the world and fled, leaving the landlord himself to deal with the freak. Everybody in the pub, apart from Ian and Heather, was watching to see what happened. I decided that if he was thrown out I was going to go with him, as a declaration of solidarity and adoration.

Words were exchanged. The landlord was known as a plain-speaking sort who wasn't afraid to use certain techniques acquired during a spell in the army if required; we'd seen many people propelled through the front door for brawling, necking or 'looking like gypsies'. I just prayed that he wouldn't hurt Gideon's precious face, and had visions of him lying in the gutter, a trickle of blood vivid against his pale hair and face, me mopping his brow with a lace-trimmed handkerchief.

Then, amazingly, the landlord smiled, pushed the glass he was holding not into my beloved's face but against the vodka optic, money changed hands and Gideon was returning to our table bearing drinks. I started breathing again, and the rest of the pub's customers, disappointed there wasn't going to be a fight, continued with whatever conversations they'd been having before.

'Well then there now,' he said, like James Dean in *Rebel Without a Cause*. 'So what do you think of the new image?'

'You look like a right pair of weirdoes,' Heather said crossly. 'You,' she nodded at Ian, 'look a mess. What *possessed* you?'

I picked up my pint. I'd never drunk beer without lemonade before, and I'd never drunk anything out of a pint glass, so it took all my concentration not to spill it all over my batwing top. The taste was rancid: I couldn't imagine how people knocked this stuff back with such apparent enthusiasm.

I was so absorbed in mastering the art of drinking a pint, that it took me some time to notice that Alison had gone off to the toilet, Heather and Ian were engaged in their version of a heated argument – in which Heather told Ian what she thought and he good-naturedly agreed with her – and Gideon was looking at me. I thought his green eyes and dark eyebrows looked even more beautiful contrasted with his new hair.

'Do *you* think I look like a weirdo?' he asked me.

I put my pint glass carefully on the beer mat, wondering how to respond. 'You look . . . heroic,' I said, and felt myself going the deepest shade of red.

He gave me that grin again. 'Excellent,' he said, finished off his pint in one impressive flourish and added, 'I'm only doing it to irk my parents.' He was the only person I knew who would have used the word 'irk' just there, and it made me adore him even more.

'And has it irked them?'

He smiled gleefully. 'Oh, yes. They are what you could describe as well and truly seething. Which is a puzzlement, because it'll grow out in a couple of weeks and I'll look quite normal again.' *As if*, I thought. 'It's not permanent, like if I got a tattoo, or a piercing . . .' He thought for a moment. 'Hey, Ian,' he called to his friend, 'd'you fancy getting your ear pierced?'

'No, he does *not*!' Heather responded on his behalf.

'No, I do not,' Ian echoed affably. Under Heather's ministrations his hair was now parted on the opposite side to usual in order to hide the bleached streak; this gave him the appearance of a friendly but not-too-bright puppy.

'Come on, then, Cass.' Gideon stood up and held his hand out to me. 'I need you.' Everything went a little blurred for a second and I had to remind myself to keep breathing, then I picked up my coat. Heather was looking at me, amazed. On our way out of the pub I saw Alison coming back from the toilet, and her expression was the mirror of Heather's.

Although it was still light as we stepped outside, the air was beginning to feel chilly. He was still holding my hand, and it made me feel so happy I thought I might fly away to heaven, and at the same time it was the only thing anchoring me to the earth. He walked fast, and I trotted along beside him, relishing the stares we were getting from people we passed; indeed, a couple of people crossed the road to *avoid* passing us, and a man of about my dad's age muttered something about 'freaks' as we walked by. I was in seventh heaven.

'Are your mum and dad at home?' Gideon asked. I shook my head. My dad was away on business and Mum would be out with the 'girls' from work. 'Okay,' he said, 'let's go to your house.' I swallowed hard. It appeared he had seduction on his mind, and he hadn't even kissed me yet. I was suddenly nervous: I felt like I'd been shoved out on a stage to take part in a play, and I'd never seen the script.

It was like a scene from the Marquis de Sade. Side by side on my parents' kitchen table I placed, as instructed, a lighted candle, a tray of ice cubes, a packet of sewing needles (Newey Dorcas dressmaking pins having been rejected as 'somewhat feeble-looking'), a cork, some cotton wool and a bottle of antiseptic.

I was feeling more than a little queasy.

'There's nothing to it,' he said encouragingly. 'You just sterilise the needle in the candle flame, get the ice cube—'

'Where do I put the needle while I'm doing that? It'll get unsterile.'

'I'll do the ice cube,' he said, 'then you put the cork at the back of my earlobe, and wham the needle through in one nice, firm movement, just where I made the little dot. Piece of cake.'

'I don't think I can,' I said. 'I'm a bit squeamish.'

'Don't worry, it won't bleed because of the ice cube,' he said confidently, and shook off his leather coat, tossing it across the back of my mum's favourite armchair. Underneath he was wearing a hand-knitted, black mohair jumper that was unravelling at the sleeves and bald in places. The neckline was wide and gaping, and hung slightly off one shoulder; his white skin was stretched tight over his collarbone. I wanted to plant devoted kisses along every centimetre of it, but at that moment I had other things to think about.

On the walk home he'd been adamant that he wanted his ear piercing *now*, and he couldn't possibly wait until Hair By Marjorie opened the next morning to have it done 'quickly, painlessly and hygienically'. I was terrified at the idea of doing it, but there was no way in the world I would have refused.

My hand trembled as I held the needle close to his ear. I was about to mutilate permanently the person I loved most in the world, but it was inexpressible joy to be so intimately close to him. Squeamishness and lust fought for the upper hand, with lust just about edging it. I took a deep breath to calm both and, as instructed, I attempted to wham the needle straight through his precious flesh.

'Aagh! Fuck! What kind of needle is that?' It hadn't gone through, and when I looked at it I realised it was a darning needle, with a blunt, rounded end. I apologised and hurriedly chose a sharper one, waving it into the flame of the candle.

This time the needle went clean through, but by then the effect of the ice cube had worn off. Blood trickled from the newly made hole in my beloved's ear, down his neck and along that wonderful collarbone, mingling with the mohair fibres of his jumper.

'Oh, God, I'm sorry . . .' I said, dabbing at him with the cotton wool and praying I wasn't going to faint.

Gideon sat there unconcerned, his only comment being, 'It's just as well I only wanted one doing.' Once the blood flow was more or less staunched, however, there was another problem. 'I don't have anything to put in it,' he said. 'No earring. Shit. The hole's just going to scab over and heal up. Haven't you got an earring I can borrow?' I thought I'd died and gone to heaven: he was asking to wear something of mine; it would be like a love token.

I dashed up the stairs to my room, and rummaged in my jewellery box. It was one of those musical ones where you open the lid and a ballerina pops up and spins round to the tune of 'Lara's Theme' from *Dr Zhivago*. I gripped the pink plastic ballerina and mashed her down flat while I rummaged: I would have been mortified if the sound of 'Lara's Theme' had betrayed just what a soppy girly I was. I rejected numerous pairs of earrings as too naff (including those shaped like hearts, flowers, cartoon characters and various types of sea life), and eventually chose a plain silver star hanging on a tiny hoop.

I cast embarrassed eyes around my virginal bedroom. The wallpaper, chosen by my parents years earlier, was pink and flowery, although it was mostly covered up by posters of the Human League, Spandau Ballet and Duran Duran and an old, yellowing one of Adam Ant that I couldn't bear to part with. Although Adam Ant had said ridicule was nothing to be scared of, I decided, imminent seduction notwithstanding, that I had to keep Gideon away from this room at all costs. I resolved to speak to my mum about a change of décor as soon as the opportunity presented itself.

I dashed back down the stairs, and was amazed all over again that the subject of so many of my daydreams was actually sitting at our kitchen table; in fact, the room seemed to be filled with his skinny black outstretched legs. He'd blown out the candle, I noticed with a trace of disappointment, and the smoke was spiralling upwards.

'Will this do?' I held out the earring.

He inspected it. 'Perhaps a tad subtle, but it'll do.'

I left it to him to get the silver hoop through the raw hole I'd just made, afraid again that I'd faint if I tried to assist. He stood in front of the mirror that hung on the chimney wall, wincing slightly as he pushed the metal through his earlobe. I winced in sympathy.

'You should have waited till you could have it done at Hair By Marjorie, with one of those stud-gun things,' I said.

He shrugged, apparently unconcerned by the pain. 'Wanted it doing now. There.' He turned round from the mirror to show me the effect.

'It looks good.'

'It does, doesn't it?' he said. 'And the Doctors Harker are going to do their nuts.'

'Why are you so bothered about annoying your parents?'

There was a pause before he replied, long enough for me to

54

wonder if he'd heard the question. 'Isn't it what we're all supposed to do?' he said eventually. 'Teenage rebellion. I bet you do it as well.'

'No,' I said, sincerely. I rather doubted that there was anything in the world I could do to annoy my parents. Most of the time I didn't think they remembered my existence. I put the kettle on to make some coffee. 'Your parents getting mad at you – it shows they care about you.'

'Well, I wish they cared a bit less,' he said, with feeling. 'Anyway. Sorry, I don't really have time for coffee. I've got some stuff to do at home.' He stood up and started to pull on his leather coat, which as well as looking like an old Bible also smelt like one.

I went with him to the front door, and just before he opened it he flicked tentatively at the silver star hanging from his earlobe.

'Thanks for this,' he said. 'You're a mate.' He was standing really close to me and I waited breathlessly for him to kiss me, as he surely had to. I closed my eyes for a second, then I felt the cool summer evening air on my face and he was already half-way down the garden path.

He turned back at the garden gate and blew me a kiss, then stalked off towards home, like a tall skinny crow.

The Passenger

I heard a car toot outside, and glanced out of the window. A dark metallic blue Range Rover was crouching outside with its engine running. After a moment, the driver's door opened, and a stocky figure with thinning hair got out and walked to the front door of the house; his breath was cloudy in the cold, damp afternoon air. I grabbed my holdall and handbag and ran down the stairs. By the time I'd got the front door unlocked, the balding figure had been joined by a female who was his exact replica, only with somewhat more hair.

When I'd contacted Judith Bardsley, who was organising the reunion, to tell her I was coming, she'd suggested that I could get a lift up north with a couple of our old schoolfriends, Sharon Goodchild and Philip Oliver, who were now married and living in Croydon. My own personal finances being as tight as those of Coltsfoot Hall, I couldn't turn down the offer of a free ride, though I did have some misgivings about travelling all that way with people I hadn't seen in so many years, particularly as they were both accountants, which didn't bode well for amusing in-car entertainment. I remembered Philip Oliver as a friendly, freckled boy who played a lot of practical jokes, while Sharon Goodchild had fully lived up to her surname by being one of those incredibly hard-working people in whom sheer diligence makes up for a lack of natural brilliance. Oliver and Oliver, as they were known professionally, sounded like a circus act and looked like one, too, as they stood on the front steps of the Hall. Both stocky, rounded, baby-faced and freckled, they didn't seem to have changed since school; only Philip's dearth of hair gave any indication of time passing. And, of course, the Range Rover and their obviously expensive smart-casual apparel.

Sharon gave the shriek that I was to learn in the next forty-eight hours was *de rigueur* for greeting long-lost schoolfriends. 'Cass!' she screeched, flinging herself at me and depositing a kiss on each cheek. She then stepped aside while Philip did the same, although admittedly his shriek was in a lower register. He grabbed my bag and threw it into the back of the car.

'Well, you've done very well for yourself!' he remarked, as we fastened our seat-belts. Even though I was sharing the back seat with an assortment of Louis Vuitton hand luggage, I resisted the invitation to say that obviously they were doing well, too.

'It's a bit the back of beyond, though, isn't it?' Sharon added, smiling winningly at me over her shoulder.

'Not specially,' I said, defensively. 'Where was it Judith said you were living?'

'Croydon.'

'Mmn. Lovely.' *Hardly the seething metropolis, is it?* I thought, already beginning to wish I'd caught the train.

'We like it,' Sharon said. Then we lapsed into silence: there really wasn't anything to say. I was beginning to remember why I hadn't bothered to keep in contact with any of these people when I went to university.

For better or worse, however, I was squeezed into the back seat of Philip's four-wheel-drive pride and joy cheek-by-jowl with the Louis Vuitton for the next four hours, being propelled to further embarrassing encounters with people I was likely to have nothing in common with. There was no conversation between us until we were safely on the M1, as Sharon was occupied with screeching navigational orders at her husband. I couldn't remember her being so loud at school, where she'd appeared to be a successful product of the seen-and-not-heard school of child rearing.

Things didn't improve when Philip popped on a Dire Straits CD. Greg had interviewed many footballers over the years, and he estimated that around ninety per cent of them named Dire Straits and Simply Red as their favourite in-car entertainment. And footballers are not known for their good taste.

'Would you rather have something else on?' Philip asked, jiggling his eyebrows at me in the rear-view mirror. 'I've got Simply Red . . .'

It was late by the time we got to the hotel Judith had

booked for us. It was in a town about five miles away from where we grew up, and had been built in the years since we left, so I didn't feel the expected burst of nostalgia or even recognition as we got out of the car. My main sensations were aching cramp and tiredness, and sheer relief that my enforced incarceration with the Olivers was at an end. I wanted a bath and bed.

Philip pushed open the door of the hotel and stepped back, mumbling, 'Ladies first.' I squeezed past his paunch and walked into the small lobby. There was room for only a vestigial check-in desk and two armchairs arranged at either side of a coffee table, on which there were two glasses. A lone woman was sitting in one of the armchairs, and she stood up when she saw us, her shoulder-length white-blonde hair shining in the lamplight.

'Bacardi and Coke,' Heather Alderman said, indicating one of the glasses. 'If you don't mind breath like Zip firelighters.' Her pretty face broke into the broad grin I hadn't seen for so many years, and I dropped my bag and rushed to give her a hug.

Girls Just Want To Have Fun

Seeing Heather made me forget my tiredness, and after the Olivers had gone off to bed ('They look like a matching salt and pepper set,' Heather observed), she and I stayed up late, drinking our way down a bottle of single malt whisky she'd brought with her, and catching up.

As she poured me a drink I noticed that she was wearing engagement and wedding rings. 'Heather! You're married!'

She looked up and grinned. 'Oh, yes. My mother is very

proud that her daughter married a surgeon. Can you believe the glamour of it? You've never seen anything sweeter in scrubs, believe me. Better-looking than anything on *ER*.' Heather and Pierre had been married soon after he qualified. He worked at the same hospital where she was a radiographer, though there had been talk of relocating to Montréal, which was Pierre's home town.

She took another swig of her whisky and sighed distractedly.

'Is anything wrong?'

She regarded me for a couple of seconds, as if trying to decide whether the adult me could still be trusted with confidences, and apparently decided I could. 'Don't say anything to any of the others – not even Alison – but things aren't all that brilliant at home.' She told me that Pierre was keeping unpredictable hours, even for a doctor; he was often defensive and guarded when she talked to him and, as she put it, 'Sex is as rare as an Appalachian mountain stoat. Honestly, Cass, I've started to feel like Ingrid Bergman in *Gaslight*: nothing he says to me seems to quite match up with how he behaves. It makes me feel like I'm going nuts.'

'You think he's seeing someone else?'

'Frankly, everything points that way. I've even thought of hiring a detective, but then at other times I just think I'm being paranoid.'

There wasn't much I could say to comfort or commiserate with her, not knowing the other party and not really knowing Heather or much about her life any more, so to cheer her up and reassure her that she wasn't the only one with a less-than-perfect relationship I told her about the last birthday present I'd had from Greg.

'I think that's quite a sweet idea,' she said, sounding unconvinced.

'Sorry, no,' I said. 'Books, jewellery, flowers, weekends in

Paris: those are sweet ideas. Sponsoring the kit of an under-sixteen footballer is *not* sweet.'

Heather laughed. 'How sad are we? We haven't seen each other for fifteen years and here we are, preoccupied with useless men just like we were when we were seventeen. Come on,' she picked up the whisky bottle, 'it's time we got seriously pissed.'

Life In A Northern Town

As a result of our enthusiastic execution of this plan I stumbled downstairs the next morning to find I was too late for breakfast. The proprietor of the hotel, a small, solid woman whose perm stood rigid on her head like a bubbly helmet, grudgingly agreed to provide me with a cup of coffee, and I was drinking this when Heather appeared. 'Oh, another cup of coffee, Mrs Chainey, *please*,' she said, and our hostess shuffled back to her kitchen muttering to herself.

The reunion was that evening, which left the day free. Heather suggested that we go for a grand tour round our old haunts. 'Which means,' she said, revving the engine of her ancient car noisily, at which Mrs Chainey's disapproving face appeared at the hotel window, 'first stop, the Duke of York, springing-off point for many a night of debauchery and lust!' She swung the car out into the road and we headed off in the direction of what used to be somewhat over-optimistically referred to as 'the town centre'.

'Debauchery and lust for you, maybe,' I said, referring to how she and Ian would always, at some point in the evening, wander off together, quite often disappearing during the walk home when they'd been overtaken by passion and had to jump over a hedge into a field, leaving anyone they'd been walking with (usually me) to carry on discreetly without them.

Heather laughed. 'He was a dirty little beast, that Ian Kane,' she said. 'Under that sweet fluffy exterior there was an insatiable shag-monster just waiting to get out.'

'And, of course, you were happy to oblige.'

'Of course. Which way is it now?' She peered left and right. 'They've changed all the roads.' It was true. Apart from us the area seemed to be almost totally vehicle-free, which was just as well given the erratic nature of Heather's driving. A frenzy of road building had clearly taken place since we'd lived there: the landscape was barely recognisable, criss-crossed with roads that didn't seem to lead to anywhere. After three separate encounters with the same mini-roundabout, we eventually found a road we recognised.

I was of little help with the navigating. My main preoccupation that morning was that at this very moment Gideon Harker might be somewhere near by; at any second we could drive past him. I couldn't imagine how I would feel when I saw him again.

Heather slowed the car as we passed the Duke of York. There was no doubting it was the right place: the building was more or less the same. But the bullseye glass windows had been replaced by industrial-looking black shutters, making the place look blind and derelict. The only indication that it was still in some sort of use was a sign above the door in lurid purple and gold lettering, proclaiming it, pretty unbelievably, to be the 'Casino Royale'. In smaller letters was the warning, 'Strictly Over 21s'.

'I wonder what the under-age drinkers do now?' I said, staring at the place for clues.

'Probably spend their evenings alone in their bedrooms, having cyber-sex on their computers,' Heather said grimly, and released the handbrake with a crunch.

The high street, such as it was, looked much as I

remembered it, though about half of the shops seemed to have been turned into houses. The Queen of Tarts bakery my mum had worked at was still there, and the chemist's from which the 'rougher' girls at my school used to shoplift makeup. Beyond the high street, a new housing development had been built over the area where my granddad's house used to be.

I felt my throat tighten as I thought about my granddad. He'd been such a lovely man. Every morning he'd gone out to buy a newspaper, during which quarter-mile round trip he would manage to find out all the local gossip. He could spend hours just talking to people in the street, but not in the Ancient Mariner, buttonholing sort of way that some old people have. People were always pleased to see my granddad and would cross the road to have a word with him. In the afternoon he would read his paper or potter in his garden, and his evenings were spent watching television or at the pub (the Red Lion: he would have found the Duke of York far too noisy and youthful).

This ordered, routine life had suited him well, which made it all the more amazing that he'd so happily had it disrupted by offering to take on full-time responsibility for a teenage granddaughter who, one day, inexplicably took to wearing nothing but black clothes.

I was orphaned in 1984. Which is not strictly true, in the sense that both my parents are, as far as I know, still alive, but that's how it felt at the time. Right in the middle of my A levels, as if anyone had cared about that.

I remember my dad as a vaguely disturbing presence, in the sense that his infrequent appearances in my life would always be accompanied by a disruption to the usual routine and the atmosphere in general. For example, Mum never watched *Crossroads* when Dad was at home, because he couldn't stand it and she would be too busy trying to cook him dinners from recipes she cut out of the *Family Circle*. Cooking was not my mother's forte. When Dad wasn't there my mum and I would sit in front of the TV, or she would watch TV on her own and I would sit upstairs with Radio 1 and my homework. Dinner typically consisted of soup and bread rolls she brought from the bakery, or she would bring fish and chips on her way home. She didn't bother trying to cook, which meant we avoided a great deal of stress and anguish. I avoided a severe vitamin deficiency by supplementing this diet with a serious apple habit, like Jo March in *Little Women*.

I suppose I always knew that my parents didn't have the happiest of marriages; I never defined it or put it into words even to myself, but whenever I got to that famous line in *Jane Eyre*, 'Reader, I married him', I always felt vaguely uneasy on Jane's behalf. Just stay as you are, Jane: marriage means a mad wife in the attic or a cold silence across a scarcely edible steak and kidney pudding.

My dad was usually away on business trips. His business was some kind of insurance, not selling policies door to door like the man from the Pru but something to do with insuring big companies. He had to travel a lot, and we were used to him being away; preferred it, in fact. Until the day he came home and said he was moving to Warrington. He'd met someone, he said. He wanted a divorce.

It turned out that he'd been having what's known as 'an affair' with this woman in Warrington for five years. She was the 'love of his life', according to him, but although that was the sort of language that would normally impress my romantic heart, unsurprisingly this didn't. When I was very little, I'd once bought Dad, with my own pocket money, a keyring that said 'Drive Safely Daddy': it seemed an appropriate gift for someone who was hardly ever there. He took it from me as if it was the most precious thing in the world, and fixed his car keys to it proudly. He had it for years, though I can't remember if he still had it when he moved out. I couldn't help wondering whether it had ever given him a twinge of conscience while he was driving across the Pennines to Warrington to meet his other woman.

This is going to sound very selfish, but I honestly don't know how upset my mum was about him leaving. If she cried, she did it in private, because I never saw her in tears. I think she was eighty per cent relieved that her sham marriage was over; her only comment was, 'The bastard could have had the decency to leave ten years ago when I still had my looks.'

But she did still have her looks; she was quite a young woman (not much older than I am now, in fact), and after a while she realised it. That's how I ended up living at my granddad's house. Not long after my dad had finally packed up his suits, three dark blue and one black (for funerals), his golf clubs and his collection of Bert Kaempfert LPs, my mother began wondering whether she should have made more of an effort to lure Paul McCartney away from Jane Asher: after all, Linda had managed it. She sat me down to make an announcement. 'I'm going to Motown,' she said.

'Motown?' I echoed blankly.

'Mo-town. Motor-Town.' I was still looking blank. 'Detroit, *Michigan* – what do they teach you at school? Then I'm going to Duluth, Minnesota, where Bob Dylan was born, and Memphis, Tennessee, of course, home of the King. Wichita, because I need a small vacation. Galveston, San José, Phoenix, Tucson. California Dreaming. I'm going to be a rock-and-roll pilgrim and visit all those lovely places people sing about.' She closed her eyes and I imagine now that she was seeing deserts and sparkling blue seas and miles and miles of freeway. At the time I thought she was totally unhinged. After a while she reverted to a more practical, less dreamy voice and said, 'Anyway, it's about time I lived a little bit. We were saving up to go on a cruise as soon as we got you packed off to university, but that was always your dad's dream, not mine.' She pulled the face she always pulled when forced to acknowledge that I had a father, an Elvis-like sneer.

'So I've talked to your granddad, and he says you can stay there till you've finished your A levels.'

I could have said, 'Good for you, Mum, you deserve some happiness after all these years of doing your best at being more or less a single parent, only to be kicked in the teeth.' But I was a teenager, and that's not how teenagers think. All I could think of was that at the age of sixteen I was being abandoned by both my parents. 'Why do you have to go so far away?' I wailed. 'You don't have to go that far to be a rock-and-roll pilgrim. What about "Waterloo Sunset" and "Ferry Across the Mersey"? You could do those as day trips.'

My mum was not to be persuaded. 'Don't think for one minute I'm going to let you rain on my parade, miss,' she said. 'I've got you this far. You can manage by yourself from here.' And that was it: end of negotiation.

She left a few weeks later. It was like my first day at infant school all over again: I snivelled and made a fuss to begin with, but she hadn't been gone too long when I shrugged metaphorically and got on with my life.

As if she'd read my mind, Heather asked, 'What are your parents up to now?'

'Presumably Dad's still in Warrington. I don't really know and I don't care. And my mum is walking in Memphis.'

'She's what?' Heather laughed.

'Walking in Memphis. Like the song. She's working as a tour guide, showing people round sites of Elvisly historical interest.'

'Did she ever get married again?'

'Yep. He's another Elvis fan – his name is Dwight.'

'An Elvis fan called Dwight, eh? How very *Jerry Springer*.'

'He's nice. A lot nicer than my bloody so-called father, anyway. He talks like a country-and-western singer – you know, he makes "end" rhyme with "begin", as in "Where the Sidewalk Inds, the Road Begins".' Dwight was, as they say in his part of the world, Good People: a kind and quiet man who cherished my mother as if she was Miss Tennessee.

We were leaving the high street, and Heather turned right, heading for Middleton Road.

And suddenly, right in front of us at the top of the hill, there was the house where Gideon Harker used to live: the kind of large, 1930s semi-detached house that's sometimes described as a 'villa', standing high above the crossroads with a flight of steps leading up to the front door flanked on either side by a rockery. I stared at the left-hand upstairs window, where I knew his bedroom used to be. There were pink striped curtains there now, and an assortment of fluffy toys were ranged along the window-sill. A child's room. The Harker family had moved away years ago.

'What are you staring at?' Heather asked, and followed my gaze. 'Oh, God! Punky Harker's house! You had such a thing with him, it was so funny.'

'It wasn't *funny*,' I snapped.

Heather looked at me. 'Oh,' she said, for once lost for words. She jerked the car into a sudden right turn, and stopped next to the small park. 'Come on,' she said. 'If we're going to have a nostalgic girly talk about boys, we have to do it in the proper manner. Since the Duke of York seems to be no more, we'll go for plan B: the swings.'

She led the way to the playground, which was deserted on this wintry morning, and jumped on to a swing. I perched on the one next to her, clutching at the cold chains. I've never liked swings, they always make me feel dizzy, so I sat and watched Heather as she swung higher and higher, her amazing bright blonde hair gleaming like chunks of sunshine. With her broad face, strong cheekbones and that hair, it was obvious that her genes must have arrived in the area long ago on a Viking longboat. Apart from a few traces around the eyes, and the shorter hair, she looked like the same Heather with whom I'd shared so much at Middleton Road.

Eventually she slowed down, and we sat side by side, the swings swaying gently.

'You and Punky Harker,' she said, her voice amused, 'you were practically joined at the hip. I was quite jealous.'

'Of him or me?'

'Both. I was jealous of him because I hardly saw you once he was on the scene, and I have to admit I was a bit jealous of you, too – he was pretty gorgeous.'

'He was, wasn't he?' I sighed. 'Do you want to know something funny? I miss him.'

'What? You *miss* him? After all this time?' Her face was incredulous.

'I don't mean I pine for him every single moment,' I said defensively, 'but when I heard about this reunion, it started me thinking about him again. And I do miss him: he was special.'

'At the *time*, maybe,' Heather said.

'Maybe. That's what I want to find out. All I know is I've never felt again like I did when I was with him, but I don't know if that's just because I'm older now and I felt like that because I was young, or whether there really was something special between us.'

Heather reached into her pocket, pulled out a small silver hip flask, unscrewed the top and offered it to me.

'Heather! It's only eleven o'clock in the morning!' I took it anyway, and drank a good mouthful of the same whisky we'd been drinking the night before, feeling it settle in my stomach in a ball of warmth. I passed the flask back to her.

She grinned. 'There is no wrong time to drink a decent single malt,' she said.

We sat in silence for a minute or two, looking round the park that had seemed so large when I was a little kid. It had shrunk: I didn't remember being able to see houses all round the edges of it before, but perhaps that was because I only remembered it in summer when leafy trees hid them. Now the

67

trees were bare, and the park was little more than a smallish square of grass.

I remembered sitting with Gideon on these very same swings, on a hot summer night full of the smell of cut grass; from somewhere the sound of Cyndi Lauper singing 'Time After Time' drifted on the air.

Gideon's hair was now dyed blue-black and he was wearing black jeans, Dr Marten's ten-eyelet boots and a black T-shirt. He'd had his ear pierced again and a red feather had joined the little silver star. We were probably on our way home from the Duke, as I remembered feeling quiet and mellow, as if a few drinks had probably passed my lips earlier, and as always happy just to be with him.

'Cass,' he said.

'Mmn?'

'Why does everyone call you Cass?'

'It's my name.'

'No, it isn't. Your name is Catherine.'

I explained that when I was a baby and first learning to talk, my earliest attempts to say my name had come out sounding like 'Cass'. My family took to calling me that (my mum specially liked it because of Cass Elliott: she was a big Mamas and Papas fan and 'Creeque Alley' had been in the charts when I was born), and as I grew older it just stuck.

'Well, it doesn't suit you,' he said. 'It's too hard and too modern. You were born to be a Catherine and that's what I'm going to call you.' He jumped from his swing and knelt in front of me on one knee, his hands clasped to his chest. 'My lady Catherine,' he said, taking my hand and kissing it.

I seemed to see him in front of me, down on one knee on the sun-parched grass, his black-lined eyes and pale face giving him the look of a hero in a silent movie. I smiled, but Heather didn't notice.

'Punky Harker . . .' she was saying. 'The stuff he used to wear. All that black, and that leather-coat thing and the big boots.'

'Oh, please. You sound so *stuffy*! And I liked it, anyway, it was part of what made him different.' I shoved my hands deeper into my pockets. It was really too cold to be sitting outside, and I wanted to be back in Heather's warm car or, better still, at the hotel with a cup of tea.

'Wouldn't it be awful if he's there tonight and he's fat and bald like Philip Oliver?' Heather said. 'With a cardigan! That would put a strain on your romantic visions. Or he might have a loathsome wife who does stencilled borders and likes lots of swagging at the tops of the curtains, and a couple of whingey kids.' She was hitting her stride now. 'Or he could have got religion and be wandering around with a guitar singing "Oh, Lord, kumbaya" all over the place.'

'Oh, stop, please! It might all be true, and I don't think I could cope with the stencilled borders. Or the wife. Especially not the wife.'

Heather sat looking at me for a minute, her face wearing an expression of uncomprehending concern. 'Aren't you taking this a bit seriously?' she said. 'After all, you were only seventeen last time you saw him. Everything seems so important when you're seventeen, but when you look back it wasn't, not really. And now you're a fully grown-up woman, you've got your job and you've got your relationship with – what's his name again?'

'Greg.'

'Well, what's *he* like? Did you say he's a journalist?'

'He's a football reporter.'

She snorted. 'A football reporter? Does that mean he has an entire wardrobe of sheepskin coats?'

'Not a single one, actually. He's quite presentable.'

'And?'

And indeed, I thought. What to say about Greg? He was just a fact of my life. He didn't make my heart beat faster. He wasn't a romantic hero, not Mr Knightley or Mr Rochester, and he was a million miles from Heathcliff. Emily Brontë would not have been impressed.

'He's nice,' I said. 'Sort of warm and sweet . . .'

'You make him sound like a doughnut,' Heather said.

Youth

After lunch, Heather wanted to visit Alison Stoker (*née* Mutch) who was staying at her parents' home not far away. I cried off this plan: I wanted some time to myself.

I sat in my hotel room, which was small, square, functional, and totally devoid of anything that Eleanor Yarr and her Associates could have described as a 'period feature', or even 'detailing'. The window looked out over several of those new roads that seemed to go nowhere and were only bothered by the occasional vehicle. I felt a twinge of annoyance towards the mad planners who'd decided to Tarmac over the fields of my youth. Stubby black leafless hedges bound the few fields that remained unscathed; news of spring hadn't yet reached this far north, and no fluffy white lambs skipped between the dirty grey sheep.

I lay back on my bed and stared at the ceiling, which was closer than a ceiling had a right to be: at Coltsfoot Hall the ceilings were high enough to accommodate a decent-sized trampolining troupe. Being back in my home town had affected me more than I'd expected, and in unexpected ways. I thought I'd be able to feel a sense of coming home, but so far I hadn't felt anything like it. That wasn't surprising, when I thought about my childhood.

I remembered the time I'd asked my mum what it had been like falling in love with my dad; I was so naïve in those days, I'd taken the heroes in *Jackie* magazine as templates for real-life romance. They were always described as having 'floppy hair' and 'crinkly eyes': I think the *Jackie* office must have been plastered with inspirational posters of David Essex, because I couldn't think of anyone else to whom that description would apply at the time.

Looking back now, I don't even know if my parents had *ever* 'fallen in love'. What they *fell* for was me, and in the north of England in 1967 there wasn't much choice. My dad did the right thing, they got married and there they were: up the junction.

My mum had married beneath her: I heard this phrase from my grandparents (her side) and her friends at regular intervals throughout my childhood. Granddad was a bank manager, Granny had stayed at home clipping the privet and painting her toenails; they went on package holidays to Marbella and the neighbours called them 'posh'. I think my mum only went out with my dad as a little gesture of rebellion before settling down: if she couldn't have Paul McCartney and a jet-setting rock 'n' roll lifestyle, she'd have a fling with Jim Thomson, who at the time was an apprentice car mechanic. She still imagined that when she got married it would be to someone called Simon or James (who would *never* shorten it to Jim). But my arrival put paid to that.

Just as I had my escape in books, my mum took her refuge in music. One of my earliest memories is of her listening to *Rubber Soul* by the Beatles. She would play 'Norwegian Wood' over and over, sitting in a trance till the last note died out then jumping up to shift the needle back to the start of the track.

When I was small, my mum used to refer to me, in her most indulgent moments, as the little thing that was sent to try her, but as I grew older and increasingly self-sufficient, she found me more tolerable. She was more like an inoffensive, pretty much self-absorbed flatmate than a mother, and we each had our own territories, to which we generally kept. This didn't mean I liked the arrangement: I longed for a normal family life, with everyone round the dinner table in the evening, exchanging news, private jokes, gentle teasing, even a bit of fighting. Like Alison's family, in fact. I adored Alison's family: they were almost a different species, a real-life version of *The Waltons*, and such a contrast to my life that visiting them was as painful as it was wonderful.

I remembered visiting Alison one Saturday not long before Christmas when I was about fourteen. The house was full of people, noise and festivity; her parents were putting up the Christmas tree, Alison's mum proudly showing me decorations that Alison and her brothers had made at infant school that were lovingly preserved and brought out every year. Her dad laid out the tree lights, plugged them in to test them, and at first nothing happened. He and Alison spent the next fifteen minutes methodically unscrewing and rescrewing each tiny bulb to find the faulty one, until suddenly the chain of lights blinked into life like a little carnival parade on the living-room carpet. The brothers, one older and one younger than Alison, made so much noise that it was hard to believe there were only two of them: they seemed to be permanently running up and down the stairs. When the whole family sat down together for their evening meal, sharing news and good-humoured teasing, it was all so cosy I could hardly bear to leave and go back to our house, where Mum would be listening to the Temptations or Bob Dylan while getting ready for her evening out with the 'girls' from work.

But since the maths lesson in 1981 Gideon had been a presence in my life, in my imagination anyway, as my guardian angel and the object of my affection. The day he bleached his hair blond and asked me to pierce his ear, he became real.

I'd hardly dared to hope that being singled out for the task of mutilating my beloved would be the start of something, but the day after Gideon had appeared in the Duke of York looking like an anthem for groomed youth, he appeared on my doorstep. It was a Sunday: Mum and I were in the kitchen; she was reading the *News of the World* over her usual breakfast of instant coffee and cigarettes, and I'd just finished my Weetabix. The doorbell rang, and Mum looked at me suspiciously. 'Who could that be at this hour?' she asked, as she invariably did, whatever the hour happened to be. Obviously I had no idea.

'Well, answer it, then,' she said testily. 'I've only got my dressing-gown on. If it's anybody trying to interest us in God, tell them to piss off, it's Sunday.' I went towards the front door, and she hollered after me, 'Or tell them you're Jewish. Let them try to argue you out of that!'

Gideon was already grinning as I opened the door. 'Don't tell me,' he said, 'you're Jewish.' I blushed furiously and made a mental note to kill my mother. 'So I can't interest you in a copy of the *Watchtower*, then?'

'The what?' I was blithering like a fool, dying inside because I was wearing some sort of awful pink jumper and really horrible, shapeless jeans, Sunday stuff, and on my doorstep was the most perfect man imaginable, if you discounted the red, scabby-looking earlobe.

'Who is it?' my mum yelled from inside the house. I looked at Gideon. Who was he? How could I describe him? There was no precedent for this at all.

'Tell her you've got to go out,' he suggested.

'I can't go out in *these*,' I said, gesturing at my clothes.

He laughed. 'You're right. God. I'd best come in, then, while you get changed.'

He followed me inside. It was unbelievable: twice in two days. At this rate he was in danger of becoming a regular visitor. Then I was treated to the sight of six feet four of bottle-blond teenage sex god towering over five feet four of dressing-gowned, unmade-up mother. The look on her face was a picture: she tried about fifteen different expressions before settling on no expression at all, a stunned blank.

'This is Gideon,' I said.

'Is it?' She pulled her lemon dressing-gown tighter round herself. Then she took the cigarette out of her mouth, presumably because it would have dropped out anyway while she stared at the Thing that had appeared in her kitchen. I decided the best plan was to leave them to it, so I muttered something about getting changed, and dashed off to my room, where at high speed I tried and rejected four outfits, finally settling for black Spandex leggings under a blue-green shirt-dress.

When I reappeared Gideon smiled approvingly. He was sitting at the table next to my mother, with a mug of coffee in front of him, and they were poring over a page in the newspaper. Cecil Parkinson had resigned from the government following revelations about his affair with Sara Keays.

'It beggars belief how that man can get *one* woman to sleep with him, never mind two,' my mum was saying, offering Gideon a cigarette. He shook his head, as if people's parents offered him cigarettes all the time.

'Ready, Cass?' he said, smiling at me.

My mum finally noticed I was there. 'Good grief,' she said, when she saw my clothes. 'Legs like a couple of sticks of liquorice!' I shot her an evil look.

We went for a walk. He walked fast, like somebody escaping from something, which it turned out he was. 'I needed to get out of the house for a while,' he said. 'My parents just never stop.'

'Were they mad because of your ear?'

He grinned. 'Oh, yes. They hadn't quite recovered from the

hair, but the ear certainly upset them. First I had the illustrated lecture about infection, then the one about how you can't have doctors with earrings because it wouldn't inspire any confidence in the patients and they're a breeding ground for bacteria.'

'I didn't know you were going to be a doctor,' I said, panting with the effort of keeping up with his pace, and dead impressed at the thought of him in a white coat, healing the sick: it fitted my view of him perfectly. Disappointingly it didn't fit with his view of himself.

'I've told them there is no way on the *planet* that I'm going to be a doctor, but they won't give up. That's why I had to get out this morning. My dad started on one of his the-advantages-you've-had, the-sacrifices-we've-made numbers.'

We weren't walking towards any particular destination, it was more like we were simply trying to put space between Gideon and his parents, but as we got further away at least he slowed his pace down.

At one point, we found ourselves walking behind a woman on her own. We were in a tree-lined lane and there was hardly any traffic.

'Let's cross the road,' Gideon said, tugging at my hand.

'Why?'

'Because she might think she's being followed. It might frighten her. And no one should ever have to be frightened.' He said this with such conviction that I glanced up at his face, but he was turned away from me checking there was no traffic before we crossed the road.

At the far end of town was a church, and a service was currently in progress: we could hear a hymn being sung, the doomy one about those in peril on the sea. We sat down on a bench in the churchyard. It was a beautiful morning, with a wide blue sky; birds fluttered between the headstones, which were old and lichen-covered, with long grass and dandelions growing in between. There was a distant sound of lawn-mowers and bees.

Again, this was unprecedented. I was sitting in a church-yard on a Sunday morning with a boy. Not just *a* boy: *the* boy. It was wonderful: the blue sky, the sunshine, the muted sound of hymn-singing and a faint whiff of peroxide still lingering on his hair. Tongue-tied, I tried to witter something topical about Cecil Parkinson.

'The odd thing is that anyone's surprised,' Gideon said. 'The whole lot of them are hypocrites and liars.'

'So are you going to vote Labour when you're eighteen?' Which was still a year away for him and even longer for me.

'They're no better,' he said. 'There's one or two, like Tony Benn or Ken Livingstone, but the rest of them are just like the Tories.' I only had a vague idea of who Tony Benn was, and none at all of Ken Livingstone. My mum often said, 'What do they teach you at school?' What they taught us was Magellan's circumnavigation of the globe and the main topographic features of a glaciated highland. School was for stuff like Archimedes' principle, but things like politics, how the world really worked, I was ignorant of all that.

Whereas it seemed to me then that Gideon knew every-thing. At school, he was the golden boy; he couldn't help himself. He was good at everything: academically there was no idea that was outside his grasp, and he often asked questions to which the teachers had no answer, forcing them to go away and find answers to save face. They even turned a blind eye to his increasingly non-uniform appearance, viewing it as an outward manifestation of his genius. He was also remarkable at drawing and painting: he could accurately draw anything put in front of him, which was a skill I admired hugely, though he dismissed it, saying that just being able to draw didn't make you an artist. The only area where he didn't excel was sport. He was uselessly non-competitive at team games and seemed to be overtaken by natural inertia whenever called upon to do anything athletic.

'Why do people think if you've got long legs it qualifies you as a high-jumper?' he moaned. 'It just means I've got more length of leg to get tangled up with that damn bar. I don't want to end up with a broken nose tripping up on that thing.' He had always had a fear of breaking his long, straight nose.

The church doors opened, and a man came out. He was small, middle-aged, angry-looking, wearing an ugly brown suit with wide lapels and a nasty green tie. He saw us sitting at the end of the churchyard and came stamping towards us. 'What you two doing?' he demanded.

'We're just sitting enjoying the weather,' Gideon said.

'Probably planning how to rob the lead off the church roof,' the man said.

'We're not doing anything wrong,' Gideon said.

'Mate, have a look at yourself in a mirror. You just *are* wrong. Blokes in makeup, bloody freak.' He turned to me specifically. 'You look like quite a nice lass,' he said. 'You don't want to be hanging round with his sort.'

'Oh, I do,' I said fervently. Gideon gleefully squeezed my hand.

The man looked exasperated. 'In that case, both of you had better bloody clear off before I call the police.'

He stamped back in the direction of the church, from which the congregation was now emerging, blinking in the sunlight like creatures just out of hibernation.

'People are strange,' was Gideon's opinion, and I had to agree.

I lay on the bed and wondered what he was doing right now, right this minute. Was he nearby, on his way to the reunion? What was he thinking about? Me? Or just how to keep the kids quiet in the back of the car?

Suddenly I felt really lonely, and picked up the phone to

call Greg. After several rings his answering-machine clicked on, and I looked at my watch: four o'clock. He'd still be right in the middle of a football match; in fact he probably wouldn't be home till almost midnight, as he'd most likely go for an after-match drink or several. I left a quick message to say I'd arrived safely and was missing him, which I wasn't sure was strictly true, and hung up.

Party Fears Two

I have to admit, I was starting to feel more than a little nervous. To be honest, I was terrified: my usual pre-party shyness, combined with the thought of stepping back inside that school made me feel like heading for the hills. The worst part was that I'd spent so much of the day thinking about Gideon, and running various scenarios through my mind of what meeting him again would be like, that I really didn't know how I would react; there was a serious possibility that I would scream, faint or just start cackling alarmingly like mad Mrs Rochester.

No, I couldn't cope with it. I shouldn't have come at all: why stir up a reasonably happy life with all these memories?

Back at home (because it *was* home: I hadn't found anything in this place yet to make me change my mind) I had a beautiful house to save from Randall Robertson's big chopper, some good friends, and my 'scrumptious journalist boyfriend', as Jackie had described him. It had been nice seeing Heather again, but as for Gideon Harker, he was just going to have to stay in the past, where he properly belonged. I decided to escape.

I grabbed my bag from the top of the wardrobe, and began to throw my clothes into it, wanting to be well away before

Heather returned from visiting Alison's parents. I'd leave her a note, she'd understand, and now we'd met each other again we would keep in touch, I told myself. I hadn't brought many clothes, so I was soon ready.

The last thing I packed was the dress I'd been going to wear for the reunion. It was simple, dark green silk: I'd bought it specially, spending more money than I meant to because the expensive cut made it cling to just the right places and skim the rest. I knew exactly how Gideon would look at me in a dress like that – or, rather, how the Gideon I had known fifteen years earlier would have looked at me. I'd never know what he might think of it now. Or what he'd think of *me*.

I folded the dress carefully and laid it across the top of the other clothes. Maybe I would be able to get a refund if I could keep it uncreased.

I was about to close my bag when there was a knock on the door. It was so abrupt in the silence that I jumped almost out of my shoes. It must be Heather, back early: maybe Alison's family hadn't been at home.

'Cass!' someone called. 'Are you in?' It wasn't Heather; it was a man's voice. My mind was all over the place. *It must be him, what if it is, how did he find me, what if it isn't?* My first impulse was to run away: I even glanced at the window to see if there was any chance of escaping through it. Then the door handle turned, and I had a half-second to compose my face and try to look a little less like the madwoman in the attic before it opened.

It was Philip Oliver, standing in the doorway in a Paisley dressing-gown, behind the satiny lapels of which a white T-shirt was visible. The dressing-gown fell just shy of his round knees, which were extraordinarily hairy, as if the hair that had vanished from his head was migrating south.

'There you are,' he said, as if I needed to have my location pointed out. 'I *thought* I saw Heather go out without you.' He glanced at my fully packed bag. 'Not unpacked yet?' he said chidingly. 'Sharon always gets everything out as soon as we get to our room. Otherwise it all looks slept-in, she says.' He continued to stand there in the doorway, looking at me expectantly, as if I'd summoned him to my room for a purpose I was yet to reveal.

'Did you want anything in particular?' I asked him, and this seemed to be the cue he needed to close the door and come right in. He parked his ample backside on my bed and crossed his legs, the better to show off his hairy knees.

'I've been thinking about what you said in the car on the way up,' he said confidentially. What thing was that? I wondered. *Please turn off Dire Straits immediately before I'm forced to leap from this vehicle and land in a bloodied heap on the hard shoulder? Or, Do tell me where you and Sharon purchase those lovely his 'n' hers Argyll socks.* I looked at him blankly.

'You said you'd been getting into dire straits,' he prompted.

'No,' I said, appalled. 'I bought "Sultans of Swing" when it first came out, but . . .'

'Oh, Cass, you were always so funny,' he said, gripping a fuzzy knee with mirth. 'That's one of the reasons why I liked you.'

'Pardon?' No, on second thoughts, I didn't want any explanation of that remark at all, but it was too late.

'Ooh,' he practically moaned, 'I had a massive crush on you! *Massive*,' he emphasised, and leaned forward conspiratorially. 'Though, of course, Sharon doesn't know anything about it.' I glanced at the window again. Maybe three floors wasn't too high to jump.

'Look, Phil,' I said, 'it's been very nice having this chat, but as you can see I've got a lot of unpacking to do, so . . . '

'Just go right ahead,' he said. 'Work round me.' It seemed I had no option, so I started to take things out of the bag again and put them back on hangers. My underwear I just balled up into a heap and shoved into a drawer: the last thing I wanted was to inflame Philip Oliver further with a sight of my scanties.

It was a very unnerving experience, particularly when after a minute or two's silence he said, 'I've come to make you an offer.' I waited for him to elaborate, feeling that to say anything might give him even more encouragement. 'I think you could benefit from my skills,' he said, settling his buttocks a little more comfortably on the bed. 'And Sharon's, of course.'

Sharon's? What kinky Croydon plan had they been hatching all the way up the M1? 'I don't think . . .'

'No need to be embarrassed,' he said. 'I remember how you were always pretty bad at maths, poor love.'

'Sorry?'

'Don't be. Some people have an aptitude and others don't, that's all. Which is why I think I can help you with your little problem.'

'What little problem?' He'd completely lost me now.

'Your stately *home*,' he said, with the air of one whose patience is finally running out. 'You said it's in financial difficulties, and Sharon and I are accountants. If you know what you're doing there are always ways and means. If you get what I'm saying.'

'Oh,' I said, the light finally dawning. So he was simply offering his (possibly bent) professional services, as one old schoolchum to another. 'That's very kind of you.'

'Not at all,' he said. 'It'll be my pleasure.' He then gave me the most lascivious look imaginable and patted the space on the bed next to him, like Jason King and that breed of old-style TV smoothie. Only balder. 'It'll be a chance to get to know each other better,' he said. This man had a seduction technique straight from a seventies sitcom.

Then, to my intense relief, the door flew open. Philip leaped about six inches off the bed and his cheeks flushed scarlet: he looked like Noddy. He obviously thought Sharon had caught him out, but it was Heather, bearing an industrial-size makeup bag, her outfit for the evening, a portable cassette player and a full bottle of whisky. Saved by the Bell's.

'I've come to get ready in your room. It'll be just like old times,' she announced, then realised Philip was there. 'Oh, hi, Phil,' she said, without missing a beat. 'Sharon's looking for you.' She peered at him suspiciously and I shot her a *get rid of him!* look, which she understood as perfectly as if we had still been at school.

'Come on, then,' she told Philip briskly, plucking at the fabric on the shoulder of his dressing-gown. 'Mustn't keep your wife waiting.'

As he turned to leave he said to me, 'Think about what I've said.'

I smiled winningly at him. 'I've thought,' I said, 'and I'll be getting the train back home.'

As the door closed, Heather said, 'That dressing-gown had shoulder pads.' She shuddered. 'Were you about to be *seduced* just there? He looked well furtive.' I recounted the conversation I'd just had, and she roared with laughter.

'Who would have guessed?' she said. 'Polly Oliver was your secret admirer all those years? Perhaps it was him who sent you that red rose on Valentine's Day when we were in the fourth form.' That was a depressing thought, particularly as it was more than likely true; I'd always harboured a fond notion that it might, despite his later protests to the contrary, have been from Gideon.

'Poor Philip,' I said, 'but if he hadn't come in just then, I might have been half-way to the station by now.'

'What do you mean?'

'I was going to go home,' I said. 'I've gone off this reunion idea.'

'Is this because of Punky Harker?'

'Partly.'

'Oh, for heaven's sake,' she said. 'Look, if he's that important to you, surely the best thing would be to see him. I bet once you've set eyes on him again you'll wonder what you ever saw in him. And if you don't go, he'll still be in your mind like Mr Punky Perfect, and you'll always wonder. For the rest of your life,' she added for emphasis, and I knew she was right. She looked at me, knew that I was going to stay, and poured us each a glass of whisky.

'Personally I can't wait to see young Ian Kane again,' she said.

'Won't it be a bit odd, seeing him?'

'Not really,' she said, zinging her mascara brush in and out of the tube like the magazines tell you not to do. 'I'm sure I can handle seeing someone I last shagged when Madonna was still wearing ra-ra skirts.' She leaned forward and inspected her face in the mirror. 'Thank God for eyelash dye.' She wielded the loaded mascara brush at her already chemically enhanced lashes. 'To be honest, I forgot about him more or less as soon as I went to university, there were too many other things to think about. I can't say I've really thought about him at all. But I'm interested to see how he's turned out, same as I am with everyone. I can't wait to see if Punky Harker has turned into Middle-aged Punky: he might have a pramful of punky babies with cute little pastel-coloured Mohicans.'

I changed the subject. 'How was Alison?' I asked her.

She rolled her eyes. 'That husband,' she said, 'has as much personality as a load-bearing wall. He's called Pete. Not Peter, mind, Pete: as in Pete Bog.' We collapsed in fits of giggles, even though it wasn't that funny: it was just two best schoolfriends, getting into the party spirit. 'I've been *dying* to say that all afternoon!' she said, checking that all the laughing hadn't made her mascara run. She pressed the play button on the cassette player, and Duran Duran whisked us straight back to the eighties.

'D'you remember how it would take us an entire afternoon

to get ready for a school party?' I said, accepting the toothmug of whisky Heather handed me.

'It was important to get it right,' she said, like the voice-over on a documentary. 'You might just have one good crack at that gorgeous fifth-former you'd been lusting after for months. Only one chance for him to see you *not* wearing a school tie and looking like some kind of dykey prison warder.'

'Speak for yourself.'

'I was speaking for Mary Weldon, actually.'

'Ugh. I'd forgotten her. I wonder if she ever did become a prison warder in the end?'

'According to Alison, she's working as a hairdresser,' she said.

'Imagine letting *her* loose on your hair.'

'She'd have you looking like an inmate from *Prisoner: Cell Block H* as soon as look at you.'

'Anyway,' I said, returning to the subject, 'it was all right for you at those parties: they were queuing up to dance with you.'

'You had your share of admirers,' she said, pouting at herself in the mirror. 'Should I have washed my hair, do you think?' I shook my head: if her hair was any cleaner and shinier it would pose a hazard to aircraft. I racked my brains, trying to think who this share of admirers had been, Philip Oliver aside, and came up with only the embarrassing tally of two: Kevin Davis (the ugliest boy in the school) and Gary Coningsborough (the most boring boy in our year).

School parties, if you weren't Heather Alderman, were mortally embarrassing. I remembered how we'd had to sit, boys on one side of the room and girls on the other: that old Middleton Road gender-divide thing again. The music would start and the boys, who for some reason had the duty or privilege of asking the girls to dance, never the other way round, would make a dash for Heather and the rest of the

84

A-list fanciable girls. I was usually one of the ones left sitting, apart from during a very embarrassing phase when an ugly child from a year below us had a crush on me (ah! baby makes *four* admirers, then). Occasionally a well-meaning teacher would grab the hand of a wallflower and drag her across the room, dodging through the ungainly throng essaying the Gay Gordons, to where some hapless boy would be sitting desperately trying to retract his head into his jacket.

The next party would still be looked forward to and prepared for with as much enthusiasm as the last: hope sprang eternal. And for the last couple of parties when I was in the sixth form, I simply sat in a corner all night with Gideon, getting surreptitiously and inevitably drunk on smuggled-in alcohol and bitching about everybody else in the manner of Stadtler and Waldorf, the two cantankerous old men on *The Muppet Show*.

'You're not wearing *that*, are you?' Heather had shimmied out of the *en-suite* bathroom wearing a dress my mum would have described as a 'frontless, backless evening strap'. She gave me a twirl.

'Why not?'

'It's outrageous!'

'Oh dear.' She sighed dramatically. 'Do you think people will stare at me? Do you think the men will be staggering around in a state of painful tumescence all evening at the mere sight?'

'Probably, yes.'

'Sounds perfect, then. Now, where's that lippy?'

We spent the next hour trying on each others' makeup, agreeing that Martin Kemp was far better looking in *EastEnders* than he had ever been in Spandau Ballet, and arguing about who had the most cellulite; of course I won that one.

'Cellulite,' Heather mused. 'They didn't *have* that when we were at school.'

'I think I had it.'

'No, I mean we didn't have a name for it, it wasn't an issue.'

'Like we didn't have *feng*-bloody-*shui* or the ozone hole.'

'We didn't even have *ozone*.'

It was like being teenagers again, except we were getting gradually pissed on whisky rather than the contents of Heather's parents' cocktail cabinet.

'We should really be drinking apricot wine and Advocaat,' I said, sentimentally.

'With a Sanatogen chaser!'

Happy Hour

We certainly didn't want to be among the first to arrive at the reunion, so we decided to pay a visit to the Duke of York – or the Casino Royale, as it was now styled. Mrs Chainey was prevailed upon to give us the number of a taxi company.

'Why don't we ask the Olivers to join us?' Heather said. For a second I thought she was serious and rushed her out to the cab before she could carry out the threat.

We were dismayed but not surprised to find that we obviously passed the Casino Royale's 'Strictly Over 21s' test, and found the interior to be even more depressing than the outside. The walls were painted dark red, and the lighting was so dim it was like being in a photographer's darkroom, except that instead of the pungent smell of developing chemicals there was a stink of old beer and tobacco with a faint underlay of vomit. Fruit machines, which flashed and bleeped all along one wall, represented the casino element, but there was nothing at all to suggest 'royale'. Even the converted treadle sewing-machine tables and other quasi-rustic pub furniture that had been so much a feature of the Duke of York had been replaced by even nastier plastic tables and stools.

The barman confided in us that this was because they caused less damage when thrown. 'I haven't seen you two ladies in here before,' he said, coming on like Tom Cruise in *Cocktail*. He looked very much like Tom Cruise, only taller of course.

'We used to come here all the time,' Heather said, 'when it was the Duke of York.'

The barman, whose little gold-coloured plastic name badge identified him as Jack, shrugged and looked mystified. 'Never heard of it,' he said. 'Are you sure it was the same place?'

We nodded. 'That was quite a while ago,' I said. 'We're here for our school reunion.'

'Oh, yeah. What school?' It turned out that he himself was a Middleton Road alumnus, though he looked frankly appalled when we told him what year we'd left.

'Shit,' he said. 'I was *ten* then.'

Heather sighed. 'And to think there were only three channels on television when we started at that school,' she said.

'Three?' he repeated wonderingly.

'Only four by the time we left. No satellite dishes, e-mails or mobile phones either.'

'Wow.' He obviously had us down as being pretty damn ancient but, even so, he was giving Heather a look that seemed to indicate that being practically as old as the Queen Mother hadn't ruled out her chances for the evening.

Like pigeons who always return to the same roost, we sat down with our drinks in approximately the location of our regular table in the corner, Heather facing the door as she had been on the night Gideon turned up transformed by peroxide.

Apropos of nothing, except perhaps reading my mind, Heather said, 'I used to wonder if Punky Harker was gay.'

'What?'

'Well,' she said, looking slightly embarrassed, or as near to it as she would ever get, 'you were always with him, but as far as I knew you were just mates. No shagging.'

'So you thought he was gay?'

She nodded. 'Ian thought he might be, too. I mean, it isn't normal at that age, is it? And all that dressing up. Like a transvestite who didn't quite dare to wear dresses.'

'Transvestite isn't the same as gay,' I pointed out.

She brushed aside that distinction with a brisk hand movement. 'We have *heard* of Eddie Izzard in Birmingham, you know.'

'Anyway,' I said, 'he never wore dresses or anything, he just dressed to please himself. And who says we didn't get physical?'

'Well, *you* never said you *did*.'

'I didn't tell you everything,' I said.

'Oh, my God!' she squealed. 'I could kill you for this! Come on, then, girl, *dish*.'

It had been true that for a long while we got no further than holding hands, but holding hands was such bliss, and fitted with my idea of romantic courtship so perfectly, that I couldn't have been happier anyway. And somehow it was all too pure and lovely to spoil it by talking to anyone about it, even my best friend.

When I was with Gideon it was as if we had a little bubble around the two of us, and nothing else was significant. We would talk for hours about books and films and music, and it was as much fun talking to him as it was talking to another girl. Obviously I didn't say this to Heather, as it would only have fuelled her suspicions regarding his sexual orientation.

Like his dress sense, his taste in music was not exactly mainstream. While everyone else was listening to Duran

Duran and my almost-namesakes the Thompson Twins, Gideon liked bands no one else seemed to have heard of, with names like Hula and Chakk. He would come round to my house (we never went to his) with a stack of records under his arm, which we could only listen to when we had the house to ourselves, because he insisted on them being played *loud*. They were quite alarming to begin with. My favourite music at the time was the jazzy pop of the Style Council, so I was unprepared for those thunderous slabs of unmelodic machine noise. I would probably have shrieked and turned it straight off if it hadn't come so highly recommended, but I listened to it and fairly soon we were both ordering obscure twelve-inch singles by mail order from stores in London, and I started wearing nothing but black. It was like being in a club of two, which is exactly what you want when you're sixteen – or maybe at any age.

One day Gideon asked if I wanted to go and see one of our favourite bands play live. The most exciting thing about this concert was that it was in a city that was a couple of hours away by train: there was no chance we would be able to get back home the same night. Gideon already had a plan: we would sleep in the railway station, get the first train the next morning and be back in time for school. When I was sixteen and in love, the thought of sleeping on a cold station platform was wonderfully appealing and romantic, though these days I don't go anywhere unless *en-suite* facilities and drinkable tap water are guaranteed.

I told my mum (this was before the lights of Cincinnati called her back home) that I would be staying at Heather's for the night. I don't think Gideon told his parents anything: staying out all night was as good a way as any to get up their noses.

I got ready in my newly adopted all-black uniform, to which I added an old raincoat from Oxfam. I covered my mouth in dark purple lipstick, and was pretty pleased with the result.

My mum looked up from her magazine as I was leaving the house. 'It's not Hallowe'en already, is it?' was her hilarious comment, then she carried on with the article she'd been reading.

I'd arranged to meet Gideon at the station, and was glad he was already there when I arrived. It was very dark and cold and I'd already been at the receiving end of a couple of muttered abusive comments on my way down the road. It was that kind of town: even looking modestly 'alternative' was seen as dangerous. He was standing waiting for me in front of the ticket office, looking like a dark angel. Under his ever-present long leather coat he was wearing black leather trousers, black shirt and Dr Marten's ten-eyelet boots.

'Well, look at you,' he said, giving me the usual bear hug, which was as physical as we ever got. We were a mutual-appreciation society, and ignored the disgusted looks of our fellow passengers.

It was a different story when we got to the venue. I suddenly felt under-dressed and small-town dowdy in the company of people who were dressed to thrill and with the confidence to match. It was total bliss.

My mum had once told me that she'd been to that same venue before I was born, to see the Walker Brothers. There wasn't much in the way of amplification in those days, and what with all the girls screaming and jumping about, my mother and her friends had been unable either to hear or see the lovely Scott. They left after half an hour in disgust. I wondered what they would make of this: sound amplified so loud you could feel the vibration through your entire body; so loud that bits of plaster were falling from the ceiling.

It was fantastic: the lights, the people, the music, the heat. In the middle of it all, I suddenly felt so overwhelmingly happy that I turned to Gideon and threw my arms around his neck, giving him a big hug. His arms went around my waist, and somehow we were kissing. In the middle of the bouncing, shoving crowd, the noise and general mayhem, we were the still, calm centre while everything went crazy around us; there was only the feel of his arms around me and his mouth on mine, his soft, soft tongue gently moving in my mouth, a kiss that lasted for ever while the world swung in slow motion around us and the deafening noise became just a background buzz. Then the lights were going up and we stepped away from each other, watching each other's eyes and grinning fit to bust.

We walked out of the concert hall hand in hand and there were hundreds of people around and no one else in the world. Outside in the cold air he kissed me again, as we stood ankle-deep in discarded flyers in the noisy darkness. Most of my purple lipstick had transferred to his mouth, but it just added to his habitual look of contrary decadence.

'So then you spent all night shagging each other senseless in the railway station, right?' Heather said, which was exactly why I hadn't told her about it at the time: it had been such a pure and perfect thing that to talk about it would have felt like sacrilege.

'No, we didn't,' I said, defensive even now. She pulled a face. 'It was the waiting room of a main-line railway station!' I protested. 'There were other people there.' We'd spent the night with our arms wrapped tightly round each other, and I'd felt happier than I'd ever been before.

Our glasses were empty, and Jack the barman spotted this and sauntered over. He was Tom Cruise, all right, but in *The Color of Money*: all he was missing was the pool cue. And Paul Newman, of course.

'Can I get you ladies anything else?' he asked.

'Waiter service in here now, is it?' Heather asked him.

He gave her one of those northern-boys-on-the-pull smiles

that I've never found convincing, and said, 'Only for our very favoured customers.'

Having dispatched the eager Jack to the bar with our order, she turned to me and said, 'He's quite cute, isn't he?'

'He's a bit young though,' I said, 'and *you*'re married.'

She pulled a face. 'Theoretically. Anyway, it's only a bit of flirting, and Pierre's safely in Birmingham. Where's the harm?' Normally I would have believed her, but there was something brittle about Heather that weekend that made me worry for her.

When Jack returned he said, 'Is it invitation only, this school reunion?'

'Yes, it is,' I said, a tad sullenly. I was starting to remember why a night out with Heather wasn't always such a great laugh.

'But you're invited,' Heather added, with no shame at all.

'Cool!' Jack said. 'I get off here at eleven. D'you reckon it'll still be going then?'

'Should be,' Heather said.

'If all us oldies aren't tucked up with our Horlicks by then,' I added, but they ignored me.

'Cool,' he repeated. 'I'll see you there, then.'

'Cool,' Heather said approvingly, to his youthful rear end as he returned to the bar.

The Art Of Parties

As the taxi pulled up outside the school, the odd thing was how small it looked. It was hard to imagine how scared I'd felt the first time I'd walked in there, how the corridors seemed to go on for miles and were full of people who, although they were dressed in school uniforms exactly like mine, looked to all intents and purposes like adults. I remembered a sixth-former who'd shown me which room I was supposed to go to first: she had bright red hair, a large nose, glasses, and a pair of fully developed breasts that thrust her school tie out at an angle to her body. I was torn between being terrified of her and wanting to hide behind her cardigan until Mummy came to take me home.

But the memory that came to me first whenever I thought of that school was a smell. It must have been a certain kind of furniture polish or something, a strong, acidic, somehow biblical smell, that was always very noticeable on the first day of term. And I always picture a particular tract of corridor outside the vast dining room, where the polish smell gave way to a stink of overboiled greens and nasty meat, and the walls were covered in glass trophy cabinets with silver cups and wooden plaques bearing the names of people who'd been pupils of the school before it was even in its present building.

We stepped inside, with me hovering behind Heather. The entrance hall had changed a lot since I was last there – posters proclaiming the 'After School IT Club', 'Tae Kwon Do' and, most bizarrely, 'MixMaster Mr Wells' Drum'n'Bass Workshop' replaced the cabinets of football and cricketing trophies – but the smell was exactly as I'd remembered.

A sturdy, heavily pregnant woman with the kind of hairstyle favoured by Rod Stewart in the mid-seventies was wedged into a chair next to a small table. She waved enthusiastically when she saw us. 'You made it, then!' she yelled, over 'Too Shy' by Kajagoogoo. I guessed this must be Judith Bardsley, matriarch of the Bardsley clan and self-appointed school archivist. The three of us exchanged hugs and kisses, which was the first time in my life I'd ever had physical contact with her. 'Don't forget your name stickers,' she said, peeling Day-Glo orange labels from a sheet and proffering them. Heather stuck hers on her handbag and I put mine on my upper arm like a tattoo. 'You unconventional girls,' Judith chided. I glanced at the sheet of stickers: about a quarter of them still remained, and among them was the name of Gideon Harker. He was probably waiting till late so he could make an entrance: that had always been his style.

When I was very young, I remember seeing a TV series called *Timeslip*, which was about a couple of badly dressed teenagers who travelled, as the title hinted, in time. The gateways to the different time zones were invisible and occurred fairly randomly – for example, you could stumble across one disguised as a barbed-wire fence, or in a derelict house, or (during an adventure set in the Arctic) behind a small polystyrene iceberg. Today a time portal had apparently opened in what used to be known as the dinner hall, but was now labelled 'Foodish Things Restaurant': flashing disco lights and the sound of 'Ay Ay Ay Ay Moosey' by Modern Romance (now, whatever happened to them?), coupled with that smell, made it feel as if, behind those doors, the 1980s had never stopped. As Heather pushed open the door I fully expected to see the girls ranged along the left side of the room and the boys on the right, with a patrol of teachers between them trying to foster some kind of social interaction.

But the class of '85 had grown up. Now the thirty-somethings who were filling the hall were fully fledged adults, established in their grown-up lives and with a certain amount of social poise, and the room was full of interaction, people circulating and chatting with practised confidence. Polite chit-chat filled the air, and no one was left hugging the wall. It was most disturbing.

'All it needs is someone to bring in a tray of Ferrero Rocher,' I muttered to Heather.

At my first bewildered glance it looked as though the room was full of strangers, and I didn't recognise a single person. Middleton Road was a big school with people travelling in from a wide catchment area, so there were a lot of people who'd been in the same year as me whom I hadn't really known. Even though Gideon's name sticker had still been there, it was possible he had slipped in without Judith knowing, and my eyes cast about for someone tall and thin. I had to assume that the leather coat had finally disintegrated, but other than that I had no idea what he might look like.

'Oh, my *God*!' Heather shrieked, and when I turned to look, someone whom I couldn't identify other than to say he was male was gripping her in a bear hug. The bear eventually let go of Heather and turned to hug me.

'Cass! You look gorgeous too!' Ian Kane said, holding me at arm's length in that let-me-look-at-you way. 'Look who's here!' he shouted, over his shoulder, to a nearby group of men in suits. They looked up like meerkats sniffing the air and came over to us. My heart was having trouble keeping pace, as each new face aroused a tiny shock of hope and disappointment. None of them was Gideon, but who were they? I suddenly realised I couldn't remember anyone's name, but Heather was equal to the task.

'David Archer, Fishy Salmon and Purple Hayes!' she yelled. 'It's raining men! Hallelujah!' She flung her arms out wide. Trust Heather to be word-perfect on the boys' names. Hugs were exchanged, Fishy brought us all a drink and then everyone launched into exactly the kind of small-talk Greg had predicted. As always, Heather was the centre of attention, much to the annoyance of Steven Salmon's wife and Gary Hayes' girlfriend, who were introduced and then more or less ignored. I knew that I was also very much a supporting feature to the star act, so I chatted to the spurned partners for a few minutes before realising that they'd prefer to bitch about Heather without the inconvenience of having one of her friends present. After a while I wandered off on the pretext of getting something to eat, stepping through little moonbeams from the overhead mirror ball as they chased across the stiletto-pocked parquet, all the while looking for Gideon.

There was a long trestle table loaded with a buffet, and a few people were filling up plates with prawn cocktail, Coronation chicken and vol-au-vents garnished with little clumps of parsley and zigzag-edged tomato halves. A woman with dead straight, shiny dark hair and glasses looked up as I approached.

'Hi,' she said. 'I know you. I *know* I know you.' She tried to peer at the Day-Glo sticker on my arm.

'Cass Thomson,' I said.

She didn't look any the wiser for a second, then a lightbulb went on and she put out the hand that wasn't holding a pineapple chunk on a stick to shake mine. Of course,' she said. 'Sarah Jones – Rowland as was. We used to sit at the same table for domestic science in the fifth year.' Oh, God, domestic science. If I'd inherited anything from my mother it was her lack of domestic skills. I was one of those girls whose Victoria sponge came out of the oven with the look and feel of a frisbee, and as for needlework, I was banned from touching a sewing-machine for an entire term because I somehow managed to cause two to explode in a single lesson.

'Sarah. How lovely. And what are you doing now?' I asked politely, though I couldn't really have cared less. All I could remember about her was that her partypiece at school was being able to do an uncanny impression of a kookaburra. She gestured with a sweeping motion across the buffet table. Well, *obviously*, we were both eating; that was fairly self-evident, I would have thought.

'No, I meant job-wise,' I said.

She slid the pineapple chunk off the stick with her teeth. 'I'm a cook,' she said. 'I run a small catering firm. I did the buffet.'

'Oh, I see. Very nice,' I said, nibbling a vol-au-vent with

polite enthusiasm. 'Great food. And it was a clever idea to have an eighties theme to it.'

'How do you mean?' She looked genuinely puzzled, and I experienced the horrible realisation that this must be her standard party buffet, whatever the occasion. Maybe we were in a timeslip after all: I sensed that the words *ciabatta* and *sashimi* wouldn't be found in her vocabulary or Nigella Lawson on her bookshelf. I tried to resist feeling superior and metropolitan, and failed. She was still looking at me in that puzzled way, and I was about to employ the old toilet excuse and escape, but she hadn't finished with me yet.

'You were a punk rocker,' she said inaccurately, looking at me as if I might be about to gob in the coleslaw. 'I was a bit scared of you,' she admitted. 'You and that what's-his-name, the tall, lanky one with the hair. Is he here too?' She peered around as if he was possibly concealing his rangy frame behind a tray of sausage rolls.

'I don't know,' I said, hoping it came out like *and I don't care, either.* 'Anyway, I'd better circulate. If I stand here too long there'll be none of this yummy food left for anyone else!'

'Here,' she said, as I turned to leave. She tossed me something gold and spherical. 'Take a Ferrero Rocher with you.'

I walked back across the room to where I'd left the others, the whumpa-whumpa-whumpa-whumpa bassline of 'Relax' by Frankie Goes To Hollywood vibrating in my chest.

Heather had found yet another man; she was clutching at his arm and laughing like a maniac at something he'd just said.

'Cass! Look who's here!' For an unsettling second I thought it was my dad: he was about the same age my dad had been when I'd last seen him. 'It's Sex God!' Heather shrieked, and she and the bloke started having hysterics again. 'We all fancied *you*,' she said to him. '*You* did, didn't you, Cass?' It would have been marginally less embarrassing if I could have worked out who on earth he was.

'Of course,' Heather continued regardless, 'Cass knew there was no future for you and her. She could never have married you: she'd have been Cass Castle, and that sounds more like a speech impediment than a name.' Light dawned: it was Mr Castle. As in third-year physics. And, yes, I had fancied him a bit; most of the girls did, because he looked a lot like Richard Beckinsale in *Porridge*, and we *had* called him Sex God. I wondered nervously how much more embarrassment Heather could possibly cause me.

The evening wore on. We were joined by Alison and her husband, and various other people appeared, introduced themselves, chatted a while and moved on. Everyone was getting pretty drunk, and when the DJ played 'Come On Eileen' by Dexy's Midnight Runners, Heather grabbed my arm.

'Come on!' she yelled. 'Let's dance!' She yanked at Alison, and the three of us took up position in the centre of the dance-floor area and commenced dancing around Alison's handbag, with me still keeping a close eye on the door watching for any tall newcomers. We were joined by Ian and his mates, Sex God and a couple of other people I vaguely recognised, all moving in the self-conscious, stiff-jointed manner of people who haven't danced in a long time.

The record finished, and the next one was 'Don't You Want Me' by the Human League, the DJ having realised that his audience was ready for participation. Heather and Alison started enthusiastically to sing the girls' parts, but I left them to it and went to find a drink.

I sat down in a corner half hidden by a stack of chairs, and looked around at my former classmates. It was so strange seeing them all, because when you think about people you haven't seen for a long time they stay preserved in your memory exactly how they were when you last saw them, but here they were, all grown-up, drinking and smoking quite blatantly in front of the teachers, socialising and scoffing quiche Lorraine, getting pissed. I imagined the conversation I'd be having if Gideon was here.

'What's that thing called that Janet Cooper's wearing?'

'I believe it's known as a shrug.'

'A shrug? It looks like two sleeves in search of a cardigan.'

Someone sat next to me: David Archer. I'd always liked him: at school he was thoughtful and quiet, a shy person who seemed always about to apologise for his presence. He'd certainly improved with age: compared to Ian, who was getting slightly jowly, and some of the others, David seemed to be the kind of man who, like Martin Kemp, gets better-looking as he gets older.

'This is a bit odd, isn't it?' he said. I nodded. 'Heather seems to be on good form,' he observed. I wondered privately how good Heather was really feeling, and whether at least some of this *joie de vivre* was a smokescreen because things were less than brilliant in her marriage.

'And how are you?' I asked him.

'Oh, you know, busy,' he said.

'What is it you do again?'

'I'm a doctor,' he said.

'You're kidding?'

He shook his head. 'I'm trying to keep it quiet,' he said. 'Otherwise I'd spend the whole night listening to people telling me all about their ailments. I've had many a good party ruined that way.'

I laughed. 'But wasn't it you who fainted in that biology lesson when we had to test a blood sample?' I asked him. He looked a teeny bit embarrassed and nodded. At school, if we'd had a vote for the person least likely to become a doctor, David Archer would have won it. He was horribly squeamish, and because he came alphabetically first in the class, he was always first in line for injections. Invariably he would faint and have to be carried out of the nurse's office, past everyone else queuing for their turn. I imagine a few bets were lost among the careers teachers when *he* went into medicine.

'You can't let something like that spoil your life,' he said, or rather shouted: the competition from the Human League was pretty stiff. 'Even though I was a bit of a softie, I always wanted to be a doctor. I decided the only way to get over it was to see as much gore as possible, so Harker sorted me out a job at the hospital, through his parents.'

'Did he? I never knew that.'

'Oh, yes. I spent a glorious summer washing surgical instruments and catheter tubing.'

'How fragrant.'

'It was disgusting, but it did the trick.' We watched our former classmates dancing for a minute; the song playing was 'Agadoo', which involved a lot of imaginary pineapple-pushing and tree-shaking. Heather's hair shone in rainbow colours in the disco lights.

'So have you seen him? Harker?' David asked.

My heart flipped. 'Is he here?'

'I don't know. I don't think so, and that's not what I meant, really. To be honest, I didn't think he would come,' he said. 'He wrote to me a couple of times when he was at Cambridge, and he didn't seem to have very fond memories of this place.'

I felt doubly stung: that he'd written to David Archer but not to me, and that he didn't have fond memories of Middleton Road. What about me? What about all the things we'd done together, everything we'd shared? It might not have ended so well, but surely he'd had plenty of fond memories, like I did, like I'd been having all day. I felt such a fool. I'd come to this reunion, I had to admit it, with the express hope of seeing him again; maybe I'd thought that there would still be something between us, that he would still be my steadfast Gabriel Oak, my guardian angel.

Idiot.

'Do you still hear from him?' I asked David, not sure if I really wanted to know.

He shook his head. 'Not for years. Just a couple of letters when we were both in the first year at university. I've no idea where he is now, or what he's doing.'

'At university, was he . . . seeing anyone?' I don't know why I needed to know this, but I did. David gave me the sort of look I suppose he gave to patients before he told them they had something incurable.

'First year at university?' he said. 'Weren't we all?'

Steppin' Out

Needing to be alone and finding somewhere to do it are two different things when there's a party in progress. The toilets were fairly obviously out: by now they'd be full of women retouching makeup and bitching about how badly the other women had aged. I thought maybe I could sit down for a while in the deserted cloakroom, but as I approached I overheard: 'It's his bowel habits I can't tolerate. He does these turds that remind me of those hillbillies in *Deliverance*: they hide round the bend and wait to pop up and terrify you when your guard's down!' I kept walking, and ended up outside.

The night was cool and breezy, making goosebumps stand up on my arms. I made my way to a particular spot at the edge of the playing-field. Schoolgirls are creatures of habit: in the same way that we'd always sat at the same table in the Duke of York, on hot summer days we'd always sat in exactly the same place in the school field. It was about fifteen feet away from the boundary wall, far enough away from the building to prevent teachers sneaking up on you and near enough to the boys' side to afford a good view. Every Tuesday lunchtime we'd rushed there after attempting to eat the disgusting offering that had been presented to us as 'lunch', turned on the radio that Alison always carried in her red PVC tote bag and listened to the Radio 1 charts, which we took very seriously indeed. As I sat there I could almost hear the ponk of tennis balls hitting rackets and the screeches of the little kids playing chasing games; could picture the boys, and one in particular, in white school shirts, with their collars open and sleeves rolled up on long, hot summer days.

It sounded as though the party was going well; the DJ was now mining the rich and horribly irritating seam that was *Stars on 45*, and the occasional high-pitched squeal or laugh broke through the ambient din, indicating that the class of '85 was getting well and truly plastered.

Living even on the periphery of London you hardly ever see a sky full of stars; usually the night sky is a sickly yellow colour and it's never really dark at all, but here the sky was clear and amazingly starry.

Okay, Harker, I thought, *so you weren't bothered about seeing me. I guess it's finally sunk in after all these years that you've gone.* I was never going to see him all grown-up and maybe it was better that way: he could stay in my memory, a thing of beauty and a boy for ever.

I was shivering; the air was cold and the green silk dress was designed for glamour rather than warmth, but I wasn't ready to go back inside. I folded my arms tightly around my knees, in a manner that my former biology teacher Mrs Potter, also known as 'Bones' (due to her resemblance to Dr McCoy on *Star Trek*), would have described as 'reducing the surface-area-to-volume ratio'.

You only start being bothered about the cold when you get

older: teenagers don't feel the cold at all, or they manage to ignore it, at least. When we were very young and had nowhere to go because even the Duke of York drew the line at thirteen-year-olds, we used to spend a lot of evenings just walking around the streets. Alison, Heather and I would stay out in our sleeveless summer tops and shorts until we were freezing cold, but somehow we didn't feel it. The excitement of being out as the evening turns to dusk, left to our own devices, was far more intoxicating than the under-age drinking turned out to be; of course, even that excitement soon paled in comparison to being in love.

I remembered Gideon walking me home on a frosty night years later, and how quiet it had been. The cold was penetrating my Oxfam raincoat and I was walking slowly and carefully in suede ankle-boots. Gideon was more practical in his combat boots and was planting his feet confidently on the slippery ground with that big, lolloping stride, and I hung on to his leather-covered arm for balance. Street lights threw shadows of thin twigs of tree branches across the path, making the pavement look like it had shattered into pieces with the cold, and everything sparkled with frost. The sky was black and full of stars, like now. And like now there was a taste of alcohol in my mouth, but along with it a giddy feeling from the alcohol and the cold night and hanging on to his arm and laughing so much and stopping every few yards because we couldn't go a step further without kissing each other. He stopped to pluck a late rose for me from someone's neat front garden, leaning out across the little knee-high wall, in his slightly drunken state leaning a bit too far and falling over into the rose bush, climbing back out with his hands scratched with thorns and holding out to me one perfect cream-coloured bloom.

I realised someone was walking towards me. It was Alison.

'Thought you'd be out here,' she said, sitting down next to me. She took out a cigarette and lit it.

'You didn't used to smoke,' I said.

She laughed, blowing out smoke. 'I didn't, until I found out just how much peace and quiet it can buy you. As soon as they banned smoking in the office, and the smokers were disappearing outside for ten minutes every hour, I thought I'd better get in on that, too – it'd be daft not to. And at home I can't smoke in front of the kids, so I get to go outside and sit in the garden while Pete watches them. Honestly, I'd go mad without it.'

'A shame about the lung cancer, the heart disease and so on.'

She shrugged. 'If it's that or my sanity, I'll take the risk.'

'Are things that bad?'

'No,' she said, surprised that I could think it. 'Life's pretty good, on the whole. But till you have kids you don't realise how little free time you're going to have. It's nice to have an excuse to get away from that incessant "Mummy-Mummy-Mummy". But look at you – you're freezing.' Sensibly, she'd put her coat on before coming out, and she was also wearing a scarf, which she now took off and placed around my shoulders. It was warm and smelt of smoke and Opium perfume. 'So *I'm* out here on a fag break,' she said. 'What's your excuse for sitting here freezing your bum off in your posh frock?'

'Reminiscence trip,' I said.

She sighed. 'I know. It is a bit weird, isn't it? The funniest bit is introducing Pete to everybody, like two completely separate parts of my life have somehow collided. It's kind of how I imagine my funeral would be, if that doesn't sound morbid. All these people who'd never met each other before, all together in the same place just because they knew me at some point in their lives.'

'Pete seems nice,' I said, because I thought it was probably expected of me.

'Yeah,' she said, indulgently. 'He's a sweetheart and he's

brilliant with the kids.' She told me about her two boys, and about her job as a legal assistant, and I told her about my job, and about Greg, and hugged her scarf more tightly around my shoulders. We sat in silence for a few minutes, and I realised that even while I was talking about him, Greg didn't seem quite real. Out of sight, out of mind, as we used to say.

'You'll never guess what?' Alison said eventually. 'I was just talking to our old geography teacher – you remember, Miss Finbar? – and apparently Okey-dokey's dead.' I was shocked, and couldn't think of anything to say in reply. 'He had cancer, Miss Finbar said. Died last year. Only fifty-five.'

I felt unexpectedly sad, maybe not so much for the real Okey-dokey as for the myth that I'd made of him in my mind: it was like Tweety-pie hearing that Sylvester the Cat was dead. I wondered whether I would still have those nightmares of being lost on the way to one of his classes. 'It's funny to think how much power those teachers used to have over us,' I said. 'They were like an alien species.'

'But so were parents,' Alison said, 'anybody who was old. And now I'm a parent, and I don't feel any different from when I was a pupil at this place. I don't feel like I've joined the aliens.'

'I certainly don't feel like I've joined the *teachers*,' I said. 'I still can't quite bring myself to treat them like equals.'

'Heather can. She's all over Sex God.'

'Sex God always was a bit of an exception, though.' We lapsed into a little silence while we contemplated the loveliness that used to light up third-year physics.

Then Alison said, 'Is Heather all right?' I pretended not to know what she meant. 'Well, she was always a bit wild, but she seems, I don't know . . . not very happy. Like it's all for show.' I'd forgotten how perceptive Alison could be.

'I think it's all a bit strange,' I said.

'Is that why you're out here freezing to death on the school field?'

'I told you,' I said, 'I just wanted to be on my own for a minute.'

Alison regarded me with her huge dark eyes. 'I suppose I ought to be going back in,' she said eventually. 'I left Pete talking to Purple Hayes about motorbikes, so he quite possibly hasn't noticed I'm not there, but I shouldn't leave him too long.' That was Alison, always looking out for other people. 'Are you coming too?' I nodded: I was so cold my teeth had started to chatter. Alison took my arm and we walked back to the school. As we got to the door she turned to me and said, 'The first cut is always the deepest, Cass. But even the deepest cut heals.'

It's very worrying when your old friend starts coming over all P.P. Arnold at you. I've always found that phrase particularly nonsensical anyway: why *should* the first cut be the deepest? But I squeezed her arm, and we walked back to the party.

One Step Beyond

Back inside, a few people were dancing to Madness. I could see my former admirer Gary Coningsborough, who hadn't improved with age, attempting to do a 'nutty' dance, and failing spectacularly. Alison rejoined Pete and I looked around for Heather but hadn't managed to locate her before I was accosted by a tall, freckle-faced woman who was smiling at me broadly with teeth so small and regular her mouth looked like a rack of Travel Scrabble letters.

'Louise Dunn,' she announced, and we kissed each other on the cheek. It was odd how practised I was getting at embracing people I'd never touched before. Louise, with whom I had been quite friendly at school but hadn't thought of since, was apparently something of a local celebrity.

'You might have seen us on TV,' she said, referring to herself and her partner Craig, who was replenishing his plate at the buffet table. I replied that, sadly, I hadn't. 'Oh, yes,' she said, as if I'd been doubting the truth of her words. 'We were on *When Good Holidays Go Bad: 4* on satellite.'

'I don't have satellite.'

'Oh, that's a shame,' she said sincerely. Craig joined us, and I took an instant dislike to him in his too-tight shirt, which seemed designed to show off his bulging muscles and tree-trunk of a neck. 'Sweetie, I was just telling Cass – this is Cass, by the way – about the time we were on *When Good Holidays Go Bad: 4.*'

Craig launched into an unnecessarily detailed description of the nightmare Caribbean cruise that he'd been clever enough to capture on video. 'We were damn lucky,' he concluded. 'Ended up with the cost of the cruise plus almost a grand in compen. *And* we got to meet Carol Vorderman.'

'She's ever so nice,' Louise added warmly. 'Totally natural, just like she is on *Countdown*. No side to her at all.'

'She would have come for her dinner with us, except she said she had to meet her agent,' Craig said. Quick thinking on Carol's part, I assumed.

'She did say she hoped we would enjoy our meal, though,' said Louise proudly, wrapping up an exciting tale of life among the glitterati. Perhaps she'd noticed that I was less than gripped by her brush with the rich and famous, because her eyes seemed already to be searching out the next person who hadn't heard the story; she wasn't looking at me, at any rate.

'Is that who I think it is?' she hissed to Craig, who immediately responded by squaring his shoulders and making a bobbing motion with his head, like a chicken. These are gestures that in the working-class male generally indicate that a fight is in the offing. I turned round to try and make out the intended target.

'It's that little shit who works at the Casino Royale,' Craig muttered, shoving his paper plate towards Louise and advancing towards Jack the barman, who had just appeared in the doorway.

'He's got no business in here,' Louise said.

Jack was peering through the smoky fog, trying I suppose to locate Heather, ignorant that he was being advanced upon by a brick-shithouse northern bloke in fight mode. I started after Craig, thinking I ought somehow to intervene, as I had at least been present when Jack was invited to the proceedings.

Louise was right at my heels, twittering, 'Don't interfere, Cass. Let Craig sort it out.' Which was exactly what I didn't want Craig to do.

A second before Craig and his fists were about to arrive at their destination, Heather appeared from nowhere. She placed herself neatly between Jack and the advancing Craig, took Jack's arm and bore him off in a manner that left Craig and his adrenaline all worked up with nowhere to go.

'What the hell is *she* playing at?' he wanted to know, which was a fair question under the circumstances, but I was spared having to answer by a sudden outbreak of squealing at the other end of the room. The DJ turned down the volume of 'House Of Fun' to ask if there was a doctor in the room, and I noticed David Archer reluctantly materialise from a group that included Ian Kane, Gary 'Purple' Hayes and girlfriend, Steven Salmon and wife, Alison and Alison's Pete.

I couldn't resist following him to see what was going on, and was greeted by the sight of a tableau of women crumpled on the floor clutching variously at ankles, knees and elbows. It appeared that some of the erstwhile members of the school's gymnastics team, encouraged by excessive alcohol consumption, had decided to re-create their past glories and perform some of their old moves. Unfortunately it had been a bad decision to attempt the splits in kitten heels on polished parquet, with legs that weren't as flexible as in their heyday. Two had suffered only an embarrassingly clumsy topple to the ground, but the third, whom I recognised as shrug-wearing former form captain Janet Cooper, was evidently in some agony. The assembled crowd watched with interest as David attempted to pop a dislocated kneecap back into its socket accompanied by Madness playing 'One Step Beyond'.

Wake Me Up Before You Go Go

I was woken the next morning by an insistent tapping on my door. I eased myself out of bed, feeling a little dehydrated and headachy, and opened the door a crack. Heather was standing in the corridor in a pale green dressing-gown that almost exactly matched the colour of her face, clutching her handbag to her chest.

She went straight to my bed and got into it, leaning her head back against the pillow with a sigh; the handbag was abandoned on the floor. I sat down on the chair next to the bed; it was like visiting someone in hospital.

'Good morning,' I said pointedly.

'Could you possibly bring me a glass of water?' she croaked, without opening her eyes. I went dutifully to the bathroom and ran the tap to let the water get cold. 'Not so loud!' I heard Heather moan. I brought her the water and a couple of paracetamol (I never travel anywhere without paracetamol). She drank the water slowly, testing its impact on her stomach, then subsided back into the pillow.

'I didn't know if he was the kind to steal the family silver, so I brought my bag,' she said.

'Pardon?'

'Jack. I've left him in there still asleep, but then I thought I'd best bring my money and car keys and so on because, after all, I don't really know him from Adam.'

'You spent the night with Jack?'

Heather opened her eyes and gave me a look. 'Please tell me you're not going to "do" moral indignation,' she said.

'Of course not,' I said. 'It's none of my business anyway.' Though I did wonder how you could trust someone with your body if you couldn't trust them with your handbag.

Heather yawned. 'He's one of those people who sleeps all sprawled out. I haven't had even one minute of sleep all night.' I thought she'd nodded off, but then she said, 'How did you get back, then?'

'Alison and Pete gave me a lift,' I said. 'We looked for you, but we couldn't find you. I guessed you'd gone off with Jack.'

'We were already back here, probably,' she said, and stretched again, turned on to her side and promptly fell asleep. In my bed, which I hadn't been quite ready to get out of myself.

It was so early I would actually be in time for Mrs Chainey serving breakfast, so I had a quick shower, dressed and went downstairs. Too late, I noticed that the Olivers were already at their table, looking as usual like a pristine version of Tweedledum and Tweedledee. Sharon insisted I join them, and there was no option but to do so.

'Are you sure you won't be coming back with us?' she wanted to know.

Philip looked as embarrassed as he had a right to be, and said, 'Darling, I *told* you Cass wants to visit relatives on the way home.' So that was the excuse he'd come up with, the little hairy-kneed creep.

'Who was that toyboy I saw Heather with last night?' Sharon asked, in a transparently mock-offhand manner. I feigned ignorance, though I had the horrible feeling that Jack was going to descend the staircase at any moment in search of Heather, breakfast or both. 'She made a complete show of herself,' Sharon said, rather tactlessly considering she knew well that Heather and I were friends.

'Not as much of a show as Janet Cooper.' Philip waded in with what, for him, was an impressive display of diplomacy.

'Still, I always think a party isn't a party until the ambulance turns up,' I said, and then there was a silence while they devoured their boiled eggs. I didn't feel up to anything except toast and coffee, and it was making me somewhat queasy to watch Philip dunk his bread soldier into the yolk of his egg.

As soon as I could I went back upstairs. I wanted to catch the earliest train possible: I'd had enough of this place and just wanted to be back in my little flat at Coltsfoot Hall.

Heather was in the bathroom washing her face. 'That's better,' she said. 'Now I'm off to boot him out so I can get dressed.'

'I'm leaving in a minute,' I said, 'as soon as I've packed.'

Heather sat down on the bed, running her hand through her mop of shiny blonde hair. 'Did I behave very badly last night?' she asked.

'The general view seems to be that you did,' I said, 'but it doesn't matter what other people think.'

'It does. It matters what you think.'

'I think . . . Well, you're obviously not very happy, the way things are at home and so on.'

She nodded carefully, as if vigorous nodding was out of the question. 'That's true, I'm not happy. And don't expect me to feel guilty about last night, because I don't.' She rubbed her nose with the back of her hand, like she used to do at school if she was in any kind of trouble; she'd had to make a conscious effort to stop doing it when she started wearing makeup because it brought the foundation off her nose. 'Okay, so I do feel guilty. A bit. I mean, last night would never have happened if I wasn't feeling all insecure about Pierre.' She looked at me. 'But at least I managed to enjoy myself, just for a short time, and didn't spend the whole day moping around like a wet Wednesday like some people.'

'Meaning me?'

'Of *course* you. Look at yourself,' she said. She pulled her dressing-gown tighter around herself in a way that reminded me of my mother, though even with a matching green face and dressing-gown, Heather still managed to look beautiful. 'You came here for one thing only. It wasn't to see me, or Alison, or to see if the old home town looked the same. You came to see Punky Harker.'

I sat down on the bed. 'You know, through all of my parents' divorce and everything, he was there for me,' I said.

'Well, he's not there now,' she said, realistically but not unkindly.

'Still . . . it's funny, but I always thought I'd see him again.'

'You have to be realistic,' she said. 'You always were given to over-romanticising things. Gary Numan, for one.'

'That wasn't me, that was Annette Gillingham.'

She considered this for a second. 'Yeah, that was Annette. You were more into Adam Ant and Paul Weller, and then all that techno rubbish.'

'It wasn't techno and it wasn't rubbish,' I countered, but had no energy for a debate on my former musical tastes. 'Oh, Heather,' I said, 'I feel like such a twit. Coming here has made me realise that I so much wish I could see him again. Even if it's to meet his wife and kids, or find out he's fat and ugly, or he's a serial killer, I've got to get him out of my system. For all I know, Greg could be Mr Right – it's not as though I have any serious objections to him – but I've got this idea of perfect love, and until I drag it out into the real world, no one else is going to ever match up.'

Heather put her arm around my shoulders. 'Before I met Pierre,' she said, 'I would have laughed at you and said you were just being over-romantic as usual. You mightn't have liked Gary Numan, but I've never known such a girl as you for having heroes. I could never have understood how you feel about Harker if I hadn't felt the same about Pierre. But by now I've realised that Pierre isn't as wonderful as he seemed. And, let's face it, no man is. They look perfect at the time, but if you could see them a couple of years down the line you'd find they were destined to go wrong some way or other. Look at Philip Oliver. Or even Ian. Time was when I could never go near him without wanting to fiddle with his hair – he had that kind of cuteness about him. But it's all gone now, and last night I just couldn't see what I'd found so attractive about him. Cunningly, Harker stayed away, so we never got to see how boring he is now, and I can practically guarantee that he *is* boring. Honestly, Cass, do you really think after three years' studying economics at Cambridge he's going to be Mr Punky Rebel any more? I don't think so. He'll have a decent job, and drive a nice car and have a wardrobe full of matching ties and shirts and a nice house full of nice kids. Forget about him. Be happy with what you've got.'

Passionate Friend

I sat on the train back to London, not sorry to be leaving the countryside that I had grown up in, even though this time I knew I would probably never be going back there again.

Heather had given me a lift to the station. We hugged each other tightly on the platform, both wishing we weren't going off in separate directions, she to the Midlands and I to London. At least one of the bonds of my youth was still strong.

'Keep in touch!' she yelled, as the train pulled out of the

station. 'And don't forget, if you ever want an X-ray, give me a call!' I waved out of the window at her until I could no longer see the bright flash of her hair.

Sinking back into my seat, I closed my eyes and let my mind go where it wanted to, which happened to be the winter of 1984–5, when the Band Aid song 'Do They Know It's Christmas?' was on the radio every fifteen minutes; the last winter of my school life. I was taking my A levels in a few months and, assuming I'd pass, I would be going to university in London.

Which university you were going to had been the hot topic of conversation in the sixth-form common room for months. We pored over prospectuses, comparing the photographs in them, judging places on the basis of the advertised facilities of the students' union and the hairstyles of the students in the photographs: 'I want to do computer science! Look at him – he's gorgeous!'

Of secondary importance to most of us was the academic information. I was only ever going to study English literature, so my choices weren't narrowed at all by my chosen field of study, not as if I'd wanted to do something obscure like marine biology. As to *where* I would study, I quite fancied somewhere picturesque like Bath, but the choice at that time seemed simple: I would go wherever Gideon was going.

As a final rebellion against his parents' ambitions for him to become a doctor, he'd decided he was going to study economics, and, in his phrase, 'become a capitalist bastard'. 'If they think I'm going to be a hypocrite like them, they're wrong,' he muttered. 'Pretending they're in it to help people. They're just making money, like everybody else, and that's what I'm going to do, except it won't be dressed up in a white coat. And I'm going to London: that's where everything happens. I want to live in a street where nobody gives a fuck what I look like or what I'm wearing or who my parents are, and nobody cares.'

'It sounds like it could be lonely,' I said, feeling that it wouldn't be him who was lonely – he'd always manage somehow – but it would be so lonely for me without him.

He gave my hand a reassuring squeeze. 'I'll be okay,' he said, 'because you'll be there too. Even if we don't apply to the same college, as long as you're somewhere in London, we won't be far apart. We can see each other all the time.' Somehow I felt like it wouldn't turn out quite like that, but I was mollified a little anyway.

He walked me home from school on a dark, stormy-looking January afternoon. The grey sky was so low it looked as if you could reach up and poke it with your finger, and that if you did the rain would come pouring out and never stop.

We paused at the gate. Sometimes he came in with me and we had some tea with my granddad, who despite initial horror had rather taken to the 'weirdo' I was always hanging around with. On days when he didn't come in for tea he would give me a kiss at the gate and go off to do some revision.

Kissing Gideon was the loveliest thing in the world, but it was getting harder and harder to let him go. I was starting to wonder how I could let him know that I wouldn't mind more than just kissing. On this subject the magazines that were my main source of relationship information were no help at all. Their agony aunts always counselled that if a boy was worth having, he would respect your right to wait until you were 'ready'. Being 'ready' was assumed to be so far down the line into womanhood that it was beyond the scope of those magazines. They had no advice for a girl who was ready, and steady, and twitching to go. And yet again there was no one to ask, because even though I strongly suspected that Heather and Ian had long ago graduated past the snogging stage, nice girls just *didn't*. Talk about it, that is.

That day he was going to go back to the library, and he bent down to kiss me before he left. I loved the feel of his mouth on mine and tried to communicate as much love as possible for him through my lips, willing him to understand. He hugged me, my face pressing into his shoulder. My back was to the house, so Gideon was facing it, and he suddenly said, 'That's funny.'

'What is?'

'There are no lights on in your house.'

'Granddad must be out somewhere.'

'But the front door's open,' he said. I whipped round to look: he was right. My heart contracted with panic.

'Stay here,' Gideon said, and went to the door.

'Shouldn't we get the police?' I said. 'There might be a burglar or someone inside.' But he was already disappearing into the dark house, a tall, skinny shadow.

A couple of heart-stopped seconds passed before I heard him shout, 'Catherine! Quick!' I rushed inside, my hand automatically reaching for the light switch in the hallway as I did so. Nothing happened: no light. I made my way to the living room, which was empty, and then to the kitchen, where I could see two figures on the ground.

One looked up. 'Looks like he's had a fall,' Gideon said.

As my eyes got used to the darkness I could see my granddad lying on his side, very still. I knelt down next to him.

'He's unconscious,' Gideon said, 'but he's breathing. He'll be all right, Catherine, don't cry.' I hated going to pieces like that, but there wasn't anything else I could do, with the only member of my family I had left, the only one I really cared about, lying so still on the kitchen floor. Gideon stood up, and I heard him running upstairs.

He came back with a blanket, which he tucked round my grandfather. 'Where's the phone?' he asked me. I pointed back out into the hall. He disappeared again, and I could hear him talking to the emergency services and it felt like he was far away in another country and there was only me, and this unconscious old man who was probably dying, sitting on the kitchen floor in the dark.

'Fifteen minutes is too long,' I heard Gideon say. 'We need someone now.' A short pause then he said, 'Fine, okay,' and hung up. Then I heard him dial another number. 'Dad?'

I don't know whether having the lights on made things better or worse. If I'd been able to think about it at all, I suppose I would have assumed that there was a power cut, but Gideon had realised that some of the other houses nearby had been showing lights, and the street-lighting outside was on. Apparently a fuse had blown, and Granddad must have fallen while he was attempting to fix it; a stool was lying on its side on the kitchen floor. Gideon was tall enough not to need the stool anyway, and he quickly had the fuse changed and the lights back on. I was dazzled by the brightness and couldn't see for a second or two. Then when I could open my eyes properly I saw how bad Granddad looked. His face had a sickly grey-blue tint and a sort of collapsed, defeated look, his breathing was shallow and ragged, and he hadn't shown any sign of waking up since we'd been there. I was no use at all, and just sat holding his hand, crying, thinking how small and old he looked, and wishing he'd waited for Gideon to change the stupid fuse.

There was a peremptory knock on the door, and I had a second to notice Gideon's face set in some peculiar way, simultaneously defensive and something like defiant, then a tall, grey-haired man walked in carrying a doctor's bag.

'This is my dad,' Gideon said. His father resembled him only vaguely – I wouldn't have been able to pick him out in an identity parade – but oddly his face was wearing exactly the same defensive and defiant expression, and he and his son barely glanced at each other. He nodded at me, and squatted down next to my grandfather, taking his pulse, feeling his limbs gently for breaks, lifting his eyelids. 'How long has he been unconscious?' he said. I had no idea how long we'd been there.

'We found him about ten minutes ago, maybe a bit longer,' Gideon said.

'You've called an ambulance?'

'They said they'd be here in fifteen minutes.'

'Well, go outside and wait for them, then.' Gideon looked for a second as if he was going to refuse, as if disobedience came automatically, but he went outside anyway, and a short time later returned with two ambulance men.

Dr Harker rattled out what he knew about the 'case' then told the ambulance 'boys' that he would leave them to it. 'Do you want a lift back with me?' he asked Gideon, who looked disgusted at the idea.

'No, thank you. I'm going to the hospital with Catherine.' He looked at me. 'If you want me to?' Of course I did. I managed to mutter a thank-you to Dr Harker before he disappeared, and then we were in the ambulance, Gideon gripping my hand so tightly I thought he might crush my fingers.

Granddad was suffering from concussion, and they said he would have to stay in hospital at least overnight so they could keep an eye on him although he'd recovered consciousness in the ambulance. A kind-looking doctor said that it was lucky we'd found him when we had, as he could quite easily have had hypothermia: he'd been very chilled. I remembered Gideon going upstairs for a blanket, and wondered if I would have thought of that if he hadn't been there.

We left the hospital after seeing Granddad installed on a ward. I kissed him goodnight, and told him I'd be back to see him in the morning.

'Don't use this as an excuse to avoid your revision,' he said weakly, adding, 'Thanks, pet. And say thank you to Gideon.'

His eyes looked tired. 'Don't cry, Cass. I'm tough as old boots.' But even old boots wore out eventually, I thought, and I couldn't stop the tears.

Once again we were back outside the house.

'I'll come in with you,' Gideon said. 'You're still upset.' I realised that even though it was probably still very early I felt incredibly tired, as if I could sit down exactly where I was and go to sleep, but that I wouldn't have been able to bear going back into the empty house by myself.

He made us some tea and some toast and we sat down in front of the television; we watched *World in Action*, or maybe it was *Panorama*, some programme about the miners' strike. This precipitated a half-hearted political rant from Gideon, but we were both too preoccupied with the evening's events.

'I was glad to see that ambulance,' he said.

'I was glad to see your dad.'

'I'm never glad to see *him*.' His voice sounded so bitter, so completely unlike his usual voice. 'But he's a doctor, so what else was I supposed to do?' I'd learned not to ask him about his parents: most of the time he acted as if they lived on a different planet. It was something I half understood, having parents who for all practical purposes didn't exist, and I thought I understood the bitterness in his voice because it was the way I felt when I allowed myself to think of my father. It was just something else we had in common – parents who didn't particularly care about us.

'I suppose I should try and ring my mum,' I said, while we were on the subject of parents.

'Wait and see,' was Gideon's advice. 'There's no point in alarming her for nothing.'

We sat there for a while. I was conscious that Granddad's usual chair, closest to the gas fire and directly opposite the television, was empty, and I felt as if I might start to cry again.

'You should go to bed,' he said gently, stroking my cheek with his long fingers.

'Will you come, too?' I found myself saying. Without replying, he turned off the table lamp next to him and we went upstairs.

I felt him get into bed behind me; he put his arm across me and his breath felt warm as he kissed my neck. He snuggled tight against me, making me shiver wonderfully. I could feel the heat from his body and his heart beating hard against my back; his arm was comfortably heavy across my shoulders. I felt more warm and wrapped up and taken care of than I ever had in my life.

'Go to sleep,' he whispered. I wouldn't have believed I could have slept in such circumstances, would have thought that sleep would be impossible, but I felt an overpowering tiredness and a deep feeling of peace, and I felt myself drifting away.

Very early in the morning, for a few seconds I felt disoriented; I couldn't work out why I couldn't move my arm. I'd woken up next to him once before, in the station waiting room after the Cabaret Voltaire concert, but this was different: we were in my bed, and we were alone in the house. My first impulse was to sneak away, get dressed and respectable, pretend nothing was going on. Then vanity overtook me and I wondered if I could get up without disturbing him, clean my teeth, brush my hair and so on, and return to bed before he woke up so he wouldn't see the gruesome reality that was the early-morning me.

Instead, I couldn't help watching him while he slept, his hair flattened on the side of his head, his eyelashes perfect dark curves against his cheek. I loved looking at him, and even enjoyed the stomach-churning feeling I was experiencing as I waited for him to wake up.

Then he stirred and opened his eyes, and they were the purest green I'd ever seen, and he put his hands in my hair and kissed me.

I can't say that the earth moved and the stars sang a song just for us. We were shy with each other at first, and clumsy, all elbows and bony hips and too many arms, but we laughed a lot, and we were full of love, and even though it wasn't perfect we knew that with practice it would be. And we firmly intended to practise.

Is There Something I Should Know?

Coltsfoot Hall glowed in the late-afternoon sunshine like a basking cat, sure of its place in the scheme of things. It gave off such a feeling of endurance and permanence and, more importantly than that, it felt like home. My trip north might as well have been a dream, and it was already fading like a dream does as soon as you open your eyes and start looking at something that's real.

The front door was open for business, and I went inside. There were a few visitors wandering around, mainly elderly couples and families with kids. Stan was sitting behind the little information desk, and I went over to him.

'You're back, then?'

'How's it been?' I asked him.

'Not bad,' he said, after the tiniest of pauses.

'Meaning not that good, either?'

He shook his head. 'It's all those Alton Towers things,' he said, the lines on his face settling into a deeper frown than usual, 'all those theme parks. People don't want local history, they want thrills and spills.'

He was sounding uncannily like Randall Robertson without the sexual innuendoes, but to tell him so would have been the worst insult I could devise, so I tried being cheerful instead. 'It'll be Easter soon,' I said. 'Maybe it'll pick up then.'

He looked at me through those grey eyes that had seen over eighty years of history and knew a lost cause when they saw one. 'Maybe it will,' he said. 'Maybe it will.'

Hearing Stan trying, and failing, to sound optimistic made me feel more pessimistic about Coltsfoot Hall than ever before, but I didn't want to show it in front of him: it just made me more determined to do something about it.

My next stop was the coffee-shop, which wasn't as busy as it could be on a weekday, because the ladies-who-lunch spent Sunday doing lunch for their families instead. Still, about half of the tables were occupied, and it looked like Jackie and her weekend helper Chloë were being kept busy. There was a cheerful noise of chatter, the jangle of cutlery and crockery, and as always the homely, spicy smell of something freshly baked. Chloë, a small, eager-to-please sixth-former, was buttering bread for sandwiches behind the counter, and Jackie was clearing some tables. I saw her stop by one and exchange a couple of words with the customer, whom I couldn't see because she was in the way. Before she turned away she leaned towards the person she'd been speaking to and kissed his cheek. Jackie had a man! She turned back to the counter and I looked at the man she'd kissed. He looked straight at me, and went an odd shade of crimson.

'Cass! You're back!' Greg said, standing up and smiling the smile of a man caught with his trousers down.

Jackie turned towards me and, without missing a beat, said, 'Hi, Cass, I'll get you a coffee,' then retreated behind her counter. I wasn't sure that she realised I'd seen what had just happened, but obviously Greg had. I sat down opposite him, so that the table was between us.

'I missed you,' he said. 'Did you have a good time?'

I stared at him, his hair that was expensively cut to look as though he'd just fallen out of bed, his charming blue-eyed good looks, and I wondered exactly how much he'd missed me, and what he'd been doing to fill in the lonely hours till my return. 'I didn't expect *you* to be here,' I said. 'I thought you would be at your place.'

He smiled a touch too brightly. 'I wanted to be here when you got back,' he said.

Jackie came over with a cup of coffee, which she put down on the table in front of me, a drop spilling into the saucer. I sipped it. It was still too hot to drink, but it gave me something to do while I was trying to work out what exactly I'd seen, and what it meant, and how it fitted in with my feelings at the reunion. For the whole train journey I'd been totally immersed in thinking about that first night with Gideon. Greg hadn't entered my mind once. But as soon as I saw Coltsfoot Hall, I was back in the real world and, for me, the real world included a boyfriend who was work-obsessed, logical and practical, someone not given to wanton expressions of emotion or romance, true, but at the very least *dependable*.

'Shall we go upstairs?' I asked him. There was no way I wanted to talk about this in the middle of the coffee-shop.

'Control yourself, woman,' he said. 'You *must* have missed me.' I shot him a look: he knew damn well that that wasn't what I'd meant.

There wasn't any point in skirting around it, so I didn't try. 'Is there anything you want to tell me about you and Jackie?'

Greg ran his fingers through that shampoo-ad hair and grinned. 'Is that why you're in such a funny mood?' he said.

'Oh, really, Cass. I suppose you think I've spent the weekend in bed with her.'

Clearly I wasn't the only one favouring the direct approach and, as he no doubt intended, it took the wind out of my sails. 'I don't know what to think,' I said sullenly.

He responded by raising his arms out at his sides, palms upward, for all the world like a defender trying to convince the referee that the bad tackle he's being yellow-carded for was nothing but an innocent, accidental trip. Honest, ref.

'How was the reunion?' he asked, slumping on to the sofa. He looked so relaxed that it didn't seem possible he could have a guilty conscience. Unlike me: I'd spent the last two days (if not most of the last twenty years) obsessing about another man.

'It was okay.'

'And what about your childhood sweetheart?' Greg asked, again pulling the conversational rug from under my feet and in the process tipping me right off the moral high ground.

'My who?' was the best I could manage.

'Your little hero from the maths lesson,' he said, smiling. 'Jackie was telling me. I think it's really sweet.' Now I wanted badly to throttle Jackie, and made a mental note never to trust her with any personal information ever again. Never to trust her, full stop. 'So, was he there?' Greg prompted.

'Do you really care?'

'I'm not jealous, if that's what you mean.'

'Why not?'

'Well, why would I be? Someone you knew practically before his balls dropped. Nothing I need to get worked up about.'

How smug can you get? I was furious. 'You have absolutely no idea,' I said.

He stared at me for a couple of seconds. 'You're saying I do have something to get worked up about?'

'I don't believe you,' I said. 'I walk into the coffee-shop to

find you and Jackie sharing what I believe you journalists
would call an intimate moment, and all you can think of to
talk about is some long-ago schoolfriend of mine who wasn't
even at the reunion anyway!'

'So he didn't turn up, then?'

All the energy drained out of me. 'Oh, just go away, Greg,'
I said.

Ever Fallen In Love
(With Someone You Shouldn't've)

'There's a bundle of simmering blonde fury at the desk, says
she belongs to you,' Zak said.

I looked up from the spreadsheet that was refusing to
balance, no matter how much I tweaked it, and saw, hovering
in the doorway behind Zak, Heather Alderman. 'I've left
him,' she said, where the usual phrase would have been
'Hello'.

'Pierre?'

'Who else? The bastard.' She realised Zak was still standing
there, looking curious, and paused in her tirade to smile
winningly at him. 'Thanks,' she said. Zak smiled back but
didn't move.

'Thanks, Zak,' I said. 'We'll let you get back to your work
now.'

'Can I get you any tea or coffee?' he asked, directing his
question at Heather rather than me.

'It's okay,' I said, 'I think we'll go up to the flat.' I led the
way upstairs.

'Don't worry,' Heather said. 'I'm not stopping. Even I
wouldn't be that rude, just to turn up unannounced. Even
though I did turn up unannounced, if you see what I mean.'

'So what's going on?' I made tea and we sat down in the living room.

'Well, when I got back from the reunion, I decided I couldn't let things drag on like they had been, so I was determined to find out what the problem was. I even asked him if he would go to marriage guidance or something but he kept insisting everything was fine.' She blew on her tea. 'But you know me, I'm the original template for that TV show *Cracker*—'

'A fat, chain-smoking alcoholic?'

'You know I don't smoke. Anyway, I kept on at him until eventually he had to be honest.' She paused, swallowed a large mouthful of tea and said, 'At which point it got more like *Jerry Springer* than Robbie Coltrane.' She assumed a bad impression of an American white-trash accent. '"I really care about you, but I've been seeing this other person," he says.'

'Oh, Heather.'

'Wait for the punchline! In true *Jerry Springer* style I'm doing my nut and saying "Bring the bitch out and I'll whup her ass," and he ever-so-casually mentions that the "bitch" is in fact another man.'

I was speechless.

'Lurid, isn't it?' she said, trying hard not to cry. She fished around in her pocket and produced a screwed-up tissue.

'So why did he marry you? Did he not know?'

She shrugged. 'I don't see how he couldn't know. He said he loved me, but I reckon my primary role was to be *le* beard, or whatever it is in French, which I never did learn, by the way.'

'Sorry?'

'You know. Make him look heterosexual.'

'That's terrible,' I said.

'You'd think I'd have learned my lesson with George Michael – remember how mad I was about him when he was in Wham!? Anyway,' she said, with forced perkiness, 'that's the good thing about working in a hospital. Never short of romantic possibilities, even if some of them are in traction.'

'So what are you going to do?' I asked her.

'Maybe I'll drop him in it with the Home Office. Let them know our marriage was just a ruse so he could stay in the country.'

'Can you do that?'

'I don't know, but if he thinks I'm going to try, it'll at least make him sweat.'

That was probably no less than he deserved, but I thought a bit of tender loving care would be better for her than throwing her energies into revenge, so I asked her to stay for a while. On a more selfish note, I was glad of the company.

I returned from locking up the museum after lunch to find Heather slumped in front of the television watching *Ricki Lake*.

'You ought to watch this,' she said. 'It's uncannily relevant. Ricki's got this psychiatrist woman on, and she's helping the people on the stage to achieve closure in their relationships.'

'Closure?'

'Rounding things off nicely. That's what I need, closure.'

'And you still reckon getting him deported will achieve it for you?'

'It can't hurt,' she said. 'As least I won't have to watch him wafting around the hospital corridors with his boyfriend like – like Ike and Tina Turner, for heaven's sake.'

'I don't think I want to know whether Pierre is Ike or Tina.'

'He's neither, to be honest. Imagine if Brad Pitt hadn't been hit by the ugly stick—'

'Brad Pitt isn't ugly!'

'Now you realise the scale of my tragedy.'

Chance

We took the only option open under the circumstances and went shopping. Since my salary at the museum amounted to not much more than pocket money and Heather described her financial situation as 'perma-skint', we concentrated mainly on browsing. Heather had her makeup done at a cosmetics counter, and came away with a bag of freebies, which she classified as a 'result'.

We passed an Internet café and Heather steered me towards the door.

'I'm going to send the bastard an e-mail to let him know how I'm getting on at the Home Office,' she said. 'Come on.'

I didn't think constantly sending Pierre messages was the best way to achieve closure, but I was cold and in need of coffee anyway, so I followed her inside. Soon we were installed in front of two frothy coffees and one formidable-looking computer. Heather tapped away confidently at the keyboard.

'How do you know what to do?' I said.

She looked at me as if I'd just stepped from a time machine. 'You mean you've never used the Internet? Where have you been, woman? This is the twenty-first century.' I told her about the interactivity conference, and how I might have to get to grips with technology fairly soon.

'Why not start now?' She pressed a button and the sweetly abusive message she'd been composing for Pierre vanished from the screen. 'There, that's sent. Now you can have a go.'

'But I don't know anyone to send an e-mail to.'

'What are you interested in, then? You can find all sorts on the web.'

'Try *Far from the Madding Crowd*.'

She gave me a look. 'Well, if that's what floats your boat.' She typed it in. The search came up with at least fifteen different copies of the entire text to read on the computer, various holiday destinations that promised to whisk the traveller somewhere 'far from the madding crowd' and a selection of photographs of Dorset and other Hardyesque locations taken by a man called Bruce.

'That's amazing,' I said.

'Want to try something else?'

'Can it find real people?'

'Sometimes, if their names appear on any web pages.'

'Try Gideon.'

'You're not still obsessing about him, are you?'

'No,' I lied. 'It would just be interesting, since he wasn't at the reunion and so on.' I tried to stay calm as Heather typed in the name and pressed the return key. For a second I was disappointed. The Thomas Hardy search had produced a massive list of entries, but this time there were only two. Heather clicked on the first, her eyes skimming the contents.

'It's him,' she said. 'It must be him. Look.' I couldn't make sense of it for a second, then realised it was a report on some conference, as far as I could make out something to do with banking. Heather clicked on the other entry. 'Gideon Harker . . . Trinity College . . . Cass, it's *him*, it's definitely him.' She reeled off a list of apparently unrelated names.

'Who are they?' I croaked.

'It's not a "they", it's a merchant bank, a very big, very famous merchant bank.'

'I've never heard of it.'

'Well, obviously that's what they mean by "No *FT*, no comment," you ignorant girl,' she said indulgently. 'But that, apparently, is where he's currently employed. Wow. He must be *loaded*! Cass, you've got to ring him.' She was looking at me intently, and I was aware of my heart beating hard.

'I think Greg's been messing around,' I said.

'As in . . . ?'

'Yup.'

'The bastard.' She said this with the real conviction of the recently cheated-on. Then, 'Are you sure?'

'No,' I said. 'I'm not sure. He denies it, and *she*'s acting all innocent.'

'Who's "she"?'

'Jackie. The woman who runs the coffee-shop at the museum.'

'Talk about getting it delivered to the doorstep. He's not just a bastard, he's a lazy bastard. So, what makes you think there's something going on?'

'She kissed him,' I said, 'right in front of me. They didn't know I was there.'

'As in a big snog?'

'Well, more like a peck on the cheek, but I never knew they were that friendly.'

There was a silence from Heather; she was pondering. Finally she asked, 'Why didn't you tell me this before?'

'It seemed kind of trivial compared to your problems,' I said.

'So why tell me now?'

I looked out of the window at the crowds of people streaming by: people who worked in shops, or museums, or as football reporters, or city bankers. You never know who you're going to run into in a city the size of London.

Heather was getting up from her stool. 'Come on, that's our time up.' I started to put on my coat. As we left the café she said, 'Ring him, Cass. You don't need an excuse. Whether Greg is being unfaithful or not has nothing to do with it. You have to deal with that separately. But you can't deny that you've been hankering after seeing Harker. Now we have his work number there's nothing to stop you ringing.' We walked towards the tube station.

'Maybe I will ring him,' I said. 'Just for closure, of course.'

A Million Miles Away

I sat curled up on the window seat of my living room in Coltsfoot Hall, like Jane Eyre at the beginning of the novel. That's my favourite opening to any book: 'There was no possibility of taking a walk that day . . . the cold winter wind had brought with it clouds so sombre, and a rain so penetrating, that further outdoor exercise was out of the question.' I love the idea of it being out of the question to go outside just because it's raining, and I loved having a window seat, where I could sit like Jane, 'cross-legged, like a Turk'. Although not quite like Jane, because I still had the phone on my lap and I don't think they had those in Jane Eyre's time. I imagine she would have communicated with distant acquaintances by means of dispatching a servant with a note. Nor would Jane have had much call for a school reunion: her poor classmates having been decimated by consumption, there weren't many of them left to reunite.

The phone seemed like a cream-coloured plastic Aladdin's lamp waiting to be uncorked. My hand hovered over the receiver a couple of times; I even got as far as dialling the first few digits of the number, then hung up. I started again, dialling 141 first this time, so if I chickened out when someone answered they wouldn't be able to dial 1471 and get my number. I can be very paranoid when I'm tense.

Part of me deeply regretted going into that Internet café at all. When I left the reunion I should have left Gideon Harker in my past. I would go on this course in Plymouth and pick up all kinds of inspiring ideas that would safeguard the future of Coltsfoot Hall for ever – maybe one day my portrait would hang in the hall to mark how great my contribution had been – and I would concentrate on my relationship with Greg and possibly even go to one or two football matches with him again, just to show willing. Of course, that had been before I thought that Greg might have been showing a bit too much willing in Jackie's direction.

Aside from that I still didn't know what I would say to Gideon if I ever got to speak to him again. The news that he was some kind of City high-flyer had come as a shock. Heather hadn't been much better clued up than me about what goes on in a merchant bank, except that it involved huge amounts of money and wasn't like a high street bank at all. 'Nick Leeson,' she said, 'all that business. Baring's is a merchant bank. I think, anyway.'

I'd seen Ewan McGregor playing Nick Leeson in *Rogue Trader*, so this was something I could relate to. The idea of Gideon trading millions of dollars and waving his arms around in one of those stripy blazers didn't fit with my idea of him at all, but Heather was adamant that there couldn't be too many Gideon Harkers graduating from Cambridge in that year, and that it had to be him.

I was trembling all over at the thought that his voice was only a phone call away.

I dialled the number quickly, and by sheer will forced myself not to hang up, though my hand was shaking so much I could hardly hold the receiver steady against my ear. After three rings it was answered by a woman with a light Mancunian accent, the northern familiarity of which relaxed me slightly.

'I'd like to speak to Gideon Harker, please,' I said, my voice coming out a little bit as if I'd been inhaling helium.

'Again?'

'Gideon Harker,' I repeated.

'Which department?' Despite her accent, this woman was not over-endowed with northern friendliness, I thought. I wondered again about just hanging up, but couldn't remember if I'd dialled 141.

'I don't know which department,' I said, and felt the need to add, 'Sorry.'

'Parker, was it?' she said.

'Harker. H for – I don't know – Humphrey.'

'Humphrey Harker?'

'Gideon Harker.'

'What was the first name?'

'Gideon. G-I-D-E-O-N.'

'Well, he's not on my list of extensions,' she said. 'Is it a personal call?'

'Does it matter, if he's not on your list of extensions?'

'I haven't been here long,' she said, as if that explained anything, which I suppose it did, in a way. 'I'll tell you what,' she said, 'I'll put you through to Human Resources. They might know.'

I then spent an excruciating two minutes – I know it was two minutes because I was staring at the brass clock on the mantelshelf, watching the seconds tick past and at each one of them almost hanging up – waiting to be put through to Human Resources. Then a woman with a polo-pony voice came on the line, asked me if I was the person enquiring about Mr Gideon Harker, and informed me briskly that he had left the bank's employment over a year ago.

I could have cried. 'Do you have his address, or anywhere I can contact him?' I was burbling, beginning to sound desperate. 'I'm an old schoolfriend.' I sounded more like a very *young* schoolfriend right at that minute: painful anticipation followed by such a severe anticlimax had left me feeling and sounding as if I wasn't quite in my right mind.

Brisk Human Resources Woman was clearly not impressed. 'It's not company policy to give out personal details of current or former employees,' she informed me. 'I'm sorry. Good day.'

Good day? It had suddenly turned into a very bad one.

Who Needs Love (Like That)

Greg had the look of someone who had just missed a penalty in the World Cup final. That look almost convinced me that there wasn't anything going on between him and Jackie, but it didn't persuade me to change my mind. We were finished.

'But why?' he wanted to know. I was sitting in the window seat again, and I turned to look out across the park that had once been the garden of this lovely old house. It was getting dark, which was the time I liked it best because there were no people in Puffa jackets or riding skateboards to remind me of which century I was living in.

Ever since my phone call to the bank where Gideon had once worked I'd been thinking about him. We used to argue passionately about politics and books and whether eating meat was murder and whether the Jam were better than the Clash (I said yes, he said no), but the arguments were as full of love as the laughter.

Once I asked him why he had picked me rather than any of the other girls.

'It's the way you sometimes look like a lost kitten,' he said, so of course I thumped him, and he laughed. 'We're fairly alike, you and me,' he said. 'We're pretty independent, because we have to be, but really we just want to be loved.'

That much hadn't changed: I still wanted to be loved, but no ordinary love. I wanted someone to love me with a passion that would light up the sky.

Whether that was a reasonable or achievable ambition, I

didn't know, but I did know I wasn't in love with Greg. It didn't even come close, and it wasn't fair to me or to him to pretend that it ever would. My relationship with him was like visiting a funfair in the daytime – the rides were all set up, the music and the smells were all there, but that indefinable magic was missing.

I turned from the window to face him. 'I think we've gone as far as we're going,' I said, wishing I had words that weren't clichés to explain how I felt. I hated doing this, and it would have been so easy to waver and go back to how things were. I tried to make myself feel stronger, tougher. 'We want different things.'

'What do you mean?'

'Well, you want a cosy routine, someone you can have a laugh with. Preferably someone who'd come to matches with you. I want something more.'

'What more?' he said. 'What do you want?'

'Well ... *romance*. Violins, crashing waves, sweeping passion.'

'I can do that, if that's what you want,' he pleaded. 'I'll take violin lessons.'

'Stop it,' I said. 'You're going to make me cry, and I'm not going to cry.'

'Well, I am,' he said, and to my dismay he looked like he might really be about to.

'I think you should go,' I said, still trying to sound determined and unyielding, and hating myself.

His face switched from tearful to sulky as he stood up.

'You've been funny ever since you came back from that reunion,' he said. He stood for a couple of seconds looking hurt and bewildered, like a striker after his goal has been ruled offside. I had to keep thinking of him in football metaphors, otherwise it would have hit me too hard that we'd been together for so long, and had had some really good times, and how I would miss hearing him cursing about the plumbing in the morning, and how even though he mightn't be terribly romantic he was dependable, warm and cuddly.

But I'd finally realised that I'd spent the whole of my life just letting things happen to me and then reacting to them. Good things or bad things, it didn't matter: hardly anything in my life had happened because I made it happen. Not this time. Hard as it was, this was at least *my* decision.

Are You Ready To Be Heartbroken?

After Greg had gone, I poured myself a glass of wine and turned up the gas fire to a temperature that he would have found unbearable. So much of his time was spent outdoors, either watching football matches or hanging around outside the stadiums waiting to interview people, that he'd become practically immune to the cold, and he was for ever turning down the heating as soon as my back was turned.

There was only my own thermostat to worry about now. I still wasn't sure I'd done the right thing. Greg was the first real, long, adult relationship I'd had. Before him there were lots of boyfriends, none of them serious, none of them lasting more than a few months. I think Greg lasted longer simply because he didn't allow any space for those where-are-we-going-what-are-we-doing conversations. Greg's sureness of his place in my life would have seemed like arrogance if he hadn't been such a fundamentally nice person. He made me feel comfortable, like a quiet harbour.

I'd hated to break up with him, hated being the cause of so much pain, and it was worse because it was a new experience for me. The only other time I'd split up with someone who really mattered, it hadn't been my idea at all.

*

136

When the A-level results came out, my place at university in London was confirmed, and I was relieved to be offered a room in a hall of residence. Although I was probably more used than most people my age to looking after myself and had even taught myself, against all the genetic odds, to cook and so on fairly competently, the thought of being alone and without friends in such a huge city terrified me. I was reassured by the thought that I would be among a lot of other students and, anyway, Gideon would be near by. It still wasn't clear exactly *how* near by he would be: he said he was still considering his options, though non-medicine related, parent-irking economics was top of his list.

Then one Sunday afternoon we caught a bus a few miles out into the countryside, and went for a walk on the hills. It had started out as a vividly sunny summer day, but after we'd been walking a while, clouds started to pile in from the horizon and the light breeze that had been blowing all day changed direction and turned from warm to cold.

'Let's go back to that village,' I said. 'There was a pub open down there, we could get something to eat, maybe. It looks like it's going to rain.'

Gideon shook his head, and pointed at the distant clouds, which were grey and forbidding. Shafts of sunlight burst through them in columns of light, like in medieval religious paintings. 'In old times they were called sun-suckers,' he said. 'People thought that they sucked up water from the earth straight into the sun, where they were converted into rain.' It was a lovely image and it made me smile. 'Come on,' he said, 'I want to walk to the end of one.' He had my hand and was striding out in that long-legged way of his. I wasn't convinced that we really would be able to walk to where the sun was shining: it looked a long way off, but as usual he swept me along, both figuratively and literally.

After an hour the sun-suckers had all disappeared and a steady rain was falling; we were getting drenched. Just when we needed it, we found ourselves walking into a small village with a pub.

Gideon got the usual stares from the locals, who found his Dr Marten's boots, leather coat, jeans and antique 'Oh Bondage Up Yours!' T-shirt (the one I was wearing in the photograph Alison brought to the reunion) more than a little disturbing. I think there were three reasons why he never got beaten up by locals who were not renowned for their tolerance: the first was his height – he looked a bit too big to take on in a fight; the second was his disarming charm; and the third was me, a more-or-less normal-looking girl.

We sat down with our drinks and a bag of crisps open on the table between us. I said something like, 'I'll miss these walks when we're living in London. It'll take us hours to get to any countryside from there.'

There was something about the way he shifted in his seat before replying that made me suddenly nervous. 'I'm not going to London,' he said. I just waited, my glass poised half-way between the table and my mouth, praying that I'd misheard but knowing I hadn't. He was looking down at the table, or the floor, or at anything but me. 'I'm going to Cambridge,' he said.

'What? But you didn't apply for Cambridge . . .'

'I did. I've been offered a place at Trinity College.'

There were a lot of words I could have used to describe how I felt at that minute, but the one that sums it up best would be betrayed. Or maybe abandoned – that was more like it, I felt as if he was abandoning me, like my parents had, and I told him so.

He looked up at me. 'I'm not abandoning you,' he said, and reached across the table for my hand, which I snatched away and on to my lap. 'Cambridge isn't far from London,' he protested.

While I know that's true now, at the time they might have been thousands of miles apart. The physical distance wasn't the point, anyway: it was the plans we'd made, the feelings we had for each other, the future. 'Why Cambridge?' I asked him. 'You said London was the only place to be.'

'If I'm going to make something of myself, I need the best education I can get.'

'Oh, hark at the rebel,' I muttered.

'I'm not a rebel,' he said. 'I'm just me. I'm tired of everyone having so many expectations of me: parents, teachers ... you. People are always trying to make me something I'm not.'

'How am I trying to make you something you're not?'

'Oh, Catherine, you want me to be your hero, like in one of your romantic novels. You want me to be your bloody Gabriel Oak, and I'm not.'

'You are,' I said.

'No. I'm an eighteen-year-old boy from a little northern village who knows fuck-all about the world and I'm never going to know anything if I attach myself to one person or one place. It's the same for you: you think you like me because I dress different and it seems kind of dangerous and risky to be going around with me, but you know really I'm the safest thing you've got. You don't *learn* anything by being safe. I'd just hold you back.'

'You're not being fair to me,' I said, and I know that sounds young, but I *was* young and I was feeling the safety of the closest relationship I had in the world – because he'd got that right – crumbling around me.

'I wouldn't be fair to you if I did anything else,' he said. 'I really do love you, but we can't be dependent on each other.'

It was the first and last time he ever said he loved me, and that was what made tears run down my face, both at the time when he said it and all those years later sitting in my window seat at Coltsfoot Hall, where I cried for Gideon and cried for Greg and cried for how lonely I suddenly felt.

A few weeks after that walk on the hills, weeks in which we hardly saw each other because every time I saw him it only

139

reminded me of how much I was going to miss him (the song I played obsessively that summer was 'Are You Ready To Be Heartbroken?' by Lloyd Cole and the Commotions, and I was – I was mentally limbering up for heartbreak the whole time), we both went our separate ways. Ironically it was me, the romantic, dreamy soul, who was going to the great urban sprawl of a capital city just recovering from a summer of rioting on the streets, while my lanky-limbed, spiky-haired lover and his Dr Marten's headed for the cloistered, ancient buildings of Cambridge.

I had his address, to begin with, and he had mine, but we never wrote and, maybe as he'd foreseen, I soon immersed myself in my new life, made new friends, went out with other men. Whenever it occurred to me to contact him, because I still thought London would have been more interesting if I'd had Gideon to share it with me, I was stopped by stubbornness or pride or pain, whatever you'd like to call it, and as time went on the impulse to call him became less frequent. I can't say I forgot about him, because I don't think a day went by without him crossing my mind for some reason or other, but I started to think that life had moved on and I didn't need to see him again.

Always Something There To Remind Me

I could have done without having to go to Plymouth for the conference that Randall Robertson had assured me would be my last chance to keep the Hall from the clutches of the coke-snorting supermodels.

Two weeks after my return we were due in front of the council's finance committee to argue the case for keeping Coltsfoot Hall open. The days before I left were spent frantically writing begging letters to charities, local businesses, and any celebrity who had even a loose connection with the area, in a desperate attempt to scrape together some money and some support. We'd been collecting signatures on a petition and had had a good response, but it felt like everything was too little, too late, and that was just how Randall Robertson had planned it.

I went downstairs to give the keys to Jackie. I had hoped that Zak would be around as I was trying to avoid her as far as possible. Predictably he wasn't, so I had no choice but to go to the coffee-shop.

The last customer had gone, and Jackie was cleaning up before leaving for the night. I handed her the keys, with instructions to make sure the door was locked again after Sheryl left in the morning and not to leave it open until Zak or Stan had arrived.

'I've opened up before, you know,' she said, steering her mop in between the table legs. 'You can trust me.'

'Can I?'

The mop stopped its swishing progress along the floor. 'What do you mean by that?'

'Forget it.'

'You blame me for Greg finishing with you, don't you?' she said.

'*What?* It was me who finished with him!'

'If you say so.' She resumed the mopping.

'Jackie, what *was* going on with you and Greg?'

This time the mop didn't pause, and she kept her head down. 'Nothing at all,' she said, in a clipped voice, squeezing out the mop with more effort than was perhaps necessary. 'See? I knew you blamed me. Maybe you should blame *yourself*, swanning off to meet long-lost boyfriends and leaving him here alone.'

I was speechless with anger, and it was worse because it was the kind of undirected anger that has so many targets –

Jackie, Greg, myself, even Gideon – that I didn't know how to start letting it out.

'Remember to keep the door locked till there's somebody at the front desk,' was what I eventually came out with, and headed back to the flat before she could say anything else.

I stormed back upstairs half-way to tears, and the first thing I saw when I went into the flat was a box of Greg's stuff. I did what you would expect me to do on an occasion like this (I think Ricki Lake's Ph.D. woman would call it 'transference') and gave the box a good, hard kick, whereupon the side split and a pile of football programmes came tumbling out.

Kneeling on the floor, I stuffed them furiously back into the box. Greg went to the home matches of all the London teams but the only programmes he collected were for Tottenham; supporting Spurs was in his blood. I didn't recognise most of the players on the more recent programme covers, it had been so long since I'd been to a match, but at the bottom of the heap was a face I knew or, rather, a pair of legs: the very hairy legs of Colin Calderwood. He'd scored the first goal I'd ever seen at White Hart Lane – I couldn't remember now which team Spurs had been playing against. Nadia hadn't even seen the goal, because she was concentrating on her beloved David Ginola whom she feared was limping slightly.

My mind suddenly went off on a different track: *Nadia*, with her Ginola addiction and her high-flying City career. It struck me that if anyone knew a way of getting around Brisk Human Resources Woman and her company policies, and finding out if there was any way I could track down a former employee of a merchant bank, it would be Nadia.

I rang her.

'Good grief! Cass Thomson! It's been aeons since I last spoke to you! What have you been doing with yourself? And how come we never see you at White Hart Lane any more?'

I mumbled some excuse about being busy.

'Typical fair-weather fan,' she said. 'Still, we hardy few keep the faith. And talking of whom, how is the lovely Greg?'

'We've split up.'

'Oh, my God! When? Why?' The 'when' was fairly easy to answer, the 'why' less so. What I ended up saying was that I thought he'd been messing around with someone else, but that had only made me realise I didn't care enough about him to care.

'Oh,' was Nadia's response. 'And I thought you two were perfect for each other. You never can tell, can you?'

'No, you never can,' I agreed, and after a respectable pause I said, 'Actually, Nadge, I rang you up to ask you for your help.' I told her that I was trying to track someone down and gave her the name of the bank Gideon had worked for.

She whistled through her teeth. 'Whew. He worked *there*? I'm impressed. Who is he, anyway?'

'Just an old schoolfriend.' I decided on a white lie. 'I've been up north, and I've got an urgent message for him. His name's Gideon Harker.'

'God, I've heard that name somewhere.'

'I need an address for him, Nadge. It's quite urgent.'

'This is sounding intriguing.' She was silent for a couple of seconds. 'Okay, I have a plan. Would you believe I've been slumming it these past months and going out with one of these motorcycle-courier chappies? Not much to write home about in the brains department, but he's absolutely adorable in his leathers. Biceps like Stuart Pearce's thighs. Anyway, he's always delivering stuff to that building so I'll get him to schmooze the receptionist for info.'

I felt this was getting more people involved than was really necessary. 'Can't you just make some calls yourself?'

'Sorry, no can do. They won't give anything out over the phone. But my darling Ben can charm soot down a chimney, and judging by the state of my bath after he's had his evening soak, that's exactly how he spends his days, love him. And I'll tell him if he doesn't get results by the end of the week I'll dump him.'

'You wouldn't, would you?'

'God, no! But he's not bright enough to work that out for himself. Anyway, it's been lovely talking to you, darling, we must get together soon. I'll call you when Ben comes up with the goods. Possibly tomorrow.'

'I'm going to Plymouth tomorrow,' I said.

'Oh, God, whatever for?' Nadia was practically allergic to anywhere that wasn't within easy reach of home or workplace by black cab.

'It's a long story,' I said. 'Work-related. I'll give you the number of my mobile.' I impressed on her again that it was very important that I get in touch with this person.

'Leave it with me, darling,' she said confidently. '*Ciao!*'

Lifeline

The train clattered out of Paddington. It had been a last-minute dash to get to the station, and I was sure I must have forgotten something. It made me uncomfortable to be leaving the Hall again at this uncertain time: I knew it would be safe with Zak, but I could have done without this wild-goose chase to the West Country.

Soon after the train had broken free of London and out into open countryside, my phone rang. Several people tutted and rolled their eyes. I tugged the offending appliance out of my bag apologetically.

'You are not going to believe this,' Nadia said, affecting a tone of high drama. 'Ben is such a sweetie-pie, I knew he could do it. It seems that your Gideon Harker hasn't worked for that company in over a year.'

'I already know that,' I said. 'The human-resources woman told me that much. I wanted to know where he's working *now*.'

'Sorry, darling, that I can't tell you. Not Ben's fault either: from his account it sounds like the receptionist was ready and willing to do just about anything for him. He's such a tart. The fact is, they don't actually know.' My heart sank. So much for Ben coming up with the goods: all he'd managed to find out was absolutely zero. But Nadia hadn't finished. 'Although I do have an address for him, if you're interested,' she said.

My throat was suddenly dry. 'Go on,' I managed to say.

'Well, *this* is the bit you're not going to believe,' she said. 'You mentioned you were going to Plymouth at some point today?'

'I'm on the train right now,' I said, and I saw a woman nearby pull a face: there'd been a stream of people making loud 'I'm-on-me-mobile-I'm-on-the-train-it's-just-pulled-out-of-Paddington' calls, and now I was doing exactly the same thing.

'Really? Well, believe it or not, you're heading towards your friend as we speak. He lives in Devon, poor bugger.'

It took a few seconds for everything to click together, for me to make the connection that Plymouth was in Devon, that I was going to Devon and that's where Gideon was. I felt for a giddy moment that all I would have to do would be to step off the train and there he'd be, waiting for me on the platform in his long leather coat. Then I realised that for all these years we'd both been living in London and I'd never seen him, so why on earth should I bump into him in the whole county of Devon? Except that Nadia had an address, which she gave me.

I burbled my thanks, and collapsed back in my seat.

'Are you okay?' the woman who'd pulled the face asked,

looking concerned. I nodded. 'Only I thought it might be bad news,' she said. 'You looked a bit shocked.'

'No, it's not bad news,' I said. 'Or it might be, I don't know. It might be very good news. Or not.' The woman contemplated me for a second or two, decided I was possibly mad but probably harmless, and returned her attention to her book. I looked at the address I'd scribbled on the back of my train ticket. The briefest of addresses: Whimbrel Cottage, Ereford, Devon.

The Future's So Bright
I Gotta Wear Shades

I'd never been to Devon before. In fact, there is a remarkable number of places in my own country I've never visited. Maybe it was something to do with having an absentee peripatetic businessman as a father: we were not the sort of family to go on long car journeys for recreational purposes, because when my dad did have a few weeks off he 'didn't want to spend all the bloody time driving'. Family holidays were usually spent in some Spanish tourist resort where the beer was cheap, the food wasn't too 'foreign' and entertainment was provided for 'the kiddies', which meant I would be packed off each morning for regimented singing, dancing and blind-man's-buff sessions, conducted by students who were either hyperventilatingly enthusiastic or bored to the point of being comatose.

In fact, until I'd bought my ticket I'd only had the vaguest idea of where Plymouth was, but when I arrived there I found a compact, pleasant town that was partly very new, munici-pal and shopper-friendly, but which had a quarter that was much more to my taste, all narrow streets and olde-worlde antiques shops and buildings that looked like smugglers' inns. Of course, it was just my luck that both the conference centre where the miracles of interactivity would be revealed to me, and the hotel accommodation that went with it, were housed in possibly the bleakest, ugliest building the town had to offer.

It wasn't an encouraging start, but I was too preoccupied to care. I'd set out that morning without much enthusiasm for what the weekend had in store, but seeing it as a good opportunity to get out of the way of any possible attempts at communication from Greg and any contact at all with Jackie. Now I saw everything through different eyes. There was something about this place that made Gideon want to live here, and I searched everything I saw for clues.

The course leader was called Brad. Everything about him was affected, from his flashy suit to his mid-Atlantic Loyd Grossman accent. I'd been on quite a few similar courses in the past and, predictably enough, we started the session with a getting-to-know-you exercise in which I was paired up with a woman named Marcia who ran a travelling exhibition on knitting through the ages called 'The Ragged Sleeve of Time Roadshow'. She looked as though she was wearing quite a few of her own exhibits; if I'd seen her out on the street I might have given her a handful of spare change.

'So. What are you hoping to get out of the course?' Marcia asked me brightly, as per Brad's instructions.

I pondered. Another of Brad's instructions had been that if we couldn't think of anything positive to say, we weren't to say anything at all, lest we 'bring down a negative atmosphere', and as I couldn't think of anything particularly positive, I mumbled something about hoping to acquire new skills, blah-blah. Then I glazed over while Marcia waxed lyrical about the technological revolution, and had I realised that even knitting machines were really *computers*, and a computer program could be likened to an elaborate knitting pattern. I could feel myself mentally unravelling even as she spoke.

'You don't seem entirely present with us,' Marcia said, reminding me once again of the Ph.D. woman on *Ricki*.

'Sorry,' I said. 'It's been a difficult week.'

Marcia dutifully reported all of this back to the group: 'This is Cass Thomson. She's running a museum that's suffering financial insecurities, and we have to go easy on her because it's been a difficult week.'

The rest of the group mumbled their concern, and Brad said, 'Thank you for sharing that with the group, Cass. However, I'd like to remind everyone that the watchword is positivity.'

I began to hate him, which I admit wasn't terribly positive at all.

Brad then gave us a lecture, complete with illustrations on his dinky laptop computer, about government policy. 'The government is urging museums to target young people,' he said. 'We should be forward-looking: we're talking about rebranding Britain, not about preserving dinosaurs.'

'Aren't museums all about preserving the past?' someone sensibly pointed out.

Brad, who was all of twenty-two and looked like he had the sense of history of the average goldfish, seemed mildly exasperated. 'Think about the success of Tate Modern,' he said, 'that's what people want to see – attendances at the more traditional Victoria and Albert Museum have been falling steadily.'

'That's since they started charging admission,' the dissenter argued.

Brad ignored this. 'Tate Modern, the Design Museum, the Science Museum: these are the examples we should be following. We have a mission to promote the contemporary.'

'The place I work at has nothing to do with the contemporary,' I said.

Brad sighed. 'I'm going to demonstrate to you this afternoon that that kind of thinking is quite misguided. If we can incorporate the present and the past, that's when we can start talking about a *future* for history.' He was talking complete bananas, and continued to do so for the rest of the day. His parting shot was: 'When we gather together tomorrow, I will impart to you the three S's of the Interactive Leisure [pronounced to rhyme with seizure] Experience.' He turned on his shiny heels and slid out of the room, leaving everyone making guesses about what the three S's could be. Stupid, stupid, stupid, was my best guess.

When I left the conference hall I turned down Marcia's suggestion of exploring local hostelries and went straight to the reception desk of the hotel and asked if they had a map of the county. One was duly produced, but even with it spread open in front of me I was none the wiser: Devon is *big*. My eyes scanned uselessly across a few place names that I'd heard of (Torquay, Exeter, Dartmoor) and hundreds of places I hadn't, places with archaic-sounding names. I'd somehow expected just to look at the map and my eyes would land on Ereford, possibly accompanied by a little heart symbol, which the key would helpfully translate as 'Residence of Former Beloved'. In the end, I was forced to ask for help.

'Do you know where I can find a place called Ereford?' I asked the receptionist.

He frowned as if I might have been speaking a foreign language, and said, 'You mean Ereford?' pronouncing it, I'm certain, exactly as I had. I nodded, and pushed the map towards him. He squinted at it for a second, then jabbed his finger at the paper. 'That's us here,' he said, his finger pointing at Plymouth, then he waved his finger in the air for a few seconds like a divining rod and plopped it back down. In tiny italic letters I could just make out the word Ereford. 'It's about twenty miles away,' he said.

Twenty miles? That was nothing. It was still early, and I could be there in about half an hour. Once I knew that, there wasn't any way I wouldn't have gone, or any way I could have waited till the next day. Why waste time wondering about what might happen, or whether it was a good idea? If I went now, I need never have another night of not knowing what had happened to him. And if I didn't go now, I would chicken out and never go at all.

The receptionist directed me to where I could find a bus, and said that there should be one in about ten minutes that I would catch if I hurried. I left the hotel without thinking about what I was wearing, how I looked, what I was going to do, whether I was mad, any of the things that you'd imagine I'd be concerned about. I'd gone through all of those thoughts so many times over the course of the last couple of weeks that now a reunion might be only half an hour away all I felt was a sort of calmness and a bubbling happiness that I was going to see him again.

In A Big Country

Twenty miles translates as twenty minutes to someone who's used to living in a city and to travelling on motorways. What I hadn't considered was how long it would take to travel twenty miles in a country bus that stopped every few hundred yards to pick up and drop off children on their way home from school.

I ended up sitting on the bus for well over an hour. I was warm and comfortable in the afternoon sun slanting through the window, as we wound our way through pretty villages with thatched roofs and neat gardens, along twisting roads that were barely as wide as the bus and bordered by hedges too high to see over. The roads were so narrow that on several occasions oncoming cars had to reverse to a place where the road was wide enough for the bus to pass.

Devon was undeniably pretty. If only Coltsfoot Hall had been in a picturesque setting like this, with lots of passing tourists, instead of being swamped by the outer reaches of a stinking city, it might have stood a chance. As estate agents are fond of saying, the three most important things are location, location, location, and Coltsfoot Hall had none of them. This landscape, on the other hand, was a setting fit for such a house.

The bus eventually stopped, apparently in the middle of nowhere. I'd been in such a reverie that I hadn't noticed I was the only passenger left on it.

'This is as far as we go, love,' the driver said. 'I'm turning round here and going back to Plymouth.'

I stood up and went to the front of the bus, peering out at the neat little cottages at either side of the road. 'Is this Ereford?'

'No, love, it's Low Cross.'

'I thought the bus went to Ereford.'

'Not on a weekday afternoon,' he said. Which would have been nice to know when I bought my ticket, but maybe he'd misheard me.

'So how do I get there?' I asked.

The driver scratched his head.

'Probably the wrong time of day,' he said.

'For what?'

'Tide's most likely in,' he explained, without explaining anything. I looked blankly at him. 'Best way to Ereford is to wade across the river at low tide,' he said. 'You can do it in a decent pair of gumboots.'

I looked down at my shoes. While they were fairly sensible

and practical for most purposes, gumboots they were not. And, anyway, he'd already said the tide was in, so that mercifully seemed to rule out the wading option.

'Is there any other way to get there?' I asked.

He nodded sagely. 'Oh, yes,' he said. 'You can walk round the main road.'

'And how far is that?'

'About five miles, give or take,' he replied. 'That's why most folks prefer to wade the river.'

'Which isn't an option because the tide is in.'

'Yup.'

'So what can I do now? I can't walk five miles. It'll be dark long before I get there.'

'There's two options, as I see it,' he said. 'Either you can stay on the bus, I'll take you back to town and you can try again tomorrow at low tide. Or,' he added, and I belatedly noticed his face was crinkling up with mirth, 'you can knock on that door over there.' I peered out of the bus window to see where he was pointing.

Outside a house painted the colour of clotted cream was a small wooden sign bearing, in pokerwork, the word TAXI.

I was brought up in a semi-rural area so, unlike Nadia, I'm not the sort to get a nosebleed as soon as I get more than a hundred yards from a cashpoint machine, but this was something else.

The taxi hurtled along narrow lanes that got ever narrower, the driver braking violently when an oncoming car blocked the road and swearing under his breath when the driver of same refused to reverse to let him through. I'd never seen such narrow roads in my life. There were very few houses visible: all I could see were high hedges and trees that in some places joined together over the road to form an arch. I looked around for any sign that we were approaching a village and, seeing nothing, began to get the skin-crawling

152

feeling that we were getting further and further from civilisation and I was about to be murdered or worse.

The whole scenario played itself out in my head: Zak would realise I hadn't returned and alert the police, and eventually they would speak to the receptionist at the hotel who remembered me asking the way to Ereford, and they would quiz the bus driver who would lead them to the taxi driver who would be thrown into prison for life without possibility of parole for his heinous crime.

I was finding the story of the investigation and ensuing trial quite interesting: it was the heinous crime itself that I preferred not to dwell on, but it seemed the hour was at hand because the car had stopped, in the middle of nowhere, at a crossroads surrounded by more of those damned bungalow-height hedges and no sign of another human soul, or even a signpost, anywhere.

The driver turned round. He didn't *look* like an axe-wielding murderer, but I don't think many of them do, otherwise they'd find it that much harder to acquire victims. 'We're here,' he said.

I stared at him blankly.

'That's Whimbrel Cottage down there,' he said, indicating a lane that was differentiated from all the others only in that it was even narrower and more overgrown. 'Easiest if you walk, it's not far.'

Feeling somewhat relieved that I'd arrived safely, I paid him and set off along the lane.

Never take country folk at their word, I soon realised: 'Not far' turned out to be relative. In a couple of seconds the comfortingly familiar sound of the taxi's engine had faded away, replaced only by birdsong and spookily rustling leaves. Twenty metres along the lane the trees overhead had formed a total canopy of foliage, blocking out what little daylight there was, and the surfaced road had morphed into an unsurfaced track. The only trace of comfort was that it looked as though some type of vehicle regularly passed this way, as two parallel tyre tracks were deeply rutted into the reddish dirt.

There didn't seem to be any alternative except to continue down the road, even though the further I went the darker and narrower it got. The trees were ivy- and moss-clad and looked ancient, like a forest in a fairy tale. I was the beautiful princess lost in the woods, praying to be rescued by my handsome prince but expecting to bump into the wicked witch at every turn. I was spooked out by the rustlings in what I couldn't help but think of as undergrowth, and the visions that I'd been having in the taxi, that I would end up dying here and my body would never be found, suddenly seemed only too plausible.

A bird of some kind suddenly clappered up out of the long grass and through the leaves; I didn't even see it, but I cried out with fright, and my heart was banging painfully. I rummaged in my bag with trembling fingers for my mobile phone: a quick call to Zak or even Jackie – anyone in the real world – just to put things into perspective, and let someone know where I was if I never made it back again. I prodded at the buttons, but was rewarded only by the message 'No Network'.

'Shit.'

I shoved the useless phone back into my bag and carried on walking, though that on its own was getting difficult, as in some places the tyre tracks were filled with water and surrounded by slopes of mud, and my shoes were slipping and sliding all over the place. My foot slid down into a puddle and the shoe filled with water. I cursed aloud, cursed the taxi driver and this stupid place and especially the juvenile insanity of chasing memories in the middle of nowhere at almost nightfall on a chilly evening, when I could have been enjoying a hot meal and a drink in my ugly but comfortable hotel.

I was giving up hope of the lane ever leading anywhere at all, when the track suddenly started to slope steeply away from me. It was even harder to keep my footing, but dimly in the distance I thought I was walking towards a break in the trees; I could see sky and the glitter of water.

A few minutes later I reached a gate with a sign that proclaimed: WHIMBREL COTTAGE. PRIVATE. NO PUBLIC RIGHT OF WAY. NO PUBLIC ACCESS TO SHORE. TRESPASSERS WILL BE PROSECUTED.

'Friendly,' I muttered, finding the sound of my own voice strangely comforting in the absence of any mobile-phone coverage. There was no sign of the cottage itself, but there seemed no alternative but to brave the strictures of the PRIVATE notice and open the gate. At that moment the thought of being prosecuted for trespassing was the least of my fears.

Closing the gate behind me and latching it (a lesson learned from ads on TV in my childhood about 'following the country code'), I found the path curved sharply to the left around a clump of trees. In front of me was a small house.

It wasn't a pretty house by the standards of those I'd seen from the bus and the taxi, being built of dark grey stone with a matching slate roof, almost cubic in shape with plain windows and no adornments of any kind, but the view beyond it was gorgeous: a broad rippling river with reeds showing through at places that must have been shallow (I remembered the option to wade across and shuddered – even if it wasn't deep, it was *wide*), and beyond it gently rolling hills on which cows were grazing, just like a picture on a carton of Devon custard.

There was a shabby estate car parked at the side of the house, a mud-spattered, unglamorous old thing with a roof-rack. It seemed unbelievable that I was at the right house: it didn't look like the kind of car a city trader would drive. It didn't bode well.

I knocked at the door with my heart in my mouth, and it was typical of my day so far that there was no reply. Remembering that people in the country are apt to leave their doors unlocked, I tried the handle, but the door didn't budge. It was starting to get dark now, and although the day had been quite warm, now that the sun had gone it was getting cold quickly. My feet were wet, I was lost in the middle of nowhere with no idea of what to do next, I was hungry and bone-tired from the long slippery walk.

A path around the side of the house led to a wide, paved terrace with a breathtaking view across the river. It was beautiful and peaceful, with no sound except the gentle lapping of water against the bottom of a flight of stone steps that led right down into the river, and the whoop of some kind of water bird. I sank down on to a wooden bench set against the wall of the house and looked up and down the river, breathing in the scent of water and damp vegetation and the ozone smell of the sea. It was so remote – apart from the birds, no sign of life: no lights, no sound of traffic – and though it sounds strange under the circumstances I felt completely calm and almost happy. I closed my eyes, enjoying the light breeze on my cheeks and the smell of the water, and the wonderful feeling of aloneness and space, a feeling like Emily Brontë must have had on the moors above Haworth.

After a few minutes I gradually became aware of another noise distinct from the sounds of the river and the birds: a rhythmical crunching sound, like the noise Greg made eating popcorn in the cinema. It was getting louder, and nearer. Footsteps: someone (it sounded like only one person) was walking along the river path from the other side of the house. I had a bizarre impulse to hide, but I stayed where I was, my hands gripping the edge of the bench, and waited.

The steps at the other side of the terrace apparently led

down to a path and not straight into the river, because it was from there that a dark shape emerged, a head and shoulders, then the body of a tall man. For a disorienting few seconds I couldn't believe this wasn't a dream, this oddly beautiful location, the twilight, the whooping of the water birds, and standing in front of me a man who was, unmistakably, Gideon Harker.

Reward

It took me a couple of seconds to convince myself that it really was him, during which time I was also overcome by the feeling that I'd made a huge, stupid, embarrassing mistake coming here in the first place. Despite the fraught journey, incredibly it was only now that I stopped to wonder why in the world I'd gone to such an effort to look for this man I hadn't seen for so many years, whose life I knew nothing about.

Those vividly green eyes, that handsome, intelligent face that I'd thought about so often, were looking at me downright suspiciously; I couldn't really expect anything else, turning up unbidden in the middle of the countryside at nightfall. Equally clearly, he was not a person to be unduly alarmed by anything.

'This is private property,' he said, stating his territory and perhaps buying time. I stood up and at the same time he took a couple of steps towards me, then stopped. 'Catherine?' he said.

I smiled, and waited for the smile to be returned, and maybe for his arms to open for a hug. He stayed exactly where he was, and his face was so guarded I couldn't read the expression. He was strikingly handsome: his face was tanned and his dark hair was cropped shorter than it had ever been when he was younger; it suited him.

'What are you doing here?' he asked, which was the obvious question, I suppose.

'I was in the area,' I said, lamely, and not surprisingly he didn't look as if he believed me.

'And how did you know *I* was in the area?'

'It's a long story,' I said. 'Is there any chance of a cup of tea? I've been sitting out here a while and it's getting a bit chilly.' He turned towards the path alongside the house and I took this as an invitation to follow.

None of the scenarios I'd been running through my head about how this meeting would go had prepared me for his apparent lack of interest in me. I felt like a complete fool: I'd built him up into the most spectacular and interesting thing since Halley's Comet, and to him I was nothing but a minor nuisance. The best thing to do would be to minimise the embarrassment by getting out of there as fast as possible. I'd have some tea, just to fortify myself for the return trip, ask him for directions to the nearest bus stop back to Plymouth and this whole stupid episode would be over.

The house was blissfully warm. The ground floor consisted of one large room, heated by one of those big oil-burning stoves. The floor was bare stone, without any rugs. Opposite the door a window framed a magnificent view of the estuary and a sky that was turning deep indigo, and the walls were covered in paintings and photographs of the sea. Under the window was a large table covered in books, paper and jars of pens and brushes, and to the right of this a huge, comfortable-looking sofa. At the other side of the room there was the stove and other kitchen fittings, with a door beyond presumably leading to a staircase.

Gideon filled a kettle and stood it on the stove, where I guessed it would take about an hour to come to the boil, and spooned tea into a pot. I perched on a corner of the sofa, feeling like the intruder I was.

The kettle boiled faster than I expected, he made the tea and in handing me a cup had no option but to acknowledge my presence. He pulled a chair from beside the table and sat almost opposite me. Even though there was room on the sofa for at least five people, he clearly wasn't in the mood for any kind of intimacy. He really was good-looking, what my sixth-form English teacher would have called 'toothsome', as in 'the toothsome Mr Darcy'. If he had come to the reunion he would have blown all the other men out of the water. No different from when he was seventeen, then, at least as far as I was concerned. He looked self-contained, serene, and very, very sexy (perhaps these were the three S's of the Interactive Leisure Experience).

'So, how *did* you find me?' he asked.

'Heather Alderman found you on the Internet.'

'You still see Heather?'

'I met her again at the school reunion,' I said.

'A school reunion? When was this?'

'A couple of weeks ago. Didn't you know about it?'

'No,' he said. 'But I wouldn't have gone even if I had.' That much had become obvious. The conversation, such as it was, ground to a halt.

'Do you live here alone?' I asked finally.

'Yes.' This ought to have been the best news I'd had all day, but evidently he wasn't about to go into detail. We drank our tea in silence for a couple of minutes, and he asked me how I'd managed to get to the house, so I told him the whole story, glad of an excuse to fill the silence with something and hoping that he would be swept into some kind of conversational exchange.

'My plan was to go back to the hotel in Plymouth,' I finished. 'I didn't realise how far away it'd be.' He didn't say anything. 'I don't suppose you could give me a lift back?'

'If I could, I would,' he said, 'but the car's knackered. I'm waiting for a new water pump.'

'Could you call me a cab, then?'

'Phone's out,' he replied.

No telephone? Now I really did feel like I'd arrived at the back of beyond. I remembered my granddad's fall, and what the consequences of that might have been if we hadn't had a telephone; and thinking about that night made me suddenly unable to look at him. I stared at my knees, and he must have thought I was worrying about how to get back to Plymouth.

'Look,' he said, speaking more gently than he had so far, 'it's nearly dark, so you'd better stay here tonight, and tomorrow I'll walk you up to the village. If that's okay.'

'That's fine. Thank you,' I said, glad of the excuse to spend more time with him; maybe after an hour or two of talking over old times he would relax a bit.

Then he stood up. 'Well, I'm going to bed,' he said. 'The sofa's pretty comfortable, there's a pillow and a quilt in that chest over there and the bathroom's at the top of the stairs. If you're hungry just help yourself to anything you find.'

And with that, he was gone: it was only about seven o'clock. Of all the scenarios I'd played through my mind over the years about what it would be like to meet him again, I'd never have imagined such absolute indifference, such a complete lack of interest in me or in anything that had happened in the years since we'd seen each other.

For some reason, I thought about my dad. I remembered a freezing Bonfire Night, the smell of gunpowder in the air, me wrapped up warmly with a woolly scarf pulled up under my nose, a hat and gloves and at least two pairs of socks keeping all my extremities warm. Dad was hunkered over a Roman candle with a wax taper. He leaned as far as he could without falling over, the flame flickering at the blue twisted-paper wick, then stepped back smartly. I remembered the background sound of rockets slashing and whistling up through

160

the air, the distant wail of a fire engine, the barking of a dog who should have been locked securely indoors as per *Blue Peter* instructions. All of these noises originated from outside our small garden, but from the firework that Dad had just lit there was no sound, nothing but a wisp of smoke. He stood back, hands on hips, a frown on his face. He'd been fooled: inanimate objects were supposed to obey, be controllable. This wasn't supposed to happen.

'Try again, Dad.' I was getting bored now.

'Go on, Jim. It didn't catch. It wants lighting again.'

My dad advanced half a step forward, half a step back. 'No,' he said. 'Best leave it. Never go back to a firework once it's been lit.'

Maybe that was the only helpful thing my dad ever said; it's a shame I remembered it too late.

Should I Stay Or Should I Go?

It was barely dawn when I woke up. There were no curtains at the window, and from my position on the sofa I could see a lightening sky with narrow bands of cloud. Someone was knocking – or, rather, pounding – on the door. I heard Gideon running down the stairs to answer it, then a woman's voice.

'Come on, lover, it's a beautiful morning.'

'Suze! It's barely six o'clock.'

'Exactly, and time's a-wasting. I've been down to have a look, and it's as good as you're going to get: almost head-high and clean.'

'I've got someone staying,' he said.

'Oh, sorry, didn't mean to intrude.'

'It's not like that. I'll explain in the car.'

'You're coming, then?'

'Of course I'm coming. I'll just grab my stuff.' I heard him run upstairs again, then a minute later there was the sound of car doors slamming and the engine fading into the distance.

Where the hell were they going in the middle of the night? And why had she called him 'lover'? Was he her lover? Or was it merely a Devon term of endearment? I hadn't seen her, and it's hard to tell someone's age from their voice, so she could have been anything from fifteen to fifty-five. She certainly sounded like she was pretty friendly with him, though. And what was this big, clean thing she'd been to have a look at?

Whatever, it was clearly more important to Gideon than his house-guest. Even though my bed on the sofa was delightfully cosy and warm there was no chance of getting back to sleep, so I got up, put the pillow and quilt back in the trunk and made a cup of tea, which I took outside.

Words have not been invented to describe how beautiful it was. The air was cold and fresh and there was no sound, except the hooting and honking of various water birds. I watched a single snow-white heron standing at the edge of the river, his head feathers ruffling in the breeze but otherwise not moving, like a delicately beautiful garden ornament. He looked so elegant and so self-possessed. Suddenly there was an absolute clamour, like a traffic jam overhead, a honking and whirring that went on and on. I looked up, startled, and saw a skein of dozens of geese whirling around above the water in a perfect curve and off again inland.

Of all the places I'd ever imagined he might be, I could never have pictured anything as lovely as this wild and beautiful place. My imagination conjured up images of sitting out here on hot, sunny afternoons, maybe going for a swim in the river if it was really hot; on snowy days when the wind whistled around the corners of the house it would be warm and cosy inside. We could sit by the fire and read and—

But considering that Gideon had barely spoken more than a couple of sentences to me and had now gone off with another woman, that was obviously never going to happen. I tried to put a lid on my romantic daydreaming, determined to salvage as much self-respect as I could out of this sorry situation.

Reluctantly I went back inside, because before Gideon's return I had at least to attempt to make myself as presentable as possible given that I'd come unequipped with toiletries, makeup or a change of clothes. A quick nose around the bathroom reassured me that whoever this 'Suze' person was she wasn't so much in the habit of staying overnight that she kept spare toiletries there; I found only what you'd expect a single man to use, including a couple of partly used bottles of very expensive men's scent, which was the only hint I'd seen so far that he really had had a previous high-earning urban existence.

The white-painted door to his bedroom was firmly closed, and no matter how curious I was I would never have breached his privacy by opening it, but anything on public display was, like the bathroom, fair game for a good old snoop (like reading other people's postcards isn't like reading their letters, because postcards are on open view). I was particularly interested in the pictures that covered the walls. They were all original watercolours, oils or ink drawings, none of them signed, but the clutter of writing and drawing materials on the table indicated that the artist had to be Gideon himself. He'd always been good at drawing, and the pictures were beautiful, capturing the sea and sky in all kinds of moods. Some were of sea birds, and there was one of a girl, the back of her head and a long, slender neck, just enough of her shoulders and back to show she wasn't wearing much clothing. I stared at that one for a long time, picturing the scene when it was drawn, wondering who she was, envying her.

I had to presume that Gideon intended to stick to his plan of walking me to the village – the thought of trying to find it on my own was not appealing – so I sat down to wait for him to come back.

At around eight o'clock I heard the sound of a car. I jumped up to look out of the window in time to see Gideon get out of the passenger side of a red hatchback. I didn't get a look at the driver before the car disappeared back off up the lane – I was too gobsmacked.

Gideon was dressed in something like a smooth black second skin, covering him from his neck to his ankles but so clinging that it was obvious even from the rear elevation that his body had matured as beautifully as his face. I experienced the same reaction as on that long-ago day in the Duke of York when he'd appeared for the first time in his leather coat with his hair bleached blond: a rush of total lust.

The door opened quietly and he came in, bringing the smell of the sea with him. He looked like some kind of aquatic superhero – Seal Man: half man, half temptingly slippery thing.

'Oh, hi,' he said. 'I thought you would still be asleep. I've been surfing. You've got to catch the breaks when you can round here.' Aha. Clear as mud. 'Have you had breakfast?' he asked.

'I made myself a cup of tea,' I said. 'I hope that was okay.' *Surfing?* I was thinking. I couldn't in a million years have pictured the sports-shy Gideon Harker surfing. But seeing him in a wetsuit I couldn't imagine why my fantasies had never come up with the idea before.

'Just give me fifteen minutes to get out of this and have a shower, and I'll cook us something. I'm starving.' He hesitated at the foot of the stairs. 'I ought to apologise,' he said, rubbing his hand over his dark, cropped hair, which was damp and spiky-looking. 'I was very rude yesterday.'

'I suppose you don't get many guests turning up unexpectedly, all the way out here.' Why was I apologising for him? I ought to make him do the work.

He smiled. 'I get quite a few, believe it or not,' he said. 'It's one of the drawbacks with a dodgy phone line and having a post-box a mile and a half down the lane. People write to tell me they're coming and they get here before I've even picked up the post.' The effect of him standing there in a damp wetsuit was disconcerting: I had a strong impulse to touch him to see if he felt as smooth and muscular as he looked. In a way it would have been the most natural thing in the world to do so, but although there were only a couple of metres of fresh air and a few millimetres of neoprene between us, there was also the small matter of fifteen years of separation.

O Superman

He came back downstairs in a washed-out T-shirt and jeans.

'I preferred the superhero look,' I said.

'What? Oh, the wetsuit. If I was a proper superhero I suppose I'd wear my pants over the top of it.'

'But do you wear pants *under* it?'

He shot me a look: this wasn't how he expected me to behave. Then he grinned. 'I do, actually,' and added, 'Chafing.'

'*Yew*. Time to change the subject. What's for breakfast?'

'Bacon, eggs, toast, coffee. You're not veggie, are you?' He plucked things out of the fridge. 'You didn't used to be.'

'*You* didn't used to surf. But no, I'm not veggie.' He poured orange juice into glasses, and he was either nervous or still wobbly from the morning's exertions, because he overfilled the second glass so that the juice quivered at the very brim.

'Meniscus membrane,' I said, a phrase from a long-ago chemistry lesson popping into my head.

'"Humm, isn't it just, though?"' he boomed, in the voice of our former chemistry teacher Mr Goulden, and we laughed, a little nervously admittedly, but at least it felt like we were getting somewhere.

'So tell me about this reunion,' he said.

Where to start catching somebody up with so much lost time? For some reason, the first thing that popped into my head was the Olivers and how they liked Dire Straits.

'*You* liked Dire Straits,' he said.

'I did not!' I protested. 'I had *one* single, that's all, "Sultans of Swing".'

'Aha! I thought you did.'

'I was only twelve when I bought it. Anyway, I stand by that one. I like those little guitar licks in between the singing. It doesn't mean I like Dire Straits as *such*.'

He looked at me for the first time with something like affection in his eyes. 'You always were very easy to wind up,' he said, putting plates of bacon and eggs on to the table. We sat down. 'I knew this guy at Cambridge who used to listen to "Private Investigation" while he was tripping, so loud it would make your ears bleed,' he said. 'He used to lie on the floor with these huge speakers either side of his head. He said it contained the secret to the universe, only when he was straight he couldn't remember what the secret was and he thought the record was rubbish.'

We ate in silence for a while, but at least it was a friendly silence, and the awkwardness of earlier had lifted slightly. I wondered what had happened to change his mood, and whether it was anything to do with seeing Suze. I felt murderously jealous of her, whoever she was. Not wanting to put him on the defensive again, I thought I'd approach the subject obliquely. 'Do you do a lot of surfing?'

He got that look in his eyes that people get when they're

asked about their favourite subject in the world. 'Every day I can,' he said. 'Whenever there are decent waves.'

'Difficult when your car isn't working.'

He was looking at me with those green eyes that never missed a trick. 'Suzanne's my surfing partner,' he said. 'I sometimes surf on my own, but we usually go together. She's pretty good. A bit mad sometimes.' Which told me not very much at all, but to probe further would have been too obvious.

I was in no hurry to get back to Plymouth: I'd hardly even thought about the conference, the real reason for my trip to Devon. I didn't want to think any further ahead than right there, sitting in Gideon's cosy kitchen. Unfortunately, he was more practical and had remembered his promise to get me back to Plymouth. Even worse, he'd organised transport.

'You'll get to meet Suzanne,' he said. 'She's offered to run you back to Plymouth – she's got some stuff to do there – so you should be in plenty of time for your lecture or whatever it is.' Oh, fine. Now I wasn't even going to have his company on the long walk back up the lane.

'The workshop finishes at three,' I said, determinedly trying to be the new assertive me. 'Maybe we could meet up later?' I told him the name of the hotel.

'Sorry,' he said. 'I'm busy for the rest of the day.'

'But we can keep in touch?' I tried to make it sound as if I wasn't bothered either way, and possibly overdid it, because he replied in the manner of someone the morning after a one-night stand who's now regretting it: 'Okay, if you like. Give me your address.' I wrote it down for him and passed him the piece of paper.

'Coltsfoot Hall? That sounds interesting.' I told him about the museum, giving him the full guided-tour spiel about what a beautiful house it was and its importance to the community, and how it would be such a tragedy if the council sold it. I realised, belatedly, that I'd been waffling. 'It's got this lovely window seat,' I finished lamely, wondering exactly how foolish that sounded. 'I love sitting there curled up with a book.'

'Just like little Jane Eyre,' he said. I nodded. I couldn't speak, because if I'd tried to say anything I might have started to cry: even after all this time he understood me. I don't know if he noticed: he started clearing the table, putting the dirty plates into the sink. Then he turned to me. 'Suzanne isn't coming for an hour or so. I could show you my beach.'

'Where you surf?' I perked up at the thought that he might be about to put on his wetsuit again.

He shook his head. 'Unfortunately my little beach is too sheltered to get much swell. You'll need to borrow my wellies – the path is likely to be a bit muddy.'

Echo Beach

He'd obviously picked up this Devon skill, as manifested by the bus driver and the taxi driver the previous day, of geographical misrepresentation. The 'path' turned out to be a virtually undetectable track that wound around trees and massive clumps of fern. At some points we had to duck low under overhanging branches or clamber over fallen tree stumps. It didn't help that I was wearing wellingtons that were at least three sizes too big for me, and following someone who was fit and knew the path well. He loped along as comfortably as if he was taking a stroll across a lawn, while I was practically wheezing with the effort. It was just as well that he didn't seem inclined to talk: I wouldn't have had the breath to reply.

Eventually the path started to descend at an alarming gradient as it emerged from the trees. I could hear the sea.

'Best way is just to let yourself slide,' Gideon advised, going down ahead of me. 'I'll catch you.' I planted my feet sideways and attempted to control my descent, like we'd been taught to ride patches of scree on a school walking holiday in the Lake District. Unfortunately the path was muddy and mud doesn't react in the same way as scree, and for the last few metres I was sliding uncontrollably, only just managing to stay upright. I landed ungracefully in his arms; he held me tight for a fraction of a second, then we both leaped away from each other as if we were radioactive.

'Welcome to my beach,' he said. It was a tiny cove, surrounded by steep rocks that looked like piles of dark grey, folded paper, the lower ones covered in gooey green seaweed and those higher up colonised by little flowering plants. Small waves broke on a beach about the size of two tennis courts, covered in fine biscuit-coloured sand. It was right at the point where the river joined the sea; to the right, where the house was now hidden behind the trees, was the river estuary, to the left the open sea. I recognised the spot from some of the paintings I'd been looking at earlier. 'This is yours?'

'It's part of my land. One of the reasons why I bought the house. On days when there's no surf, I can at least be by the sea. It's okay for swimming, too, in summer.'

We went to the water's edge. I walked in the tiny waves, watching my boots sink into the fudgy sand. It was cold, and the air smelt clean and tangy.

'What's it like, surfing?'

He stared far out to sea, as if he was picking out which wave he was going to ride. 'There's nothing like it. It's exhilarating, exciting, hard work; you can have moments of pure terror, but at the same time it's the most peaceful thing I know. When you're planing along a peeling wave, everything goes quiet. All you can hear is the ripple of the water against the board and it feels like time stops; you become very focused, and all sound disappears. It only lasts for a few seconds, but it feels like for ever. It's a wonderful feeling. Once you experience it, it gets into your blood.'

'Is that why you left London? So you could surf?'

'More or less.'

It didn't sound like much of a reason to me. 'But you were working for a merchant bank . . .'

'You *have* been doing your homework,' he said teasingly. I concentrated on watching the little slipstreams my feet were making in the water, not knowing what to say, but he carried on talking without any prompting from me, and told me about his job as a derivatives trader.

'Sounds important,' I said.

'Important? No, not important at all, in the grand scheme of things.'

'Glamorous, then.'

'Maybe. Very lucrative, and totally soul-destroying, anyway, in the sense that I was turning into a not very nice person. You have to be aggressive, ambitious, driven, all that stuff that isn't really me. I pretended to myself it *was* me, for a while, and I was good at the job, made a stupid amount of money, but in the end I got tired of being so focused on making money, and seeing nothing but tube trains and the trading floor, so I quit.'

'You don't miss it?'

'Not at all. What I liked best about that job was that chaos was always just around the corner. You'd look at all those figures on the screen and at first it would look totally confused, but you'd see a pattern, and make some sense out of it. Then you'd make your trade and sit back and watch the disorder return. The sea is like that. Surfing is literally going with the flow. When you've been smacked straight down on to bare rock by a huge wave you know your place in the scheme of things, and it isn't a place to be puffing yourself up or getting any ideas that you're more important than plankton.'

'So what do you do now, job-wise?'

'I give tourists surfing lessons in the summer sometimes, do odd jobs here and there, but – um – I don't really need to work. I've got enough money to live on, I don't need much.'

'Must get lonely.' He didn't answer, and I wondered if there was more to it than he was letting on. We were walking back up the beach towards the path.

'We ought to get back,' he said. 'Suzanne will be here soon.'

Who's That Girl?

The red car was already waiting at the back of the house. I went inside to get my shoes, and when I came out Suzanne was leaning against the car talking to Gideon. She was probably in her late twenties, very pretty and outrageously healthy-looking, exuding well-being, with skin like Miss Pears and the posture of a gymnast. I thought: If that's what cream teas do for you, make mine a double.

'You must be Catherine,' she said, and I was temporarily outraged – there was only one person in the *world* who had ever called me Catherine. But, of course, that's the name he would have told her.

She slid into the car, and Gideon kissed my cheek very lightly. It was a formal, completely unromantic kiss but it still made my knees weak. Then he said, 'Well, it was nice to see you, Catherine. Have a good trip back to London.' He followed the car as far as the gate and closed it behind us, then he turned to walk back to the house before we were even out of sight.

I felt crushed. There had been a couple of moments that morning when I'd believed that we were still on the same wavelength, even after so long apart, but obviously I'd been deluding myself.

Suzanne didn't help. In between negotiating those preposterously narrow roads, she gave me an appraising look. 'So . . . do you surf?' she asked, and raised her eyebrows high when I said no.

'No?' she repeated, as incredulous as if I'd told her I was still a virgin. 'Weird,' she said, and changed tack. 'Gideon tells me you and he go way back.'

'We were at school together.'

'Wow. *Way* back. Funny he never mentioned you before today.' This woman was clearly into scoring points, so I decided to score one of my own.

'I used to go out with him,' I said.

She didn't miss a beat. 'What a coincidence,' she said. 'So did I.' And of course he hadn't told me that, although I wasn't surprised. She inclined her head towards me in a conspiratorial manner. 'We should form a club,' she said. 'The exes of Gideon Harker. It'd be sociable, there are quite a few of us.'

'Sorry?'

'He obviously hasn't told you about all of his little surfing babes. He didn't tell *me* about some of them. The ones before me and after me, perhaps, but the ones *during* I usually had to find out about from other people.'

I didn't want to hear this, it wasn't fitting in at all with my romantic view of him, but she still wasn't finished. 'He's not the settling-down kind, I guess. Bit of a free spirit, you could say, if you were feeling kind.' After that she was content to drive in silence for a while. She drove like a rally driver, flinging the car round the tightest corners, but right then I didn't particularly care if I made it back to Plymouth in one piece. You don't particularly care about your personal safety when your dreams have just been shattered.

Fool's Game

I got back to the hotel in time to change my clothes and put on some makeup, then I had to rush straight to the conference hall, where Brad was already in full flow. You can imagine that my mind was even less on the interactivity course than it had been the day before. Marcia had kept a seat for me next to her, and when Brad left the room for a minute she nudged me in a pally sort of way.

'Where did *you* get to last night?' she asked. 'We knocked on your door several times. Sally and Bob and I went out for a meal. Bob was absolutely hilarious. He's an amazing guy, runs a fascinating archive on the history of vitamin-deficiency-related diseases in the East End of London. He kept us enthralled for hours.' I couldn't think of anything more likely to put you off dinner than hearing about vitamin-deficiency-related diseases throughout the meal, so I smiled politely and gave silent thanks that I'd missed it.

Brad swooped back into the room, followed by one of the hotel staff pushing a trolley laden with computer equipment.

'Okay, Keepers of the Holy Screeds! Prepare to be inculcated into the wonders of modern communications.'

Apparently I'd missed the revelation of what the three S's were, but the only interactive leisure experience I would have been remotely interested in involved a beautiful, sexy man who, it seemed, lived for surfing. And the perks that apparently went with it, if Suzanne was to be believed. Little wonder that I wasn't the star pupil of Brad's class that morning. I did my best to concentrate, made every effort to take notes, to join in when Brad demanded 'brainstorming', tried to work out how all this applied to my lovely local museum with its specific little treasures, and completely failed.

This was a red herring: Randall Robertson had known damn well that nothing about this course was even remotely going to apply to Coltsfoot Hall. The whole trip had been a waste of time and a huge mistake. I'd learned nothing of value to help save the museum; all I'd learned was that Gideon Harker couldn't have cared less.

After the 'plenary' session, in which about half the group told Brad how energised they were feeling about the whole interactivity thing and the other half adopted a resigned silence, Brad informed us that he had some copies of his book for sale by the exit, but we were to feel under no obligation to purchase. I declined the invitation from Ragged Sleeve of Time Marcia, East End Diseases Bob and a couple of the others to go for an after-workshop pint, and trudged back to my room to gather my stuff together for the trip home.

When I opened the door, the first thing I saw – there was no way you could have missed it – was the most enormous vase of velvet-red roses; there were dozens of them. I stepped towards them, touching the crimson petals in amazement. There was no card with them, but they had to be from Gideon. It wouldn't have been his style in 1985, but maybe it was something he'd acquired during his banking career. My heart was hammering like a thousand drums.

I'd left the door open behind me, and I heard someone tap gently on it. I turned round. Greg was standing in the open doorway.

'Greg? What are you doing here?' He came into the room, and closed the door behind him.

'I'm doing what I should have done months and months ago. Years ago,' he said. 'Letting you know how I feel.'

'I don't—'

'Ssh,' he said, 'I had to come and tell you how much I love you. I've been taking you for granted, treating you like one of the lads. But you're not, Cass, you're special. You're the most special person I've ever met.'

Oh, God.

'Aren't Crystal Palace at home tonight?' was what I finally came up with.

He winced. 'That's exactly what I mean,' he said. 'I've been putting my job ahead of you, and that's not right. I'm surprised you put up with it as long as you did. But no more. From now on you come first.' He hadn't made any move to touch me and was still standing at the door.

'Thank you for the flowers.'

'That's just for starters,' he said. 'Get your bags packed. We're going.'

'I was just about to. The train leaves for Paddington in half an hour.'

'We're not going back to London,' he said.

'Where are we going, then?'

'It's a surprise.'

'Greg!' I protested. 'I've got to get back to work. Zak's expecting me.'

'Zak knows all about it,' he said. 'It's sorted. Come on.'

I didn't know how to react. Like I'd said to Heather at the

reunion, all my adult life I'd been looking for something and never found it because I had this idea of perfect love in my head. Over the years Gideon Harker had meant more to me than any of the pop stars or actors or footballers I'd been besotted with in my youth. He'd been the embodiment of all the romantic dreams I'd ever had. I'd thought that if I met my perfect love again and saw that he wasn't as wonderful as I remembered, maybe I could start living in the real world. And relationships didn't have to be like they were in books, did they? So Greg didn't make my heart beat faster: maybe at my age it was time to get real.

I tried to forget that when I was with Gideon I'd felt exactly the same as when I was a teenager, mad-happy in love, like I was with the person I was *meant* to be with. It would have been total joy except that it clearly wasn't reciprocated: he hadn't been interested in seeing me again, hadn't even waited till the car was out of view before he'd gone back into the house. I'd been nothing more than an unwelcome intrusion into his world of surfing and everything that apparently went with it.

There was no point in trying to hold on to ghosts any longer: that was the real result of my visit. It was time to start living a non-fiction life.

'It'll take me a few minutes to pack,' I said to Greg, and then added, 'I'm glad to see you,' and let him kiss me.

I Guess That's Why They Call It The Blues

For a horrible while I thought Greg was taking me back to Gideon's: we drove off in the same general direction, but as soon as we were on to those little country lanes I was completely disoriented. Greg wouldn't let me look at the map, because 'that would spoil the surprise', so I just had to sit tight while he took frequent pauses to try to figure out where he was going.

Eventually we came to the top of a steep hill, heading towards the sea, grey and cold-looking under a cloudy sky. We rounded a bend and suddenly straight ahead of us, almost as if we could fly off the road like Chitty Chitty Bang Bang and land straight on it, a grass-covered island the shape of an inverted soup plate rose out of the sea. On the side of the island facing us was a dazzling white art-deco building. It was flat-roofed, three storeys high, and in the centre was a small tower with a blue-green top like a curved pyramid.

I pointed at it, amazed at seeing such a beautiful building in such an unexpected location. Greg nodded, grinning. 'That's where we're headed,' he said. 'It's a hotel. Agatha Christie and Noël Coward stayed there, and it's where King Edward brought Mrs Simpson to escape the press.'

'It's incredible.'

'I thought it would appeal to your romantic nature,' he said, pleased with my reaction. 'Shall we go across?'

The only way to get to the island when the tide was in was by means of a vehicle like a cattle truck but with enormous wheels that lifted it clear of the sea: 'The only one of its kind in the world', according to the driver, who presumably said the same thing many, many times a day.

Inside, the building was no less spectacular. It was like walking into the 1920s: I expected to see women in ornate Erté dresses and men with monocles and cigar holders.

'It's like *The Shining*,' Greg whispered, 'where Jack Nicholson goes into the Gold Ballroom and finds himself back in 1921. "You're the best goddamn barman in the world, Lloyd."'

Our room wasn't just a room: it was a suite bigger than most of the flats I'd lived in, furnished in perfect art-deco style, with a separate sitting room and doors opening on to a long balcony with a breathtaking view of the sea. I went outside. The weather was cloudy and cold, and the beach was practically deserted, apart from a couple of hardy souls walking dogs. I heard Greg step on to the balcony, and he stood behind me and wrapped his arms around my waist, resting his chin on my shoulder.

'Not bad, is it?' he said. I'd almost forgotten he was there, I was so preoccupied with my thoughts.

'It's beautiful,' I said. 'How did you find out about it?'

'Jackie told me,' he said. Now, why didn't that surprise me? 'And, believe it or not, that sea tractor's been on *Teletubbies*. I saw it at my sister's house the other day when the sprogs were watching it.' He squeezed me harder, and I felt his cheek against mine. 'It's a bit draughty out here,' he said, 'and in our room there's a great big bed. We could have a bit of a snuggle.' His touch was warm, familiar, and meaningless.

'Greg,' I turned to face him, 'we were *split up* just an hour ago. You can't expect me to jump straight into bed with you.'

'But you came here . . .'

'I didn't know we were going to a *hotel*. You didn't tell me.'

'You knew it was a hotel while we were checking in.' Which was a fair point. The truth was, I was confused. The events of the morning had left me feeling lost and vulnerable, then Greg suddenly appearing like that, and bringing me to this extraordinary place, had made me wonder if I'd made a mistake after all. Isn't it better to spend your life with a man who cares about you and wants to be with you than to be alone with nothing except memories? A bird in the hand and all that . . .

'I'm sorry,' I said. 'I'm feeling a bit mixed up.'

'Tell you what,' he said, 'I'll order us some champagne. We should be celebrating.' Presumably Greg meant celebrating us getting back together again after this briefest of separations. I wasn't in the mood for celebrating anything, but I thought perhaps getting a bit squiffy on champagne might help me to relax and simplify things a bit, so I agreed with him.

He went back inside to ring for room service, then I heard the television going on and the all-too familiar voices of Ray Stubbs and John Motson. How like Greg not to be able to resist watching the full-time football results while he waited for the champagne.

I stayed on the balcony, my arms folded around my body against the cold wind, looking at the sea that Gideon loved so much. As I gazed across at the sandy beach, I noticed a man in a black wetsuit with a yellow surfboard under his arm, running into the waves. It wasn't Gideon, it wasn't tall enough to be him, the hair wasn't dark enough, but I watched fascinated as he started to paddle hard to where the swell rose and crashed down. A bigger-than-usual wave suddenly broke on top of him and he vanished from sight. I stared anxiously at the spot for a few seconds until I saw him again, still lying on the board and still paddling. He floated for a minute, then started to paddle for the shore and in a quick and fluid movement he was on his feet and skimming along parallel to the beach, his knees bent, all his weight and balance pivoting in his hips, speeding along the face of the wave like he was flying.

I realised my eyes were full of tears. I wasn't meant to be here; I wasn't meant to be anywhere, because I wasn't welcome in the only place where I wanted to be.

I heard a knock on the door of the room, and Greg opened it to get the champagne. I left the balcony and went inside as he was preparing to uncork the bottle. 'Don't open it,' I said. 'If you give it back unopened maybe you won't have to pay for it.'

'I thought you wanted champagne?'

179

'No,' I said. 'I'm sorry, Greg, it was a lovely idea, but it's too late.'

'You'd rather have something else? Brandy, to warm you up?'

I shook my head. 'I'm going back to London,' I said. 'I was confused, and all I can say is I'm sorry – again – but this hasn't changed anything. We're still split up.'

He was angry now, and I couldn't blame him. 'I've gone to all this trouble,' he said. 'I'm missing covering an important match to do this.'

'Maybe you'll be able to get back in time.'

'I don't *want* to,' he said. 'I wanted to have a romantic time here with you.'

The only thing I could think of to say was that I was sorry, but I'd already said that twice so I didn't say anything.

'You're going to see *him*, aren't you?' Greg asked.

I just looked at him. 'Who?'

'Oh, come off it, Cass! Nadia rang me yesterday and told me about this long-lost friend of yours from the north, who just happens to be living in Devon.'

'What did she do that for?' I said. The whole world seemed to make it a priority to communicate my business to Greg as fast as they could.

'She thought we ought to be given a chance to patch things up,' he said.

'How generous of her,' I said, but Greg ignored the sarcasm.

'It's him, isn't it? The maths-lesson one?'

Attack being the best form of defence, I said, 'Well, what about you and Jackie?'

'What do you care, anyway?' he muttered. He slumped on to the sofa and turned the television back on.

'He's been having a horrendous season, injury-wise,' John Motson was saying.

'Aye,' Alex Ferguson replied. 'You have to feel for the lad, but you've got to bear in mind it's a physical sport.'

I picked up my coat and bag.

' 'Bye Greg.' He didn't look up.

I left the hotel quickly. The tide was going out and it was possible to walk across the wet sand to the other side. I looked for the surfer, but he'd gone.

Our House

There's hardly anything on earth more terrifying than when a group of ordinary, peace-loving citizens turns into an angry, unruly mob, baying for blood.

Or that was the plan, at least. If the genteel inhabitants of certain Channel ports could be mobilised to protest against the export of live cows and sheep, there was surely some way to muster public outrage against the imminent sell-off of a much-loved municipal treasure. Accordingly, Jackie (with whom relations were frosty, to say the least) had been lobbying her customers, serving up propaganda along with the tea and strawberry cheesecake; Stan and his troops had dropped leaflets through letterboxes all over the surrounding area; I'd written letters and phoned every newspaper, historical society, councillor and MP I could think of. Even Lady Eugenie had been agitating at her bridge club.

Everything was geared towards Friday's council finance meeting. Zak was masterminding a demonstration outside it and was sitting at the desk folding a huge pile of leaflets that Flora had run off for him on the photocopier at the school where she taught.

'We could get the Socialist Workers to provide some banners,' he suggested enthusiastically.

'I didn't think protecting stately homes came under the remit of the class struggle,' I said.

'But you see them demonstrating about anything and everything,' he said. 'They're always there at the front of any demo, and they always bring loads of those placards on sticks. If we tell them it's the little guy versus the might of the council they might go for it.'

'I don't think I *want* them to go for it,' I said. 'Even if they did, I should think the presence of the "loony left" would alienate a lot of the people we want on our side.'

The phone rang.

'Hi, am I speaking to Cass Thomson?'

'You are.'

'Hi, Cass, great to talk to you at last!' The voice was female and American, as friendly as blueberry pancakes. 'This is Carmen Dykes. From the Wyoming War Poets' Society? Is this a good time to talk about us arranging to visit with you in the fall?'

'There may never be a better time,' I said. 'It's quite possible we're not going to be here in the autumn.' I told her about the threatened – or, as it seemed now, imminent – closure of the Hall.

'Oh, my Lord,' she said. 'That's calamitous! I am shuddering in disbelief that they can do that, with such disregard for the wonderful history they have on their doorstep. What can I do?' I'd warmed to Carmen Dykes just from the sound of her voice, but that 'what can I do?', which assumed there would *be* something and that she would be prepared to do it, cemented it for me. Though I couldn't honestly think of anything that a handful (literally: as in five) of people in Wyoming could do to help.

'Maybe you could ring or write to the council?' I suggested.

'You betcha. Just give me the numbers.' I gave her the names and addresses of anyone I could think of, and then she said, 'Cass? Remember the indefatigable spirit of the War Poets. Don't give in to tyranny.'

I put the phone down. 'Carmen Dykes just told me not to give in to tyranny,' I told Zak.

'Too right,' he said.

I sighed. 'Trouble is, I don't know if I've got the heart for a fight. I mean, it seems to me that this is a done deal as far as the council's concerned, and all we're doing is shouting into the wind.'

'You mean pissing. But you can't think like that, Cass,' Zak said, getting up from his seat at the desk and stretching his back and shoulders. 'Have you ever read *Titus Groan*?'

'Years ago, when I was at school.'

'Well, think of yourself as Barquentine, the Keeper of the Ritual: these ancient stones are in your hands. Think of old Randy Robertson as Steerpike.'

'Bad analogy. I can't remember whether Barquentine ends up burned, or drowned, or both, but Steerpike definitely wins that one.'

'So he wins the battle – but does he win the war?'

'You're a real comfort, Zak.'

Living On The Ceiling

As soon as he stepped through the door we could tell that the man in the checked suit was a potential buyer rather than a normal visitor. It was the way he ignored what Zak liked to call 'the artefacts' and looked straight at the big picture – the building itself. You could see him mentally knocking down walls and dismantling things, picturing what the walls in the former drawing room would look like with a colour scheme of, let's say, cerise and aubergine.

'Enemy sighted,' Stan muttered. He eased himself from his stool behind the information desk and slid into action. 'Lovely old house, isn't it?' he said, placing himself directly in the path of the man in the checked suit who was doing his best to pretend to be a normal customer. He nodded, trying to look nonchalant. 'Of course,' Stan continued, 'in a house like this, you're always going to run across one or two problems.'

'Such as?' Checked Suit asked, *faux* casually.

Stan drew a deep breath. 'Well, where do you start? The roof wants replacing, for a kick-off, but of course you can't do that without sorting out the walls first. Timbers are rotten, in my opinion, then the whole lot wants replastering. And, of course, while you're doing that, it needs rewiring: electrics are shot to pieces. There's going to be a serious electrical incident before too long, I'm always on at them about it. Then there's—'

Almost as if they'd rehearsed it, Zak came rushing through brandishing a broom. 'Did you see it?'

'See what, lad?' Stan asked, innocently.

'The rat! Great monster of a thing, just sitting there like he owned the place.' Playing my part, I screeched in a girly fashion and jumped up on my chair. Checked-suit man was looking a little uneasy.

'A – rat?' he said.

'Don't bother us usually,' Stan said. 'We just learn to work around them. Part of the character of the place.'

'This one was bloody enormous, though!' Zak said, and carried on his pursuit into the next room, from where a moment later we could hear the sound of him giving something a good thrashing.

'Sounds like a resilient bugger,' Stan remarked.

Checked-suit man didn't stay long after that.

This effective scheme would have been put to wider use, had Jackie not gone bananas when she heard about it.

'You're telling people we have *rats*?' she stormed. 'What if he'd been a health inspector? What if he reports us? You could get me closed down, you bunch of morons.'

While there was nothing that would have made me happier than Jackie not being around any longer, I'm not vindictive and I'm not stupid. 'No more rat stories,' I told Stan and Zak. 'Or cockroaches or anything of that sort. We'll have to think of something else.'

And quickly, I thought to myself. We all had this feeling that Coltsfoot Hall was slipping out of our hands.

Labelled With Love

I have this occasional escapist tendency, which becomes more pronounced in times of crisis, to imagine I'm in a film of my own life. I find it enlivens certain mundane tasks, like dusting, or fetching the post.

Picture this: the screen completely dark to begin with, only the sound of beautiful piano music – something by Mozart, perhaps – gradually brightening to a close-up of a lily-white, unringed, very feminine hand trailing artistically down a banister carved from a deep, dark wood, burnished to a mirror-like sheen. The camera pans around panelled oak walls, dwelling for a few seconds on the portraits hanging there, stiff and solemn, ornate dresses and powdered wigs, cherubic children and ruddy-cheeked adults. Then we track along a sunlit hallway, in which dust motes hang lazily, to a door beyond which we glimpse a mahogany escritoire, tapestried chairs and an ancient grandfather clock. For a second we can hear the clock ticking slowly and ponderously, then the piano music begins to swell to a climax and we cut to a close-up of the slippered feet of our heroine (me, remember) as she treads softly down the stairs to alight on the worn, warped floorboards.

The music fades and is replaced by different music, a keyboard and guitar, which are joined after two bars by a female singer with a distinctive, quavering voice – Cyndi Lauper singing 'Time After Time'. Try as I might, at this point I can never keep Cyndi Lauper off the soundtrack. I try to turn the mental Mozart up louder but Cyndi keeps bouncing back like the Andrex puppy. As the vocals come in, we cut to a long shot of the back of our heroine as she walks from the staircase to the door in her brocade slippers and elegant, deep-blue bathrobe. She crosses the floor and bends down to pick up a pile of post from behind the door.

The next shot would have to be a close-up of me, the crazy woman who has these images of herself as the heroine of a wildly romantic novel, something by the Brontës or Thomas Hardy, or Jane Austen if only she'd let her hair down a bit more. The vapour from my breath would give a good impression of the ancient chill of Coltsfoot Hall in the mornings, and the viewer would see me dash back up the stairs at a pace somewhat faster than my languid descent, hotly pursued by Cyndi Lauper singing 'Time After Time'. Since I'd seen Gideon again I couldn't get that song out of my head.

But on this particular morning I couldn't summon the enthusiasm to pretend that I was in a movie of my life. In fact, I was deliberately *not* looking at the portraits of the ancestors, ignoring how Sheryl had buffed the woodwork to a reflective brilliance with her new high-tech dusters, shutting my nostrils to the smells of old furniture and plaster and damp. I was trying to reconcile myself to the fact that I wouldn't be living here much longer. All of our protests were falling on ears deafened by the sound of money. Barring a miracle Coltsfoot Hall was being put up for sale at the end of the month.

*

In a spirit of both resignation and desperation I'd been applying for lots of jobs, anything that seemed vaguely interesting, and I was expecting a few application forms in the post. The next thing would be to look for a flat to rent somewhere. Zak and Flora had offered to let me stay with them until I could find somewhere else to live, but I couldn't imagine that that would be a very satisfactory arrangement for anybody, and I hoped to avoid it if at all possible. The last thing you need when you're homeless, jobless and single is to be living with love's volatile young dream.

I flicked through the pile of letters. There were, as I'd thought, a couple of replies to my job-hunting queries, one as an information assistant for a national charity, the other at a museum in Kent. I wasn't even interested enough to look at them, and tossed them to one side. I cupped my chin in my hands and stared out of the window, completely disheartened.

When I finally turned my attention back to the post, the next letter I picked up had a Devon postmark. I didn't remember applying for any jobs in Devon, but this letter didn't look like a job application anyway: it was hand-written and addressed to 'Catherine Thomson'.

I stared at the writing on the envelope as best I could, given that my hands were shaking so hard. I only knew one person in Devon, and I only knew one person in the world who would address me as Catherine.

I hadn't had any contact with Gideon since the morning he'd kissed my cheek outside his house and disappeared inside as fast as he could, and with everything else going on I'd almost managed to convince myself that I didn't care if I never saw him again. If I didn't care, I wouldn't get hurt. It was such a thin veneer of not-caring that the only way I could maintain it was not to think about him at all. Any time his name or his face floated into my mind I shoved them ruthlessly away. I was getting quite good at it – it was almost like a form of meditation. And now this. My hands were trembling as I opened the envelope.

There was a note: *For old times. G.* And a cheque. A cheque for a considerable amount of money: practically more than I'd earned in total in my entire working life. It was signed Gideon Harker.

I sat with the cheque in my hand, staring at it, staring particularly at the signature, a big, confident sprawl in black ink, trying to divine somehow what had been in his head when he'd signed it. It was hard to believe that someone I'd gone to school with had that amount of money to give away, but what had possessed him to give it to me? Though the cheque was in my name, I knew that the money wasn't for me: it was for the museum, the old times that it represented as much as for our shared history. Gideon had given me the means to rescue Coltsfoot Hall. When the councillors saw this, they would at least have to put their plans on hold, which would give us the time and the leverage to fund-raise. It's a fact that most people won't give you money unless you already have some.

I rang Heather, who was now back in Birmingham. 'How are things going?' I asked her.

'Better,' she said. 'I've even started speaking to Pierre again. He might be a lying, conniving, screwed-up fuck, but I decided all that rage was bad for my karma.'

'So you didn't get him deported?'

She laughed. 'It was only ever an option. I trashed his Abba collection instead – so much more satisfying, and a service to the planet at the same time. A little *directed* rage can be quite beneficial. So what's happening in your world? Heard from the lovely Gideon again?'

I told her about the cheque.

She couldn't believe it, either. 'He must be loaded,' she said, when I told her the amount. 'He always was weird. Imagine living like a monk by the seaside, with all this cash.'

'Hardly a monk,' I said, remembering the ex-girlfriends Suzanne had talked about. 'But you know what this means? He must still care about me. He wouldn't do this, otherwise.'

'Well, that's one conclusion you could draw,' she said, 'but it wouldn't explain why he hasn't tried to get in touch since you saw him. He could just be feeling benevolent.'

That wasn't what I had been hoping she'd say. I wanted her to agree with me. But what she'd said was probably more realistic, and her realism was catching. 'Or me turning up like that has finally pricked his conscience about dumping me and he's trying to make himself feel better by buying me off,' I said.

'If you want my opinion, the most likely explanation is that his accountant has told him to shift some loot before the tax man gets wind of it.' That was depressingly likely. 'So have you cashed it?' Heather asked.

'No,' I said. 'I just got it. Anyway, I can't cash it without knowing why he sent it to me.'

Heather snorted. 'That's so transparent, woman. It's just an excuse to contact him again, isn't it?'

'Maybe.'

'Definitely. But if I was you, I'd get that cheque banged straight into the bank in case he changes his mind. Then give him a call.'

'I don't have his number and he's unlisted. And I don't want to write to him, anyway. I need to see him.'

'So you're going to go hurtling all that way down to Devon? You're off your chops, my dear.'

Tainted Love

This time I hired a car. I hadn't driven in a long time, and it took some getting used to, but once I was clear of London I zipped along the A31 enjoying the scenery and the feeling of freedom, and the anticipation of seeing Gideon again.

It was a different story once I'd turned off the main road between Exeter and Plymouth and was on to those little hedge-sentried country lanes. I'm not the most confident driver, and at every turn I expected to collide with a car coming too fast in the opposite direction; I was constantly braced for impact. My nervousness also increased with the knowledge that every mile was bringing me nearer and nearer to him, wondering whether I'd be welcome or not, at one minute encouraged by him sending me the cheque, at the next discouraged by his behaviour last time.

In the end the drive was uneventful. The worst thing that happened was that I got stuck for about half an hour behind a very slow truck carrying Calor gas canisters. The frequent stops while other drivers reversed to let us by at least gave me time to consult the map I'd brought.

After a lot of wrong-turnings in identical-looking roads that left me feeling like I was in Hampton Court maze, I at last found the entrance to the long and winding lane that led to Gideon's house and turned into it. It wasn't much of a relief: after driving for hours in a state of high anxiety the last thing you need is to have to negotiate a bumpy track barely the width of your vehicle. I could hear branches scraping along the sides and top of the car as it bumped and crunched its way along, and wondered how much of my deposit the hire company would want to retain after seeing the fine mess I'd got it into.

And after everything else, the *last* thing I needed was to see Suzanne's car parked outside the house: I badly wanted to talk to Gideon on his own. Suzanne herself was fastening a surfboard to her roof-rack. When she heard the car she turned. 'Bloody hell, you gave me a fright,' she said, as I got out. She tightened straps carefully around the board and jiggled it a bit, testing to make certain it was secure.

'Is Gideon around?' I asked her.

She looked at me as if I was mad. 'I thought you must have just come from him,' she said.

'I haven't seen him.' Belatedly I noticed that the windows of the house were all shuttered up. 'Has he gone away?'

'You might say that,' she said. 'He's done a runner. He's being investigated for fraud.'

'What?' I stared at her: this wasn't making any sense. She was still faffing with the surfboard, paying as much attention to it as if it were a delicate child.

She noticed me looking at her, and a vaguely guilty look passed over her face. 'It's my board,' she said defensively. 'He's been fixing a ding in it; nobody can wreck a board faster than me.'

'Never mind the surfboard,' I said, wanting to knock her silly head off with it. 'What did you mean about him being investigated for fraud? Where's he gone?'

'No idea,' she said. 'It's something to do with that bank he used to work for. Seems like he didn't make his fortune exactly legally. No wonder he's been holed up here all this time. You'd think he'd at least have had the sense to get further away than Devon.'

I couldn't believe this. I knew Gideon. I might not have seen him in fifteen years, I didn't know about everything he'd *done* but I thought I knew about everything he *was*, and I would have bet my life on him being honest. 'You've no idea where I might be able to contact him?'

'You're very keen,' she said. 'I mean, he's cute and everything, but . . .'

'He sent me some money,' I said, and wished I hadn't.

Suzanne gave me a withering look. 'Getting rid of the evidence, was he?' When I didn't reply she shrugged and swung her long legs into her car. 'See you around,' she said, and drove off, leaving me standing there.

I walked to the other side of the house and sat by the river. The sky was hanging low and grey. There was no breeze, only a dull, damp cold. Even though the scene was still beautiful, there was no joy in it, and everything looked cold and lonely, as if it was missing him.

Rattlesnakes

The drive back to the Hall was horrible. My mind kept going over and over everything, wondering what had happened to Gideon, whether the cheque I'd received had really been, as Suzanne had said, Gideon's way of offloading some of his ill-gotten gains. Would that have been so much worse than finding out he was just using Coltsfoot Hall as a way of avoiding paying more tax?

By the time I'd reached the outskirts of London, my mind was made up. It seemed that, contrary to my overly romantic notions, his motive for sending me the money hadn't been merely altruistic. It was even possible I was being used as an accessory in some kind of crime. But in the absence of any firm evidence either way, what I had was a very handy sum of money that might be the difference between the Hall surviving or not. It would have been insane from any viewpoint not to use it.

The next morning I rang the detested grants officer. I was looking forward to giving him the news that, despite his best efforts, the supermodels would have to look elsewhere for their rehab clinic.

'Randall Robertson, please.'

'Who shall I say is calling?' a minion answered, and I had to pity him: imagine having to see Randall Robertson every single day.

'Cass Thomson from Coltsfoot Hall.'

'Sorry, it's a bad line, I didn't catch that.'

'Cass Thomson.'

'One moment . . . I'm sorry Mizz Cuthbertson, but Mr Robertson seems to be away from his desk.'

'I'll hold.'

'You might be on hold for rather a long time. It usually takes him quite a while to . . . be away from his desk,' he said.

In other words, he was on the loo. 'I'm not in any hurry. I'll hold.' The line clicked on to the council's recorded 'on hold' music: Kermit the Frog's 'It's Not Easy Being Green'. A comment on the council's recycling policy or a cunning psychological weapon designed to make people who are on hold hang up with all possible speed? I didn't know, but I was prepared to endure the entire Muppets repertoire if necessary.

The line clicked, and the amphibious rhapsody was abruptly curtailed. 'Ms Cuthbertson? Randall Robertson here. How may I be of service?'

'It's Cass Thomson, from Coltsfoot Hall.'

'Oh.' Suddenly he sounded as welcoming as a barbed-wire doormat.

'I'd like to discuss the financing of the Hall.'

'I think we've exhausted that topic,' he said. 'Any last requests can be made to the members at the finance sub-committee.'

'Does it make a difference that I've got secure funding here for six months?'

There was a pause. 'What?'

'We've received a donation from . . . a benefactor. It covers over six months of the present subsidy. Which means that you've got no reason to sell the Hall.' There was a long silence. 'Mr Robertson? Are you still there?'

'It's a very bad line,' he said. It's true that there was quite a lot of noise on the line, but I was certain he'd heard what I'd said and was playing for time.

'Mr Robertson?'

'Look, I'll pass on the thrust of your news for the members to suck on at the budget meeting, okay?'

'Surely the meeting won't have to happen now?'

'Due process, I'm afraid, Ms Thomson, due process.'

'But the house will be taken off the market?'

'It's an option you can take up with the members. Now, I'm very busy, Ms Thomson. Good day.'

Wishful Thinking

'I ought to feel pleased,' I said to Zak, 'but why do I get the feeling it could all still go pear-shaped?' I told him about the conversation with Randall Robertson, and about Gideon's cheque.

'Bloody hell, mate! That's fantastic!' he said, flinging his arms round me and giving me a huge hug. 'I wish I'd seen his face! God, I need to ring Flora. Have you told Jackie yet?'

'No,' I said. 'Maybe you could mention it to her.'

He rolled his eyes. 'Still not made it up with her, eh? It's like working in no man's land with the hostilities between you two. Look, I'll ring Flora, then we'll both go and tell

Jackie and I'll escort you to the bank to deposit that cheque.'

'There's no rush,' I said, still hesitating at the thought of actually spending Gideon's money. Zak looked baffled. 'I mean, we perhaps ought to get some advice about how to deal with such a large donation,' I said, which when I'd said it did in fact sound like a sensible plan. 'There might be ways to invest it or whatever.'

Zak picked up the phone to call his girlfriend, but before he did he asked me, 'So what's this guy doing donating all this money to us?' I gave him the abridged version. 'Crikey. Well, aren't *you* a dark horse?' was his response. 'So your trip to Plymouth wasn't for nothing, after all.'

When he put it that way, then maybe not, but having a bit of a lift in the tension about the museum only gave me more time to think about Gideon. What was happening to him? Perhaps he was in prison, or being held in a police station somewhere. I wished I had Suzanne's address or phone number to see if she'd had any news – she wouldn't be the friendliest source of information, but better that than nothing. I thought of contacting the bank again, but if they wouldn't tell me anything about him when he was merely an ex-employee, presumably they wouldn't be very forthcoming in discussing someone who was supposed to have stolen money from them.

In the end I did nothing, because there was nothing to do.

Senses Working Overtime

I woke up abruptly, surfacing from deep sleep to wakefulness in about half a second. My heart was hammering. At first I wasn't sure what had woken me up, and wondered whether it had been a nightmare. Then I heard the noise.

I'm not easily spooked: I couldn't have stayed on my own in a museum if I had been, although it's true that I usually kept to the flat once everything was closed for the night. I was used to a certain amount of creaking from the old building as it settled down, but the sound I'd just heard was definitely not in Coltsfoot Hall's normal repertoire.

Slipping out of bed, I crossed quietly to the bedroom door in my bare feet and opened it, holding my breath while I listened. There was the noise again.

I hesitated. I knew the sensible course of action would be to call the police. The sound was coming from outside, in the Hall itself, not from my flat, so I could get to the phone and make the call and hopefully whoever or whatever was making the sound wouldn't be aware of my presence. I paused and listened again: nothing, this time. Maybe it was all in my imagination, or something as relatively harmless as mice (though Zak would be furious at the idea that mice had been trampling his beloved exhibits). Calling the police out would be too embarrassing if it was just mice. I opened the door.

It was freezing on the staircase as usual, and as soon as I was out there I realised how vulnerable I was and how stupid it was to be creeping around a deserted mansion in the middle of the night, unarmed, and with the martial-arts ability of the average duckling. As I turned round to retreat to the comparative safety of the flat, a sudden draught caught the door and it slammed hard, with me on the outside. A half second after that I thought I heard footsteps downstairs, and another bang like the echo of the door closing.

I was absolutely terrified. There was no doubt that something or somebody was downstairs, and there was equally no doubt that I'd just managed to lock myself out of the flat. The spare key and the only other phones in the house, including my mobile, were in the office.

I sat down at the top of the stairs, listening as hard as I

could, keeping as still as a statue, hardly even breathing. My mind was conjuring images of masked intruders, ghosts, rats. I heartily wished I was anywhere but there. I stayed like that for perhaps fifteen minutes or more, until I was so cold my head started to ache and my hands and feet were numb. There had been no more sounds. At last I tiptoed downstairs, ready to retreat again at the slightest sound, but there was nothing.

Gradually I started to think I'd imagined it all. Probably I'd been having a nightmare, and although my body had woken up, my imagination had continued to produce spooky thoughts, interpreting quite normal sounds as something more sinister. I padded barefoot through the rooms of the ground floor of the Hall, flicking on lights as I went. Everything was just as I'd left it, just as it always was. Weak with relief I went to the office to get the spare keys to the flat. I took the mobile phone with me, too, for extra reassurance.

What was worth stealing in this place, anyway? I thought, my gaze resting on a tapestry-covered chair that Zak had tied string across to stop people from sitting on it. There were lots of anonymous portraits, several rather beautiful but probably worthless Victorian mirrors and framed maps of the area. The only thing really worth breaking in for was a small case of Victorian mourning jewellery – with the emphasis on 'small' – which was still in its place. I looked at a carefully arranged display case labelled 'Childhood Through The Ages': a top-and-whip, pogo sticks, a yoyo that I knew for a fact Zak had bought at Hamley's, and possibly the finest collection of Clackers seen since the seventies. It was hardly the Crown Jewels.

I walked back across the entrance hall, and it was then I noticed that a stack of leaflets advertising local beauty spots was scattered all over the floor, like shiny coloured leaves. They must have blown over in one of Coltsfoot Hall's legendary draughts, maybe when my door had slammed shut.

Scooping them up into a rough pile and dumping them on a table, I hurried back up to the flat, locked the door behind me, and burrowed back down under the duvet.

Land of Make-believe

'Luigi Keith,' the man introduced himself, shaking my hand rather fiercely. '*Weekly Star and Advertiser*. We spoke on the phone.'

'Pleased to meet you,' I said. 'Would you like a coffee, or shall I show you round the museum?'

He fished in his pocket and produced a digital camera and a notebook. 'Lead the way,' he said. 'You're lucky it's a bit of a slow news week. I'm normally in court on a weekday afternoon. I do criminal stories, usually.' I refrained from saying, 'I know, I've read some of them,' and led him through the various rooms of the Hall.

'I must say it's looking pretty busy in here for a term-time weekday,' he said. 'I didn't expect it to be such a popular attraction.' Certainly there were a lot of visitors that day. The coffee-shop was bustling, and clusters of excited punters admired the various displays. I even heard someone say, 'Wow!' at the sight of the signed Beatles photograph, which I thought was overdoing it a bit. Zak and Stan were rushing backwards and forwards, making sure nothing was stolen, tampered with or otherwise touched.

They needn't have bothered, as they well knew. The 'visitors' were almost entirely bogus and included three generations of Stan's family, Sheryl, her husband Dirk and her bingo partner Elsie, Harrison the bread man and offspring, and four pensioners Stan had met at the bus stop and bribed inside with the offer of free tea and buns. I only hoped that our guest hadn't noticed that the same group of people seemed to be going round and round and never leaving.

I'd thought it would be a good idea to invite the local reporter over, treat him to a filled bap in the coffee-shop and show him around the Hall. Getting some positive publicity would be a major step forward. To present Coltsfoot Hall as an exciting, dynamic attraction was going to be trickier, but watching *The Truman Show* on video had given me an idea for a cunning plan. We would present the reporter with an 'alternative reality'.

It seemed to be working. Luigi Keith was looking quite impressed. 'I thought you were hard-pressed to get visitors here,' he said, 'but it's bustling this morning. Is this typical?'

'Oh, pretty much so,' I said breezily, wondering if he could see my nose growing, Pinocchio-like, as I spoke the words.

'And you say the council are pulling your funding?'

I nodded. 'It's going to leave us financially high and dry,' I said. 'We'll most likely have to close, and this popular' – I crossed my fingers behind my back – 'resource will be lost to the community.'

'Doesn't seem right, does it?' he said, taking a few snapshots. 'Who do you deal with on the council?'

'Randall Robertson.'

The reporter lowered his camera and gazed at me with his slightly bulging grey eyes. 'That explains it, then,' he said. 'Slasher Robertson, King of the Cuts, as we call him at the *Weekly Star and Advertiser*.'

We made our way past Harrison the bread man and his seven-year-old son Ronan, who were contemplating the 'Childhood Through The Ages' display.

'Look at that,' Harrison was saying. '"Circo The Automatic Clown. Tumbles and flips, goes upside down." Daddy used to have one of those.'

'It's rank!' Ronan sneered. 'I wanna go home.'

I shot Harrison a look, and he gave an apologetic laugh. 'He loves it here,' he assured the reporter.

Apart from Ronan, everyone played their part beautifully, and I could tell that Luigi Keith was impressed. I walked him to the front door. 'Will you be running the story?' I asked him.

'I'll try, but it's up to my editor. And, frankly, it's a bit of a non-story.'

'Not to all these people here it isn't,' I said.

Luigi Keith took a last look around the entrance hall, 'I'll see what I can do,' he said.

Just What I Always Wanted

That evening, after everyone had gone home (it took a while because the pensioners were keen to take full advantage of Stan's free-buns offer), I sat in my window seat watching the sky getting dark and the street lights appearing along the far side of the park like a string of fairy lights. There was a faint background hum of traffic and the radiators gurgled and pinged as they warmed up, but otherwise everything was quiet. After the spookiness of the previous night I was feeling jumpy, anyway, but when the doorbell rang the sudden noise in the darkness was nerve-jangling. Zak hadn't been gone long, and I guessed he must have forgotten something. I hopped off the window seat, put the light on, and went downstairs.

I never opened the door after the museum was closed without looking through the little window to the side of it. I looked out now and my heart was pounding like a steam-hammer as I unlatched the door.

Gideon smiled. 'I didn't think anyone was in,' he said. 'It looked deserted.'

Seeing him at his home had been one thing; seeing him so unexpectedly here at mine was strange, like he'd stepped out of a dream. He seemed a little bit taller, a little bit more real, somehow, than ordinary men, kind of luminous, but to me he always had. I was romantically unhinged.

'This is beautiful,' he said, as we climbed the staircase. 'Such a beautiful house.'

We sat down in my small living room. As on the night when I'd pierced his ear, I was amazed all over again at the way his long legs could fill a space. I was as nervous as I had been on that night, too, and went to make coffee to give myself a minute or two to calm down.

'You got the cheque okay?' he asked, when I returned.

'I got it,' I said, 'but I haven't used it. I went down to Devon to talk to you about it, but you'd gone.'

'Suzanne told me. She also told me what she'd said to you.'

'About you being under suspicion of fraud?'

He nodded. 'The bank think I was systematically embezzling money from them while I was working there. Not that they'll tell me anything about it, of course. All I know is that it's still an internal matter, and they'll try to keep it that way if they can, to avoid a scandal that might panic the clients and shareholders.' His voice was quite neutral: he didn't *sound* guilty, but neither was he vehemently protesting his innocence. I waited for him to say more, and wondered if I should prompt him, but he changed the subject. 'On your own tonight?'

'I was until you turned up.'

'So where's your boyfriend?' I was certain I hadn't mentioned Greg either to him or Suzanne. I glanced round the room: maybe he'd spotted some sign of recent masculine occupation, but I doubted it. Greg had moved his possessions out, lock, stock and radio-alarm.

'I live on my own,' I said. 'I *was* going out with someone, but that finished a little while ago.'

The expression on his face changed. 'A *very* little while. Like last week?'

'Gideon, what's this about?'

He sat forward in his chair, his elbows resting on his knees. 'I rang your hotel in Plymouth,' he said, 'and they told me you'd left with your boyfriend. To a romantic assignation at Burgh Island, they said. Sounds like he's got style.'

I thought about Greg whisking me off to that lovely hotel, and how all I'd wanted to do was run back to Gideon. 'It didn't really work out like he planned,' I said, searching his face for a reaction, and not getting one. 'So why were you trying to ring me?' I asked, and at last his face cracked into a smile.

'Oh, why do you think? I wanted to see you.'

'Why?'

'When I came home that afternoon and saw you sitting by the river looking like something the seagulls had dropped—'

'Thanks.'

'I'm not finished. When I saw you there, when I was sure it was really you, I realised how much I'd missed you.'

'You hid that very well,' I said, confused.

'I'm good at hiding things.' He reached over and took my hand in his. 'Do you remember the total eclipse?' he asked.

'How could I forget?' I said, the touch of his hand making me feel so dislocated and nervous that I started to waffle. 'I spent an hour standing in the car park downstairs, staring through a pinhole in a sheet of white A4 at a tiny pinprick image of a crescent sun.' I was so conscious of his hand holding mine that I felt as if all my nerve-endings were concentrated in that one place. 'Then it got a bit nippy and the sky went kind of twilight-looking. That was how spectacular the total eclipse was in London.'

He smiled and at that moment he was my old friend from

202

school once more. 'You should have been in Devon,' he said. 'We saw the eclipse properly there. It was the most incredible, awesome thing. And when everything went dark and the birds stopped singing, my first thought was to wonder if you were seeing it too.'

'Not really?'

'It sounds a bit sad, doesn't it?' he said. 'But it's true. The same as there's not a twenty-fifth of August has ever gone by without me thinking about you. I don't mean I do nothing else the whole day long – that *would* be sad – but whenever I hear that date mentioned I always think: That's Catherine's birthday.' While he was talking he'd started stroking the palm of my hand with his thumb. I hadn't noticed at first, I was too busy trying to take in what he was saying, but as he was talking I became increasingly aware of this soft, slow, even pressure on my palm. It was the most erotic sensation; I felt like I was melting.

I snatched my hand back.

'What's wrong?' he asked, looking surprised.

'I'm not having this,' I said. 'You can't just drop back into my life after fifteen years and expect me to believe you missed me.'

'As I recall, it was you who dropped back into *my* life,' he said. 'You came looking for me. What were you expecting to find?'

More to the point, what had I been *hoping* to find? If I'd ever dared to play out a best-case scenario in my mind it would have been exactly like this moment – Gideon telling me he'd been thinking of me during all those years apart, that he still cared about me; that I would find him as easy to talk to and attractive as I remembered and that he would still be able to make me shiver just by touching me. It was all there, and should have been perfect, but I wouldn't let it be.

'We don't know each other any more,' I said, but I knew that wasn't really the problem, or it hadn't felt like a problem when we were sitting at his kitchen table having breakfast, or walking on the wet sand on his beach.

'It would be nice to get to know each other all over again,' he said.

'No, it wouldn't.' And then it all came out in a rush. 'You can't just dump me when it suits you to go off and have your exciting career, then buy me back again with a big cheque and a load of waffle about the eclipse. Don't try and tell me you've been pining and celibate all this time.'

'Pining maybe,' he said, and a slight smile ghosted across his face, 'but not celibate, no. And don't for a minute think I'm trying to buy you. I was only trying to help you, and if you don't want the cheque, just tear it up. It's all the same to me.'

'Easy come, easy go, eh? Like everything else.'

'Meaning you?'

'If you like.'

'That's not how it was,' he said. 'I left *everything*. I wanted to start again where no one knew me. It seemed like the only way when I was eighteen. But that doesn't mean it was easy to leave you.'

'Oh, please,' I snapped, close to tears. 'That sounds like such a *line*. You didn't find it that difficult to tear yourself away, I seem to remember.' He reached out to put his arms around me, and really I wanted nothing more than to be wrapped up and looked after by him, but I was feeling too hurt and frightened of how strongly he was making me feel. I couldn't even cope with him being there. I asked him to leave, but he didn't move.

'I'm not going while you're upset. I don't know how I can convince you—'

'You can't.' I forced my voice to be as cold as possible. I couldn't believe how practised I was getting at being horrible to men who claimed to care about me. His hands dropped back to his sides and I could feel him looking at me even though I wouldn't meet his eyes.

After a while he said, 'Okay, I'll go. But I want you to know that I meant every word I've said to you. I'll leave you the number of the place I'm staying at in London, and if you want to you can give me a call.' He wrote a number down on one of the Save Coltsfoot Hall flyers that were heaped on the table. I didn't say anything and couldn't even look at him in case I changed my mind. I led the way downstairs and unlocked the door. He turned to leave, but then turned back. 'Just one question: when's *my* birthday?'

'November the seventh,' I answered automatically. He smiled, and walked away into the darkness.

Say Hello, Wave Goodbye

As he disappeared from view, I thought I heard something rustling in a clump of bushes about twenty yards from the house. There was something purposeful about the sound that I didn't like and I fought off an impulse to call Gideon to come back, stepped inside quickly and bolted the door. I checked every window on the ground floor, making doubly sure that all was safe and secure. At each window I looked out, half fearing that someone outside would be looking in at me. I dashed up the stairs and locked the flat door behind me.

Safely inside, I decided I was being silly, putting it down to my heightened feelings. Gideon's coffee mug was still on the floor where he'd left it. I picked it up and carried it to the kitchen, thinking that his lips had so lately been touching that very surface, and he would still be here now if only I hadn't been so . . . I couldn't quite work out what it was I had been.

Proud? Defensive? Stupid? Probably a mix of all three, at the time, but stupid was the way I felt now.

The phone started to ring, making me jump, and I put the mug down quickly and rushed to answer it.

'Gideon?'

'No, it's me, Heather. I was calling for an update, and I guess from that greeting that you have something to update me on.'

I told her what had happened.

'I don't understand you,' she said. 'You've been hankering after him all this time, and when he presents himself on a plate telling you he's missed you, you give him the brush-off.'

'But how can I trust him? He's let me down before, and this ex-girlfriend of his I met in Devon implied heavily that he'd been two-timing her while they were together, so he's let *her* down, too. Not to mention that he's being investigated for fraud.'

'So it's true, then?'

'Apparently so. He didn't actually deny that he'd done it, either.'

'But you don't really believe he did?'

'Of course I don't. At least, I don't think so.'

'You don't *think* so?'

'Well, nobody knows anyone else totally, do they?'

'That's true. I certainly didn't know I was married to someone who was more hotel than motel, or the other way round.'

'But it's not the fraud business that worries me, really,' I said. 'If I'd let things progress the way they were going he'd probably still be here now, but where would I be? Still letting myself be railroaded by some man, just like I was with Greg.'

'But you *love* this man. He's your soul-mate, you said.'

'I know. He is.'

'You're not making any sense.'

I sighed. I wasn't even making much sense to myself.

Advice came from an unexpected source. The next day a visitor appeared in the doorway of the office.

'Lady Eugenie! This is a nice surprise.'

'Nothing but blooming snooker on TV, thought I'd drop in,' she said, tottering into the room. I rushed to clear a pile of paperwork off a chair and she sank on to it, leaning her walking-stick against the desk. She was sporting one of the bluest blue rinses I've ever seen: disconcertingly, her hair was almost exactly the same colour as her eyes and her raincoat, giving her the appearance of someone who'd been coloured in by a child with only a limited number of crayons.

'You look like a wet Tuesday in Wimbledon fortnight,' she commented, and I wondered why Tuesday should be a worse day than others for a Centre Court deluge. She looked around. 'Good grief, this place could do with a lick of paint. It's no wonder you're depressed.'

'Actually, we've got reason to celebrate,' I said, and told her about Gideon's money.

She absolutely beamed at me, a radiant smile that showed what a beautiful woman she must once have been. 'I knew we were right to give you the job!' she said. 'Clever girl! Now, what about a celebratory beverage?'

'Sorry?'

'I was wondering when you were going to offer me a cup of tea,' she explained.

'Oh, yes, of course. Sorry. I'll put the kettle on.'

'I'd rather you went and got some from that girl in the cafeteria. She does a lovely pot of Darjeeling. I bet you only have tea-bags.'

I wasn't thrilled at the prospect of having to talk to Jackie. We were still one step away from handbags at dawn and I avoided her whenever possible, but nothing came between Lady Eugenie and her tea.

'It's for the dowager,' I explained to Jackie, in case she thought I was in the coffee-shop of my own free will, 'so make it a good one.'

'Nice and strong, just how she likes it,' she said, between clenched teeth, handing me the cup.

It looked as though Lady Eugenie was asleep when I returned, but she sat up bright and alert when she scented tea.

'Oh, how kind. No biscuits?'

I traipsed back to Jackie.

Once settled with tea and biscuits, Lady Eugenie switched into solicitous mode. 'I'm so glad things are looking up. It must have been very hard for you, with all those imbeciles from the council and their machinations, and then your young man deserting you.'

How word got around. 'He didn't desert me,' I said. 'I broke up with him.'

'Well, good for you, dear,' she said, sipping at her tea. 'That girl does make a lovely cup of tea. Thick enough to stand the spoon up in. Can't be doing with weak dishy-washy water.' Another sip. 'Any particular reason for it?'

'The tea?'

'For giving what's-his-name the old heave-ho.'

There was no reason to confide in this slightly batty old lady except that she'd asked, and she was there, and there was something comforting about her sensible mac and her flat, putty-coloured shoes and alarmingly bright tan stockings. 'I realised I was in love with someone else,' I said.

She reached to put the cup down on my desk; it jangled in the saucer. 'How lovely,' she said, her eyes bright. 'And is it love of an all-consuming, sweepingly passionate nature?'

I imagined a pile of Barbara Cartland paperbacks on her

bedside table and tried not to smile in case she thought I was being rude. 'I suppose it is,' I said.

'Reciprocated?'

'I don't know.'

She tutted. 'Young people these days are such chumps,' she commented. 'What you need is a war. I know they have a lot of drawbacks, but they do focus your mind wonderfully on the priorities.'

'I can imagine.'

'No, you can't. You've no idea how appalling it feels when the man you adore with all your heart has to leave the next day and you don't know if you'll ever see him again.'

'It must have been very hard for you when Sir Sheldon had to go away to fight,' I said.

'Sir Sheldon? Goodness, no. Hardly gave it a thought, what with the business and the house and the children to run.' She rummaged in her handbag, which was the same putty colour as her shoes and big enough to contain a sub-post office, and produced a creased, faded, black-and-white photograph of a young man in a tweed jacket and trousers cinched at the ankles with bicycle clips. His hair was oiled and parted at one side in an astonishingly straight line.

I looked questioningly at her, and she returned my gaze with a little smile. 'My Horace,' she said. 'He was killed in France. And, dear, let me tell you, if he was to walk in here now I would never, ever let him walk back out without me.' She gave Horace a last fond glance, put him back in her bag and picked up her tea-cup again.

So I rang Gideon on the number he'd left. 'I'm sorry,' I said. 'I don't know why I reacted like that.'

'Well, I do,' he said, 'because I reacted the same way when you came to my house.' There was a pause. 'So, what do you want to do?' he asked.

Nervously, I replied, 'I don't want to hear anything else about eclipses and birthdays. But I'd like to get to know you again, as a friend.'

'I think I can live with that,' he said 'But on one condition.'

'What's that?'

'You have to let me help you do something about that house you live in. I know it's important to you, and I'm sure I can help somehow. I don't mean money – I'm not trying to buy you. Just let me help.'

Now where had I had an offer like that before? Philip Oliver, on the day of the reunion. I smiled to myself: there was no comparison. As far as I remembered, Gideon's knees were almost entirely hair-free.

'It's a deal,' I said.

Somebody's Watching Me

Perhaps to reassure me that he wasn't going to try to railroad me into any romantic situations, when Gideon turned up the following day he was accompanied by a small entourage, if you can describe two men as an entourage. They looked about the same age as him and were introduced as Kieran and Sebastian. Gideon said they were business consultants who wanted to help with the museum.

'You could start by polishing that armoire over there,' I joked.

The taller of the two, who was still shorter than Gideon by some inches, looked aghast. 'You misunderstand. We're volunteering our services in a *consultative* capacity,' he said, in a voice so posh you could have shaved Parmesan on it.

Gideon and the smaller one cracked up. 'She's winding you up,' Gideon explained.

The three of them had met at university. Sebastian, the one who'd just spoken, rippled with energy and oozed privilege; he was a total *Brideshead Revisited* stereotype. Kieran was a small, softly spoken, sleepy-eyed Irishman with the apparent energy of a sloth on power-save mode.

'It's very nice to meet you, Catherine,' Kieran said, and I thought: After all these years of everyone calling me Cass, I've suddenly got people calling me Catherine left, right and centre.

'I've given them a bit of background,' Gideon said, 'just what you told me in Devon, but you'll need to fill us in on the details.'

'We'll need to see all your financial records, attendance figures, publicity materials and so on,' Sebastian said, looking round. 'I must say, it's not a bad little property. I've got some cousins up in North Yorkshire with a place not dissimilar.'

'We are *so* not interested,' Kieran said, good-humouredly.

We spent the morning in the office. They asked questions about every detail of the business, some things I had answers for and a lot of things I didn't, and many I hadn't even thought about. Sebastian asked most of the questions, with Gideon chipping in occasionally and Kieran making notes on a little laptop computer and regularly getting up to fetch tea: he seemed to have a serious tea habit.

While all this was going on I tried not to look at Gideon too much, doing my best to be ever so casual and treat him exactly the same as the other two, but on several occasions our glances met and the look we exchanged sent my stomach into loop-the-loop.

We had lunch in the coffee-shop.

'Who are they?' Jackie whispered. 'That Irish one has been in here for tea about five times. I thought he must be an undercover environmental-health inspector or something. I've been scrubbing that counter top like a demented woman just in case.' I toyed with the idea of keeping her in the dark and letting her keep on scrubbing all afternoon till her hands were raw; but as I've already said I'm just not vindictive enough. So I explained who they were. 'Blowing the council's precious money on business consultants? What will Randy Robertson have to say about that?'

'They're free, actually,' I said, and even though I'd resolved never to confide anything in her ever again, I couldn't resist showing Gideon off a bit. 'See the tall, dark-haired one?' She nodded. 'He's the childhood sweetheart I was telling you about.'

'*Really?* But I thought he didn't turn up at that reunion?' More information she'd got from Greg, I presumed.

'Long story. But we're just friends. He's helping me out, that's all.'

'He's very fanciable.'

I gave her a severe look. 'Don't even think about it,' I said.

'What's the problem if you're just friends?'

I moved the look up a notch into 'could kill' mode. 'Just *don't*, Jackie.'

When I returned to the others, Sebastian and Gideon were deep in conversation about surfing: the talk was peppered with rips, swells and left-handed reef breaks. Kieran was looking bored.

'Don't you surf?' I asked him.

'I have an inner-ear problem,' he said.

'He lists to starboard,' Sebastian added, and Gideon said, 'That's when he's pissed. The truth is he's too lazy.'

Sebastian agreed. 'The only way he'd manage to get out back would be if he was dropped off by a small pleasure-cruiser on the way home from a party.'

Kieran smiled wearily at them. 'Surfing,' he said, 'is all about hanging around up to your tits in icy water.'

The other two feigned looks of horror.

'Pernicious perjurer,' Sebastian muttered.

'Don't listen to him, Catherine,' Gideon said to me. 'He's an unnatural bastard who's devoid of the necessary pleasure genes. One day I'll teach you to surf and you'll find out why, if there is a heaven, it must be made of salt water.' He stopped, maybe wondering if he'd broken the new rules of our relationship by assuming we would be engaging in future shared activities, so I smiled to let him know I wasn't about to get mad at him. Privately the thought of trying to surf was about the most alarming thing I could think of.

After lunch Sebastian said he fancied a walk around the park before they started work again, and insisted Kieran join him. The Irishman's face was a study in pure inertia. 'Oh, I'd much rather just have a quiet sit-down and let my food digest,' he said, yawning. 'You go.'

'No, you don't, matey. We're off out.' Poor Kieran was more or less propelled out of the front door, leaving me alone with Gideon.

Not exactly alone: Zak was around, and Charlie, one of the volunteer guides, and even one or two visitors, but I had the distinct feeling that Sebastian had been acting under orders in taking his friend off like that.

Gideon was looking through a pile of papers in the office. When he heard me come in, he glanced up and his smile lit up the room. 'Do you have a copy of the sale agreement from when the Hall was sold to the council?' he asked.

'I've never seen one, but I can ask Lady Eugenie; she probably keeps it with her family papers.'

'It might be worth a look, if you could get it.'

'I could probably get it for you later this afternoon.'

'You'd best give it to Sebastian, then. I won't be here: I've got to leave in a few minutes,' he said.

My heart dropped into my shoes. 'You're going back to Devon?' I was just getting used to him being around, and liking it.

He smiled. 'Are you going to miss me?'

'No. I probably won't even notice if you're here or not.'

'Just as well, because I'm going to be back tomorrow. I'm not going home, I'm meeting an old work colleague.'

'Is this about that . . . business?'

'The business about me embezzling three million pounds? Yes.'

'God. Three *million*? I didn't know it was that much,' I couldn't help saying.

'Slightly more than that, in fact, but does it really matter how much it is? The point is, do you think I did it?'

'No,' I said. 'Of course you didn't do it.'

'You're right,' he said. 'I didn't. Unfortunately, there's nothing I can do to *prove* that I didn't. I don't even know officially that I'm being investigated for anything.'

'Then how . . . ?'

'My house was broken into,' he said. 'Nothing was stolen, but you know when you live alone, you get a sense when things have been moved? And later I noticed a car parked along the lane, and when I went out they drove off.'

'Could have been lost tourists.'

'So why didn't they wait to ask me for directions? No, there's been more than that and each little thing could have a perfectly innocent explanation, but all put together it's obvious I'm being watched. Sorry, that probably sounds paranoid.'

'It sounds scary. Aren't you worried?'

'Not if I don't think about it.'

'The ostrich approach always works for me,' I said, doing my best to sound as light-hearted as he had.

He stood up to go, and as he walked past me he stooped to kiss the top of my head. His hand touched my cheek briefly. 'I'll see you tomorrow,' he said. 'Make sure those two get on with things while I'm not here. Don't let Kieran spend the whole time drinking tea.'

He left. I remembered that only a few seconds earlier I'd said to him, 'I probably won't even notice if you're here or not,' and realised that I already missed him very badly indeed.

Even when you took the tea-breaks into account, Sebastian and Kieran were frighteningly efficient. They even read the visitors' book, to try to glean intelligence from the barely legible comments scribbled in it (most of them of the 'M.H. Woz Ere 20/8/97' variety).

'What we need is an angle,' Sebastian said. 'Something that sets this museum apart from all the others.'

'A unique selling point,' Kieran added. I suggested the Sassoon memorabilia, and mentioned the Wyoming War Poets Society's continuing interest and support.

'The First World War's not really "now", though, is it?' Sebastian frowned. 'It won't really be big again until 2014. Then you can start doing centenary stuff.'

'Looking at this guest book, I would say your biggest customers, apart from illiterates, are elderly people and families,' Kieran suggested.

'Okay,' Sebastian said, pacing around the room: he was one of those people who can think best while they're moving. I could see why Kieran was the one who got to use the laptop. 'I reckon we can put the elderlies to one side, since they don't have that much in the way of disposable income or political clout. Let's concentrate on families.'

'Pony rides?' Kieran suggested.

'Nowhere to keep the ponies,' I said.

'Evil animals, anyway.'

'Kieran, for God's sake!' Sebastian said. 'You can't tar every horse with the same brush because one happened to throw you off many moons ago.'

'I just don't trust them.'

'Oh, tell him, Catherine.'

'I've got no opinion about horses,' I said. 'I've never really been near one.'

Sebastian looked at me like I'd recently arrived in a UFO. 'What a sheltered life you've led,' he remarked. 'To paraphrase Adam Ant: you don't ride, you don't surf, what *do* you do?' I laughed, but Kieran said, 'No, seriously, what sort of things do you like doing?'

'Well . . . I look after this place, and when I'm not working I listen to music, go to the theatre and the cinema, and read loads and loads of books.'

'What kind of things do you read?' Kieran asked.

'All sorts, but most of all I love the Brontës and Thomas Hardy. That's one of the things I like about this house: you can imagine the people in those books living somewhere like this.' Sebastian and Kieran were looking at each other meaningfully.

'We could be on to something there,' Sebastian said, and his friend nodded slowly. 'I'm thinking themed entertainment, costume balls, that sort of thing . . .'

'Conventions. Film sets?'

'That could be lucrative.'

'Hang on,' I said. 'The whole point is to keep it so that the general public can visit. If we start renting it out to film-makers, surely they won't let people just wander around.'

'Good point,' Kieran said. 'And the tea-shop business would be likely to suffer if that happened. Film companies usually arrange their own catering. Anyone for more tea, by the way?'

It went on like that for the rest of the afternoon, with ideas being thrown around, some noted down for future pondering and others rejected outright. I left them to it, and went to sit with Zak at the front desk. He was making replacement labels for some of the exhibits, writing them out neatly. 'Always thought those typed ones looked a bit tacky,' he said. 'How's it going with your city gurus?' I filled him in on what little had apparently been achieved so far. Zak grinned. 'What I'm really interested in is your ex-boyfriend,' he said.

'Greg?'

'No, I mean whichever one of those three it is. Jackie told me one of them's your ex.'

'She is getting a mouth on her like the speaking clock,' I muttered.

'Is it the surfer one who talks like Prince Charles?'

'No, it's the other surfer one.'

'Well, that's a relief. Prince Chas was giving me such a hard time for coming from Australia and not surfing. Been on a backpacking holiday to the Gold Coast and he thinks he knows it all, the dip. So this is the guy who sent you the money?' I nodded, and Zak gave me an eyebrow-wiggling look that made me laugh. 'He must be pretty keen,' he said, and returned to his labelling.

Just before the two business consultants packed up their laptop and headed for home, I grabbed a chance to speak to Kieran, who seemed the more approachable of the two.

'How much trouble is Gideon in?' I asked him.

His habitual sleepy, hangdog expression drooped even further. 'The truth? From what I've heard he's in deep shit,' he said. 'It hasn't helped at all that he disappeared off to Devon just after this money's supposed to have gone AWOL. Looks a bit suspicious, that.'

'If he's supposed to have stolen the money, why didn't they

go after him straight away?'

'Seems it only surfaced recently. They deal with such huge sums, I guess it's hard to keep track of everything. I mean, look at what happened with Baring's. Some audit or other must have picked it up.'

'But three *million* . . . ?'

'That's nothing,' he said. 'I mean, to you and me it's a big deal, but when he was working he'd have made or lost that much – made it, usually – in minutes, seconds even.' I couldn't get my head round that idea at all. Kieran continued, 'I know this guy who used to work with Gideon and he told me he's never met anyone who kept so cool. It was like he didn't really care: he would take a huge gamble that no one else would risk, but his instincts were usually right. He was very successful.'

'What'll happen to him?' I asked.

Kieran sighed. 'Well, that really depends on whether they manage to find any proof against him.'

'And if they do?'

'I don't know, for certain. I suppose if they had enough proof they'd have to involve the police. He could end up in prison.'

'But he hasn't done anything wrong!' I said. 'I wish there was something I could do.'

'Seems to me you're already doing it.'

There Must Be An Angel (Playing With My Heart)

That evening the weather was beautiful: it had been one of those April days when you get a little foretaste of what summer will be like, and although it was cooler now, the sky was still a cloudless blue. It was far too nice to sit upstairs in my flat, even in my favourite window seat, so after everyone else had gone I locked the door from the outside instead of the inside and walked into the park. I sat down on a bench and let the last of the sun warm my face. The grass had had its first mowing of the year earlier in the day, and the smell was strong and sweet. A group of children ran around throwing handfuls of the cuttings at each other and shrieking.

I loved this view, but there was always the feeling that London was just beyond the trees. It made me think of Gideon's house, that broad stretch of river, the deep silence at night, the way it felt so removed from the rest of the world. No wonder he'd decided to make it his home.

I saw him before he saw me: it's hard not to notice a man who so perfectly fits the traditional fortune-teller's bill of 'tall, dark and handsome'. He was loping along with the relaxed-looking stride that I knew from experience you had to be fit to keep up with. He walked like he owned the ground beneath his feet; I could imagine him as the owner of the Hall and the land, coming home at the end of the day. As he passed through a syrupy band of late-afternoon sunlight he seemed to glow and I felt so happy to see him: after so many years apart from him it was total joy to have him here in the flesh.

Finally he saw me, and his face, which had been preoccupied and serious, broke into a greeting smile.

'I didn't expect to see you till tomorrow,' I said, and moved along the bench so he could sit down. 'How did your meeting go?'

'If it's possible,' he said, gazing out across the darkening park, 'I don't want to talk about any of that. I'm trying to forget about it.' He turned to me and grinned conspiratorially, like he used to as a teenager. 'Cheer me up. Tell me more about the Middleton Road reunion, and what old Purple Hayes and Archer and Kane are up to. First tell me how your granddad's doing – should have asked you that earlier.'

I was quiet for a moment. Even after all this time it was hard for me to say it. 'He died,' I said, 'the year I graduated.'

I was amazed to see his eyes fill with tears. 'I'm sorry,' he said.

'It was all quite peaceful. The last time I saw him he said to me, "I'm looking forward to getting to heaven, Cassie. There's someone there I can't wait to see."'

'Your granny?'

'That's what I thought, but then he said, "Eric Morecambe."'

'He always did like *Morecambe and Wise*. Bless him.'

I told him the funniest things I could remember about the reunion, including Philip Oliver's visit to my room, Janet Cooper's gymnastic accident and Sarah Rowland's catering pack of Ferrero Rocher. About Jessica Finn (whom I'd once suspected him of fancying), who was now a nursery nurse and had a permanent stoop caused by bending over at tiny tables and chairs all day, and how she'd greeted her fully-grown peer group with a hearty cry of, 'Eh-oh!' like a Teletubby. About Gary Coningsborough trying to nutty-dance and moonwalk and still smelling of fried food like he always used to, and how Sex God looked like an ageing cherub at the grand old age of forty-five. He asked lots of questions and we laughed a lot.

'What about Okey-dokey? Did he turn up?' he asked, and I told him what I'd heard from Alison, that Okey-dokey's reign of terror was finally over.

'That's sad. You mightn't believe it but I always quite liked him,' he said.

'Easy for *you* to like him – you were his star pupil.'

'True. But don't forget he gave me that great chance to show off to you that time.'

'Pardon?'

'I'd fancied you since the first time I saw you,' he said, 'but I was too shy to say anything.'

'Oh, bless! That's the sweetest thing I ever heard,' I teased. 'Even if I don't exactly believe you.'

He looked wounded. 'You still don't trust me, do you?' he said.

'I *want* to but I can't, because you're going to go back to Devon and I'd only be letting myself get hurt again.'

'I know I let you down once,' he said, 'but I was a lot younger then. Young men aren't very good with relationships, and when you're eighteen, and male, you'd rather poke your own eye out with a stick than admit to any strong feelings.'

'It's not just you,' I said. 'I suppose with the background I've got, what happened with my parents and everything, I kind of *expect* to be abandoned.'

He turned round on the bench to face me. 'You can't keep digging that up for the rest of your life,' he said. 'There has to be a time when you decide you're an adult and how your parents are, or were, doesn't have any bearing.'

'All right for you to say. Your parents didn't go off and leave you . . .' I started to protest.

'I'll show you what my parents left me,' he said, and pushed up his sleeve. In the fading light I could make out a faint white scar on the brown flesh of his arm, a difference in texture as well as colour, the skin stretched and smooth. 'The thing with my parents being doctors,' he said, 'is that they usually knew exactly how hard they could hit before it left a mark, but occasionally they didn't get it right.'

I stared at him, not knowing how to react. 'Your parents hit you?'

He sighed to the bottom of his lungs. 'They dished out discipline like they dished out antibiotics: take at regular intervals, finish the prescribed course. Nothing I could do pleased them or even satisfied them: they always set me one more goal, made me try a bit harder. Then when I ever did achieve anything they'd put me down for being too big for my boots. Eventually I realised I *was* too big, and too clever, and I didn't have to put up with it, so I stopped trying, and started doing whatever I wanted.'

For a moment I was speechless. What he'd said made sense of the way he was always trying to annoy his parents but at the same time how much freedom he seemed to have. It also explained why I'd never been inside his house, and had only met his father on that one occasion when my granddad was ill.

'I asked you about that scar once. You told me you did it falling off your bike when you were ten.'

'I didn't want you to feel sorry for me. You'd never have looked at me the same way again. You'd always have seen the kid who got beaten up by his parents, the victim, someone to feel sorry for. You wouldn't have seen *me* any more.'

'I couldn't imagine anything changing how I felt about you,' I said, deliberately speaking in the past tense, even though all I wanted to do was love him for ever.

'Well, at the time it changed how I felt about *you* – or, rather, how I behaved. I wanted to get right away from anyone who knew me, so I could start again, and stop wasting all my energy trying to prove I didn't care. It didn't work, though, not at first. Everything I did up to the point I moved to Devon was to some extent a reaction to how I was brought up: going to Cambridge, working in the City . . . Turning rebellion into money. But I wasn't going to talk about that, was I?'

We didn't know each other again well enough that we could be sure of each other's reactions. When I was seventeen I would have known what to say or do. Or maybe he was right, and anger on his behalf and pity for him would have changed everything.

'Anyway,' he said, 'after that shock-horror revelation, do you know what would be really good?'

'No,' I said quietly.

'To be somewhere warm,' he said. 'It's freezing out here.'

We walked back towards the house. The security light above the front door blazed into life when we got close, the glow spilling out across the path as if the house were greeting us.

I said, 'Do you remember all those walks we used to go on, miles and miles over the hills?' He nodded, smiling, and took my hand. After a second's hesitation he pressed my fingertips to his mouth, his lips like a soft sea creature and his breath incredibly warm. Without knowing I was doing it, I managed to communicate a response in my fingers, the tiniest gesture that we couldn't have put into words but both understood, and he leaned towards me and kissed me.

For some men, kissing is a mere prelude to the real action. For Gideon, it had always been an art form in itself. That boy had always been a seriously good kisser, and I was delighted to discover that age and experience had only improved his natural talent.

I just about managed to remember to lock the door behind us and, not even bothering to go up to the flat, we sank on to the same antique *chaise longue* in the hall that I'd mistakenly sat on waiting for my interview, joined at the lips like some mythological creature. It was like kissing someone for the very first time, and finding out that they're as familiar to you as your own fingertips.

We'd reached the point where hands had begun to slide beneath clothing, where lust takes over from any rational senses and any sensible control we might have had was seeping away.

I screamed.

'What?' he said, in panicked bewilderment. 'What did I do?'

'There was someone looking through the window!'

We both stared at the blank window for a second, then Gideon was off the *chaise longue* and heading for the door.

223

He flung back the bolts, turned the key, and ran out into the darkness.

Undercover Of The Night

I thought about ringing the police or setting off the burglar alarm, which would have brought them anyway, but while I was still thinking about it Gideon reappeared, only slightly out of breath. 'Lost him,' he said. 'Probably had a car. Are you okay?'

'I'm just a bit shocked. Should I call the police?'

'I wouldn't bother,' he said.

'But there was a peeping Tom, a pervert!'

'I doubt it,' he said, fastening all the bolts and locking the door. He handed me the huge iron key. Under the circumstances he looked so unruffled I couldn't believe it. Then light dawned. 'He was watching *you*?' I said.

He nodded. 'Probably.'

'Oh, this is too mad. This doesn't happen in *England*, innocent people being spied on.'

'You always were a tad naïve,' he said, not at all unkindly, and it was true, but this was another world, a scary one.

Gideon did his best to reassure me. 'It's an annoyance, that's all,' he said. 'It's only a matter of time before they find out I haven't got their stupid money. If they would only let me into the building I could sort this out for them in minutes.'

We went up to the flat and sat drinking coffee. The interruption and the feeling that someone had been watching us had blown the romantic mood. Irrationally, it was Gideon I was most angry with, for bringing this intrusion and anxiety into my life. Before he'd managed to get on my mind and then back into my life, things had been going relatively smoothly. Okay, so my job and my home were about to be taken away from me, but at least life was calm.

Who was I trying to kid? No amount of calm could compare to being with him. All the same, I was shaken and upset, and he knew it.

'Let me stay,' he said. I was far too shaken to want to spend the rest of the night on my own, but I didn't think I was in the mood to carry on where we'd left off downstairs, either. He smiled, as if I'd spoken the thought aloud, and said, 'I'll lie across your threshold all night, and none shall pass.'

'If you put it that way, I would be very, very glad if you would.'

The sofa-bed was on constant standby for those nights when Flora kicked Zak out. It wasn't quite the threshold, but near enough. I started to lift the cushions from it ready to unfold it, and as I stood there, a cushion dangling from each hand, I glanced at Gideon, and the look on his face melted me. He stepped towards me, his hands slipping around my waist, drawing me towards him. The cushions fell to the floor with a soft thud.

As well as your conscious memory, your body has a memory, too: the one you use for riding a bike or swimming, the one that never forgets. My fingertips ran over the planes of his skin as if it was the surface they'd been specifically designed to explore. The shape of his body was quite different from how it used to be, changed by all that surfing into a wonderfully strong and muscular version of its former lean self, but I knew the feel of him, his movements, and it seemed as if he'd always smelt like the sea. Body-memory was working for him, too, and he was touching me like only he'd ever really been able to do. For the first time in fifteen years I had that blissful sense of being wrapped up tightly in love.

When I woke up the next morning, and realised after half a second that the soft, sleepy breaths on the back of my neck belonged to the person I'd always loved most in the world, I felt like leaping out of bed, flinging up the sash window and singing 'Who Will Buy This Wonderful Morning' at the top of my voice to whoever might be unlucky enough to be passing.

Needless to say, I kept such impulses in check, preferring to watch him sleeping. I thought that what I'd always loved most about him was his sense of who he was, his self-respect and completeness, the way he could always surprise me.

'Don't you have work to do?' he murmured, his eyelids still closed. 'Or are you just going to stare at me all morning?'

'I'm not even looking at you.'

'Liar.'

'Arrogant bastard.'

His lips curved into a smile and he finally opened his eyes. 'You,' he said, 'are gorgeous.'

Which of course meant I was late for work. Eventually I rushed down the stairs almost an hour later than I usually appeared. I came across Zak in the hallway, muttering how the bloody public couldn't be trusted to keep their hands off the displays.

'I mean, I clearly labelled this *chaise longue* just the other day so people would know it was an *exhibit* and not a public amenity, but some idiot's knocked the sign off already: it looks like someone's been *sitting* on the bloody thing as well.' I tried not to blush, recalling the passion of the night before, and tut-tutted along with him. 'I despair of people, I really do,' he said, fussing around checking that the other artefacts in the hall hadn't been similarly abused. 'And it's not only the schoolkids, either. The adults are the worst. You should have a word with those volunteers. Wasn't Charlie supposed to be keeping an eye on things yesterday?'

'We can't blame Charlie,' I said quickly. 'He can't be expected to know everything that goes on.' *Thank God*, I thought, smiling to myself.

'What's up with you this morning, anyway?' Zak asked. 'You look like the cat that got the crisps.'

'Don't you mean the cream?'

'You haven't met Flora's cat.'

I was just about to give him an edited version of the reason for the big smile on my face, when the reason himself appeared at the top of the stairs, wearing a similar grin when he saw me.

'Oh, *right*,' Zak said. 'Morning, Gideon. If you guys don't mind, I've got some stuff to do somewhere.' He hurried off.

'I think we shocked him,' Gideon said, wrapping his arms around me.

'Not quite,' I said. 'But if he knew exactly how his precious *chaise longue* got squashed he'd be ropeable, as they say on *Neighbours*.'

I realised I was starving after all the morning's activity, so I suggested getting some breakfast from the coffee-shop. We settled down with a pot of coffee and a basket of hot croissants, while Jackie pretended not to be curious.

'I'd bet on it being a good surfing day at home,' he said, at one point.

'How can you tell?'

'I put the TV news on while I was getting dressed,' he said. 'You get to know the pattern of the isobars and so on.'

'You were obviously paying attention when Miss Finbar was teaching us about meteorology,' I said, pouring a second cup of coffee. 'She'd be very proud. Do you miss being able to surf?'

'Like you'd miss your breath,' he said. 'Surfing is like – on a good day when you've got some great, rolling waves and there's nothing but you and the sea – it's as if you can sing like Ella Fitzgerald. You're doing something that's so exactly right, so precise and balanced that it feels like you're making no effort at all. You don't think, you just are. It becomes part of your soul.'

'Ella Fitzgerald? Your musical tastes have moved on,' I teased, though I suppose I couldn't have expected his allegiance to Cabaret Voltaire to follow him into his thirties. 'I never realised Devon was that good for surfing. Surely there are bigger waves in Hawaii and California, and warmer sea, too.'

'Slightly warmer sea would be nice sometimes. But I don't care about bigger and better waves: it's not a competition. That's exactly the city mentality I was trying to get out of. Where I live it's beautiful, relatively unspoiled, you get the odd day when it's classic and a lot more when it's not, but I can live with that. Once in a while you get a perfect wave all to yourself, but when it's completely flat you can always just go for a swim, or float on your board if you're feeling lazy. When it's stormy you can paint or read, whatever. It's what makes me happy; it's that simple.'

It sounded like a perfect life: perfect and solitary. He always had been self-contained, and it sounded as if his life was complete as it was. Since what he'd said and what had happened the night before, I'd been wondering how I might fit into this scenario, but now I thought maybe that had been the last thing on his mind. I might have read it all wrong and all he was after was a quick tussle on a *chaise longue* for old times' sake. I steeled myself to say something, to try to find out what he felt about me, but before I could speak Stan appeared and asked me to come to the reception desk urgently.

Who Can It Be Now?

'A visitor to see you,' Stan said. I could tell by his face that whoever the visitor might be, they weren't welcome. A small, fidgety man approached me. He had a grease-spot on his lapel the size of a fifty-pence coin. He introduced himself as Kenneth Breck, chartered surveyor, and produced a business card from the breast pocket of his suit, at which point he also noticed the grease-spot and attempted to rub it surreptitiously with his thumb.

'And what can I do for you?' I asked him.

'I've come to survey the building – have you not been informed?' he asked. It was obvious I hadn't. 'Mr Robertson from the council was supposed to telephone and let you know.' Now why didn't it surprise me that Randall Robertson had managed to overlook that detail? 'I shall need full access to the whole building,' Kenneth Breck continued. 'I hope that isn't inconvenient.'

'It's actually *very* inconvenient,' I said, thinking that perhaps I could stall him or send him away.

However, Mr Breck was made of stuff at least as stubborn as the stain on his suit, and neither of them budged. 'You'll hardly know I'm here,' he said, with what was probably designed to be an ingratiating smile. He began to take off his jacket, to reveal a reasonably clean shirt: the jacket had obviously borne the brunt of breakfast. 'Now, maybe I could start upstairs?'

'I'd be careful on those stairs if I was you,' Stan said. 'They're riddled with woodworm and all kinds of rot. You could easily fall through.'

'Ha ha,' Mr Breck said. I don't mean he laughed: I mean he *said*, 'Ha ha.' He wasn't to be deterred, at any rate, and made for the stairs with total disregard for his personal safety. Stan followed him at an indiscreet distance.

Stan had made up that stuff about the woodworm and rot, of course. To my knowledge there wasn't anything wrong with the woodwork, and if there had been we would have had to close the house to visitors anyway, for health and safety reasons, but Stan didn't like the idea of Mr Breck poking around the house any more than I did and wanted to put him off. Which as a strategy was probably as useful as trying to give a City trader the wrong change.

Right on cue my lovely City trader appeared. 'So, who was that seedy little man?' he asked me, making no attempt to keep his voice down.

'That was Mr Breck. He's a surveyor,' I said. 'I think he's working on behalf of someone who wants to buy the place.'

'Aren't you going to stop him?'

'What can I do? It's not as if it's my house. It just feels like it sometimes.'

Zak appeared from the direction of the coffee-shop, overhearing the conversation. 'I reckon we should mount a picket,' he said. Zak was turning out to be the Red under the Coltsfoot Hall bed. 'By the way, have you guys seen that strange guy hanging around?'

'That's Mr Breck, the surveyor,' I said, thinking we ought to have a banner made proclaiming, 'MR BRECK THE SURVEYOR IS HERE', then I wouldn't have to repeat it so often.

'No, I don't mean him,' Zak said. 'I meant the other one, hanging around outside. Saw him duck down behind the hydrangea when I went to put the rubbish out. Which took for *ever*,' he grumbled, 'because some cat or fox or something has been through the bin.'

'How do you know?' Gideon asked.

'Well, the lid was off, and there was a pile of stuff on the ground. Jackie's doing her nut.'

'A *pile*?'

'What's this sudden interest in rubbish?' I asked, but they ignored me.

'Yeah, a pile. Come to think of it, a pretty neat pile for a fox. Must have been a cat. A cat is a much tidier animal than a fox.'

'Even cats don't sort rubbish into piles,' Gideon said. 'I'm willing to bet it was the same man who was concealing himself behind the hydrangea. The same one who was outside last night.'

'Stop being sinister,' I said.

'I'm serious, Catherine. I told you I was being watched. This confirms it. That guy in the bushes outside is obviously keeping an eye on me to find out if this is where I've stashed the cash.'

'You mean he's a secret agent?' Zak said. 'Unreal! I'm going to go out and see if he's still there.' He went back in the direction of the coffee-shop.

'As if he's still going to be crouching in the hydrangea waiting for refreshments!' Gideon laughed.

'This isn't funny!' I said. I felt like there were alien invaders everywhere: on the staircase, in the shrubbery. Nothing was safe or normal any more. 'What do we do?'

Gideon was looking as relaxed and cheerful as if he'd just stepped off his surfboard. 'We don't do anything,' he said. 'At least, whatever we *do* do, bear in mind it's more than likely being recorded.' This comment had the effect of silencing both of us for a minute.

'You don't think we were being recorded – you know?' I said.

He gave me a reassuring hug. 'No, of course not. I hope . . .' I couldn't ever remember seeing Gideon look embarrassed before. The look on his face made me laugh, but then he said, 'Hang on. What if the seedy Mr Breck isn't a surveyor at all?'

'You mean he might be a spy too?'

'Could be just a ruse to get into the building. I'm going up to keep an eye on him. Why don't you call your council bloke to check that he's bona fide?'

Trying to get the information out of Randall Robertson was as easy as getting tomato juice out of a pineapple. 'I've told you my hands are tightly bound as to what I can divulge,' was his excuse.

'But I've got this strange man running all over the building with access to all the artefacts, and he could be anyone.'

'Well, he's not likely to be a criminal mastermind if he's interested in any of *that* crap,' was his winning comment. I treated him to one of my icy glares, but of course being on the phone he couldn't see it. After a long pause in which he was probably hoping I'd go away, he said, 'Okay, so he's a surveyor, yes, I did know about him.'

'But who's he working for? Does this mean that there are still people interested in buying the house? Why is it still on the market?'

'Don't panic! For Pete's sake, woman, you make more fuss about that pile of old bricks than Prince Charles! He's there for a health-and-safety inspection, all right? Health and bloody safety.'

At least Mr Breck had an official reason for snooping around the house, but I didn't buy this health-and-safety story for one minute.

Treason

Because of the security of Gideon's cheque, I ought to have been reasonably confident that the council budget meeting would be a formality; a 'due process', as Randall Robertson had described it. Which was just as well, because most of the party assembled at the entrance of Coltsfoot Hall were so frail that they looked as if too much excitement might finish them off. There were about fifteen people, the majority as old as Stan and Lady Eugenie, both of whom were busy mobilising the troops and dispensing cough drops. However, what the group lacked in youthful vigour they more than compensated for in cussedness. The generation that had withstood the Blitz clearly wasn't prepared to take any nonsense from their so-called elected representatives.

Gideon had insisted on coming, telling me that he had a personal stake in the future of the Hall. I couldn't be sure if he was talking about me, or simply his financial investment, and I was trying to think of a subtle way of asking when Zak and Flora appeared, with a group of Flora's pupils from the girls' school where she taught. Zak had felt that the presence of the girls would make it look as though it wasn't only the over-eighties who were interested in the future of the Hall, although they seemed mainly to be preoccupied with inform-ing 'Miss' that she'd landed on her feet when she'd met the Aussie, and casting admiring glances at Gideon.

After a lot of jostling and grumbling by the Ancients, we got ourselves into a minibus that Stan had organised and headed for the town hall. The whole thing had the atmo-sphere of a doom-charged school trip.

'It's like that film *Braveheart*, isn't it?' Stan remarked, and launched into a Mel Gibson impression ('They may take our what-his-name but they'll never take our freedom') that Mel's own mother would have been hard-pressed to recognise.

Lady Eugenie only added to the confusion. 'Oh, I *adore* Mel Gibson, especially when he does the Naked Chef,' she said incomprehensibly.

'Are you perhaps thinking of Jamie Oliver?' I suggested.

'Am I? Possibly. I always think kilts are so becoming, anyway.' I caught Gideon's eye and we grinned. Kilts were very becoming, indeed: I'd never been able to resist him when he wore his cute little Black Watch number.

Zak, Lady Eugenie and I had been nominated to appear as our own defence, but at the last minute Gideon respectfully asked Lady Eugenie if she thought his presence would be helpful.

'Helpful in what way?' she asked.

'Well, I know a little bit about financial matters,' he said, 'and I've been studying the finances of the Hall, so I might be able to make a useful contribution.'

'God, he's charming, isn't he?' Lady Eugenie whispered loudly at me, and then to Gideon, 'I don't know who you are, young man, but I'd be delighted to have you batting on our side.'

The prosecution consisted of Randall Robertson, and a couple of councillors, Ken Nettlefold and June Willis. A third had been slated to appear, but Robertson had informed me that he was the king of non-appearances at budget sub-committee meetings and not to hold my breath.

We left our mob outside the town hall, unfurling the 'Hands Off Our Heritage!' banner and generally doing their best to be unruly – in a rather genteel way. As soon as the four of us stepped inside the building a man emerged out of one of many identical doors, introduced himself as the committee secretary and ordered us to wait on some hard plastic chairs in the corridor outside the star chamber.

'The bastards are deliberately keeping us waiting,' Zak muttered.

Lady Eugenie fixed him with a stern eye. 'Young man, I have to say that we shall not get very far if you employ language of that nature,' she admonished him. Zak muttered an apology, and Lady Eugenie leaned towards me; she smelt of carnations. 'Is he another of your financial eggheads?' she asked me, in a theatrical whisper.

'That's Zak,' I explained, though the twinkle in her eye indicated that she knew very well who he was and she was just trying to wind him up. 'He's an archivist.'

'Really? He has a very antipodean manner for an archivist,' she said. Zak grinned.

The committee secretary reappeared and asked us to join the meeting. I was more nervous than I'd ever been in my life, so I forced myself to walk as tall as possible, and breezed into the room first as if I couldn't give a damn. Randall Robertson and the other two were clustered together at one end of a long narrow table, giving us no option but to sit at the other end. It wasn't a seating arrangement designed to make reaching a cosy consensus easy.

Ken Nettlefold, chair of the arts and leisure sub-committee, leaned forward with his arms folded on the table, a roll of fat oozing from the collar of his shirt. 'We've asked you here to give you the opportunity of explaining to us exactly why you think the council's resources are better placed bailing out a facility which I'm told is of only passing historical interest, when we have other pressing demands on our budget,' he said, all in one breath.

Nice to start with an open mind, I thought. I'm certain that he was reading the words from a paper in front of him; either that or he wasn't keen on eye contact.

We'd rehearsed this argument. Zak talked about the history of the Hall and particularly about the artefacts relating to Siegfried Sassoon.

'Jerry sort of name but he was actually one of ours,' Lady Eugenie added helpfully.

Zak finished by reading out a letter from Carmen Dykes, which had been signed by all five members of the Wyoming War Poets Society plus three others from their sister organisation in Michigan. The councillors, unsurprisingly, didn't look overwhelmed by this display of transatlantic support. I handed out copies of the business plan I'd drawn up and talked them through it, and Lady Eugenie presented our petition.

Councillor June Willis hadn't said anything yet. She'd been spending the time smiling generally at everyone present, the doors, the windows, her glass of water, smiling so fixedly that I wondered whether it was really a smile or if she had perhaps had a minor stroke while we weren't paying attention. When she finally spoke the smile slid off her face like paint off a greasy wall.

'This is all very well and good,' she said, 'and I'm sure we're all very sympathetic about Lady Eugenie's personal attachment to the house, but can I assure you that the new owners have undertaken to maintain the exterior as is.'

'New owners?' I started to say, but Robertson spoke over me.

'Nothing's been finalised yet.'

June Willis, in some confusion, was trying to reassemble her smile, but not quickly enough for Lady Eugenie. 'The buggers have sold it already!' she exclaimed, and Robertson attempted to make soothing noises. 'Don't you shush me, you stinking collaborator,' she said. 'Bunch of liars and thieves. If Sir Sheldon was alive today, he'd turn in his grave!' Mustering generations of Thick dignity and poise she got shakily to her feet and left the room, attended by Zak.

Gideon, who hadn't spoken yet, did so now. 'Can I ask who the buyer is?'

'And you are?'

We'd introduced Gideon by name but not given any reason for his presence. 'He's the man who makes my heart go *vavoom*!' I wanted to say, but felt this wouldn't be appropriate under the circumstances.

'I'm Lady Eugenie's financial adviser,' Gideon said.

I thought I heard Robertson mutter, 'Must give you plenty of spare time.'

Gideon ignored this. 'According to the agreement upon which Lady Eugenie sold the house to the council, she has to be fully consulted about any further sale occurring in her lifetime . . .'

'We're consulting her now, aren't we?' Robertson said.

'. . . which means she's fully entitled to know the details of any prospective purchaser.'

Robertson leaned forward with his elbows on the desk and spoke in a smug, patronising way that, once again, reminded me of Okey-dokey in his heyday. 'I believe I just stated that all negotiations are in the very earliest stages, mere foreplay. And I believe that if you look at the sale document a *little* more closely you will see that we do not have to secure any agreement or approval from the previous owner, merely consult. Which is what we are doing.'

Gideon smiled serenely. 'Your familiarity with the sales agreement is commendable,' he said. 'You must also be aware of paragraph 32e.'

'Para . . . ?'

'What's that one, then, Robertson?' Councillor Nettlefold turned to the man next to him, his chubby neck taking a few moments to settle into its new position.

'Erm . . . I'd need to look it up,' he said.

Councillor Nettlefold looked impatient. 'This lot is impinging upon my lunch hour. I've got Waste Disposal and Sanitation at two o'clock.'

'Allow me,' I said, producing a copy of the sale agreement. I began to read aloud from paragraph 32e, which said that the council agreed to make every effort to keep the Hall as a museum for the benefit of the community providing that the museum's trustees could guarantee the financial soundness of the business.

Ken Nettlefold responded to this, obviously trying to speed proceedings towards an early lunch: 'We would, of course, be happy for the place to stay in the public domain if only we didn't have to subsidise it with council-tax-payers' money.' He paused for a sip of water before continuing. 'Sadly,' he said, 'it doesn't look as though that'll be able to happen quickly enough. The main thrust of your business plan is that you couldn't manage to be self-supporting for at least a year.'

'The local authority has bent over backwards to help you, but you've really had your last stab at it,' Randall Robertson concluded.

'Didn't you tell them about the cheque?' Gideon muttered to me.

I nodded, furious.

'What cheque's this?' Councillor Nettlefold asked. I glanced at Gideon again to make sure that he was sure, then reached into my bag for the cheque, which I skimmed down the long table towards them like a glass of whisky on a saloon bar. Robertson smacked his hand down on it and picked it up. The colour had drained from his rectangular face.

'It's enough to cover the subsidy for six months,' I said.

'Lady Eugenie has a very generous financial adviser,' Robertson said quickly, 'and I really wish you'd told me about it earlier.'

'But I did!' I protested. 'I rang you about it only two days ago!'

Now Robertson, whose shoebox head was proving to be quite versatile expression-wise, had adopted a look of baffled confusion. 'You surely don't think I would have forgotten something as important as this, do you?' he said.

I was speechless: I didn't believe for a moment that he'd

simply 'forgotten'.

June Willis was still staring into space, but Councillor Nettlefold was looking at Robertson in exasperation. 'So where do we go from here?' he asked.

Robertson was recovering quickly, and he waved his hand. 'This changes nothing, Councillor,' he said. 'It's merely putting off the inevitable. They still couldn't guarantee funding beyond what they have here.' The other two were looking less sure.

'I think the business plan strongly suggests otherwise,' Gideon said.

'And at the very least this money means you do have to put off the sale,' I added.

June Willis said, 'They have a point.'

Robertson was looking like thunder. 'That's a discussion that ought to happen behind closed doors,' he said. 'I suggest that we wind up the meeting now. We'll let you know of the decision in due course.'

Gideon stood up to leave, but I continued to sit there for a couple of seconds. Then I felt his hand on my shoulder. 'Let's go, Catherine.'

I followed him, not forgetting to pick up the cheque on the way out. I was storming. 'I can't believe that man! He deliberately didn't tell them about your money. It's obvious the other two didn't know anything about it. He just wants Coltsfoot Hall sold, no matter what we do.'

'Calm down,' Gideon said. 'There's still plenty we can do, like contacting the local press and making sure it's public knowledge that the council have no need to sell the Hall.' He gave my hand a reassuring squeeze. We looked around for the others, but they'd all gone.

'Zak must have taken Lady Eugenie back home in the minibus,' I said. 'Did you see her face in that meeting? I could kill Randall Robertson for this.'

'It'll all be fine. Trust me.' We started walking towards a

bus stop, going over the meeting, speculating on what Robertson could be up to. Gideon's guess was that he was taking backhanders from whoever wanted to buy the Hall.

'So he hoped all the legal stuff would have gone through before anyone got wind of the cheque?'

'Possibly. I've no idea how we could prove anything, though.'

'At least we can get the press on his case,' I said. 'Someone at the local rag is bound to be interested in a scoop like this.' I looked behind me to see if a bus was coming. It was still early, and there weren't many people around, so there was something about one particular man, who seemed to be dawdling very slowly, that made me glance at him again. I felt my skin crawl.

'Gideon! It's him – the man at the window the other night? He's following us.' Gideon turned to look, and I expected to see the man turn and scuttle away, but alarmingly he quickened his pace and walked towards us. I was gripping Gideon's hand, wondering whether to run or scream for help.

The man stopped in front of us, and flipped out a Metropolitan Police badge. 'Gideon Harker,' he said, 'I'm arresting you on suspicion of fraud. You do not have to say anything but it may harm your defence if you fail to mention when questioned something you may later rely on in court.'

Mad World

It felt as if the ground was sinking under me. Things like this just didn't happen in the real world. Among all the preparations for the council meeting, and with Gideon being apparently so confident about it, I'd managed to put this fraud business to the back of my mind. And now he was being arrested. I felt panicked, helpless, distraught: what could I do? Thank God I had my phone with me: I would stay with him as far as I could, make sure he had a solicitor, let all his friends know where he was. I wasn't going to let this happen to him.

After a moment or two, I realised that nothing *was* happening. Gideon hadn't been bundled into a police car, or handcuffed or anything. He and the policeman were merely staring at each other. Incredibly, Gideon didn't look worried at all.

This mutual stare-out continued for what felt like ages, until Gideon finally broke the silence. 'You're not a policeman at all, are you?' he said.

The other man sighed. 'Nope,' he said. 'And you aren't under arrest.'

'Well, obviously.'

'Will someone tell me what's going on?' I said.

'Good idea,' Gideon said to the bogus policeman. 'Why don't you tell us all about it?' The other man looked unsure, until Gideon added, 'Impersonating a police officer is a fairly serious offence, I would have thought.'

The man's name was Derek.

'Sorry if I've been bothering you,' he said politely.

'It's all right—' I started to say, but Gideon said, 'Catherine, it's *not* all right. He's been scaring you witless. It's a terrible intrusion into an innocent person's private life.'

'*Two* innocent people,' I said.

'Indeed. Two innocent people. And I wouldn't say your methods are exactly legal, are they, Derek?'

Derek looked wretched. 'I'm merely using standard surveillance procedures.'

'Pretending to arrest people is "standard", is it?'

The other man puffed out his chest. 'It certainly isn't,' he said. 'I made that one up. Faced with imminent arrest, even the coolest customer is apt to crack.'

'Oh, for heaven's sake,' Gideon said. 'What about all the lurking in the bushes, going through the bins, bugging the phones?'

'Surely you weren't bugging the phones?' I said, horrified, my mind rerunning anything I'd said on the phone in the last few weeks, particularly in my conversations with Heather, and horribly embarrassed that someone else had been listening to me.

'I didn't mean to upset you,' Derek said. 'You weren't supposed to know. I would have been finished in a couple of days anyway, if only you hadn't turned round and seen me.' He rolled his eyes to heaven. 'I am in such deep shit now,' he said.

We Are Detective

I'd never met a spy before. Or maybe I had: after all, the whole point of spies is that you're not supposed to know they're spying on you. In this, of course, Derek had been spectacularly unsuccessful.

'My heart just isn't in it,' he confessed, in the pub, a while later.

'But surely you have to go through some kind of fairly rigorous selection and training process before you get into a job like yours?' Gideon asked him.

Derek nodded, wiping beer foam off his top lip. 'I still have no idea how I got through the interview. I completely winged it. Mind you, I think being in the SAS helped.'

'You were in the SAS?' I asked him.

He shrugged modestly. 'In a purely administrative capacity. Plus I have a facility for languages. *Tengo facilidad para idiomas. Ich habe eine gute Sprachbegabung.* Et cetera.'

'Must be very handy in the world of espionage,' I said. I still couldn't believe that this was the same person who'd terrified me by peering through the window. Up close, Derek was actually rather sweet. He had sandy-coloured, thinning hair, a pleasant if nondescript face and the demeanour of a normally polite and well-behaved child who's been caught with his hand in the cookie jar and has realised he doesn't like biscuits anyway.

'What *were* you doing peeping through the window the other night?' I wanted to know.

'Oh, earth swallow me now!' he said, looking mortified. 'I thought you'd both gone up to your flat. I was trying to find a way to get into the office to have a look through your files. It looked as if you might be otherwise occupied for a while . . . God, I hate being a private eye.'

'You certainly don't seem cut out for it,' Gideon said.

'I think I'm a bit too clumsy,' Derek admitted. 'You almost caught me the other night.' I remembered sitting freezing on the stairs, terrified of the sounds below.

For the first time, Gideon looked properly angry. 'Spying on me is one thing,' he said, 'but I wasn't even there! What the hell did you think you were doing, snooping around and frightening her?'

I thought he might be about to land a punch on the hapless spy, who obviously thought so too, because he put his hands up defensively. 'Not the face!' he said. 'I've said I was sorry.'

At least Derek was able to reassure us on one point. He told us that, despite following Gideon and overhearing almost every conversation he'd had in the past weeks (though mercifully my bedroom hadn't been 'wired'), he hadn't been able to find anything incriminating against him.

'I've been very thorough,' he said, as if we might be about to complain that Gideon hadn't been followed and spied on comprehensively enough. 'I've read all your letters before you've seen them yourself. I've been intercepting your e-mails—'

'I don't use e-mail. I haven't even got a computer.'

'Are you sure?'

'Of course I'm sure.'

'That explains it,' the spy said, taking another mouthful of beer.

'Explains what?'

'Well, you didn't seem to be the kind of bloke who would be that interested in Harry Connick Junior.'

'Who?'

'Exactly. I just knew you wouldn't be. You get an instinct for that kind of thing in this job. Poor man's Frank Sinatra: I've got no time for him, personally.'

'Why did you think *I* would have?'

'You subscribe to a Harry Connick Junior newsgroup.'

'But I don't have a computer.'

'No. I realise that now.'

Even though Derek had been over-zealous to the point of intercepting e-mails that weren't even for Gideon, he had failed to turn up any evidence to show that he'd embezzled as much as a paper-clip. 'I shall be filing my report, of course,' he said, 'recommending that you aren't pursued any further.' Gideon's face was generally a picture of serene confidence, but even so I could see how relieved he was.

'In fact you'd be home free,' Derek continued, 'if it wasn't for the Ben Michaelson connection.'

'Who?' Gideon asked.

Derek sipped again at his pint: spying was clearly thirsty work. 'I shouldn't tell you this, really, but he's already been charged, and I'm satisfied you didn't have anything to do with it. Ben Michaelson was the real brains behind the scam the whole time. We just needed to know who he was working with.'

'But I don't know any Ben Michaelson. Does he work for

the company?'

'He works for himself, as far as I can tell,' Derek said. 'He gets information from insiders in various financial institutions, like the one you were employed in, then makes his own trades on the Internet using the information. Shares his profits with his informants. One of your former colleagues got a bit greedy and tried to branch out on his own, which is when your lot got suspicious.'

'So how does this Ben Michaelson get the information?' Gideon wanted to know.

'Well, you're never going to believe this, but he's a motorcycle courier. Acts thick, but he's the brains behind the whole operation. Sometimes it's the dim-looking ones you have to watch out for. He's in and out of those City places all the time, so all the security people know him. Bit of a charmer, by all accounts. He gets access to – are you all right?' I must have gone a bit pale.

'Nadia's Ben,' I said. 'Oh, God, Gideon . . . I think all this might be my fault.'

He didn't hold a grudge. In fact, he thought it was hilarious that in trying to track him down I'd almost managed to get him into very deep trouble.

'Who would have thought you'd have such serious underworld connections?' he said.

'I've never actually met this Ben. I used to go to football with his girlfriend.'

'*Football?*' he repeated. 'Now, that *is* serious. I really am going to have to revise my opinion of your good character.'

Derek was listening to this exchange with amusement. 'You two are funny,' he observed. 'It's like you're living on a planet of two.'

'Is that meant to be a compliment?'

'I'm going to take it as a compliment,' Gideon said, 'although I'm not exactly happy about the methods you've used to reach this conclusion.'

'Only doing my job,' Derek said. 'Anyway, how did your meeting with the council go? I didn't manage to get any listening devices in there.'

'We should be grateful for small mercies,' I said. 'If you had been listening you would have heard us being totally shafted by our so-called grants officer.' I looked at Gideon. 'He knew damn well I'd told him about your cheque.'

Derek nodded. 'You did,' he said. 'I heard you.'

'What?'

'That's one of the conversations I listened in on.' He looked sheepish. 'It was about money,' he said defensively. 'It was a legitimate line of enquiry.'

'You didn't tape it, did you?' Gideon asked him. Derek nodded again. Gideon and I were grinning at each other. 'Derek,' he said, 'you're a star.'

Guilty

Randall Robertson's face was a picture – and, being perfectly rectangular, a picture just the right shape for easy framing – when we played him the tape.

'What's this all about?' he said, when Gideon and I walked unannounced into his office. 'I've got nothing more to say about Coltsfoot Hall.'

'But here's a little something you said earlier,' Gideon said, and clicked the tape player on. To say that Robertson went pale is a drastic understatement. He leaped up to close his office door then slumped back in his seat as if he was trying to disappear behind the desk as he listened to his own voice assuring me that he'd pass on the information about the Hall being in receipt of some new funds. Finally he shot Gideon a look of pure hatred. 'So I forgot to tell them about your blessed cheque. It's not a hanging offence.'

'You didn't just "forget",' I said. 'You deliberately misled the council members.'

'You can't prove it,' he said, sounding less sure of himself.

'If we've got this conversation on tape, how do you know we haven't got others?' Gideon asked. There followed a bit of a face-off. Robertson's eyes were searching Gideon's face, trying to work out if he was bluffing or not. Gideon's face was unreadable as far as the grants officer was concerned. I could see now what Kieran meant when he'd described how composed Gideon could be even when he was under extreme pressure. I could also see a tiny tension at the corners of his mouth: you had to know him very well to spot that he was trying hard not to smile.

'"Financial adviser" my arse,' Robertson said finally. 'You're working for the Liberal Democrats, aren't you?' No reply. 'You've been bugging the phone.'

Gideon just stared at him, unblinking. 'What kind of people would be interested in hearing these tapes?' he said.

'This is blackmail!'

'The thing about blackmail,' Gideon said, 'is that the blackmailee always has to have done something they don't want somebody else to find out about. It wouldn't work otherwise.'

'It would never stand up in court.'

'I wasn't thinking about court,' Gideon said. 'I was thinking more of your boss, or maybe the local papers. Wouldn't do your career much good, either way.' If looks could really kill, Gideon and I would have been reduced to two pairs of shoes with a wisp of smoke coming from each.

Finally Robertson cracked. 'Okay,' he said. 'What do you want me to do?'

'Go back to the committee and tell them that it's your strong recommendation that Coltsfoot Hall should remain as a museum. Make sure they're persuaded. We're not interested in the subsidy – we've got that covered – so you can still make your budget saving. That way you look good and we get what we want. I think that sounds fair, don't you?'

'Do you think he'll go for it?' I asked, as we left. Gideon grinned in reply, that splendidly wicked smile I'd always loved.

'I would bet – what? – three million pounds on it,' he said. 'We've done it: I reckon after this Coltsfoot Hall is going to be safe. We'll take Seb and Kieran's stuff to the bank tomorrow. You won't have any trouble getting a bridging loan, then it'll just be a lot of hard work filling in grant applications and things, but you'll get them.' His arms were warm around me. 'I'm really proud of you,' he said. 'You've achieved something important in saving this place.'

'It wasn't me – it was you.'

'Rubbish. I just came in at the end. You'd already done all the work. Now you can relax a bit and enjoy it.' We stepped out of the town hall, down the steps into a noisy, traffic-filled morning. It was sunny and breezy. Gideon put his hand gently on my cheek and kissed me, one of his toe-curling specials that always left me panting for more.

In my mind I was again throwing open the window and singing 'Who Will Buy This Wonderful Morning?' but celebrations were perhaps a bit premature.

Don't Dream It's Over

Any excuse is a good excuse for a party, and in this case there seemed to be a lot of good reasons to celebrate. I'd received a letter informing me that the sale of Coltsfoot Hall had been cancelled, and that the council agreed to keep the building for its present purpose. After some initial reservations – not entirely unpredictable, considering he knew the Hall's financial track record – the bank manager couldn't help but be impressed by the professional documents that I'd produced with the help of Sebastian and Kieran, and he admitted to having a bit of a soft spot for the old Hall. Funding was agreed.

My job and my home were safe and, perhaps more important to me at that moment, I had Gideon back in my life. Everything was as good as it could be.

I rang Heather to tell her the good news. I'd hoped she'd be able to come to the party, but she had other plans. 'I'm going to Montréal with Pierre,' she said.

'What? Are you back together?'

She laughed. 'Good grief, no. Unless you mean am I back in my old role as *le* beard, in which case the answer is a provisional yes. The hypocritical toad has been summoned to the demise of his *tante* Marguerite, and of course the lovely Barry would not be welcome at the bedside, so I'm playing the devoted wife, for one final grand performance.'

'Whatever for?'

'Free holiday in Canada. After I've done my duty I'm free to wander off into the wilds, at his expense. I've always fancied Vancouver.'

'I don't believe you sometimes.'

'I don't believe myself, but what can you do? Anyway, what's happening with you and Le Punky?' she asked me. 'I'm practising French like mad, by the way, so I can comfort the soon-to-be-bereaved. Is he staying or going back to Devon or what?'

'I don't know,' I said. 'We haven't talked about it. I mean, I daren't ask him.'

'You daren't ask him? What's happened to the assertive new you that pursued him half-way across the country?'

'She's disappeared inside the new desperately in love me who's terrified of losing him.'

'Oh, good grief. Get a grip on yourself, woman. This is the year two thousand, not one of your Victorian novels. If he *does* go, if he never wants to see you again – which from all the evidence seems unlikely – there are plenty more surfers in the sea.'

'You're a born cynic, Heather.'

'No, I'm not,' she said. 'I was as mad in love as you are, remember, but the good news is that I've survived losing it. It hurts, but it doesn't kill you.'

'You make me sound totally dependent. If I was just a sad, clingy female who couldn't live without a man I wouldn't have chucked Greg, would I? But for me, there is only one man. There always has been, and it's not that I haven't tried any others. I wish you could see him, Heather. He's special. He shines.'

'I wondered what that glow was on the southern horizon.'

I never had birthday parties when I was a child. My mother thought even one small, quiet child was headache enough and wouldn't have contemplated me adding any more to the house. Alison and Heather had had loads of parties, and the *soirée* we had at Coltsfoot Hall was oddly reminiscent of those I'd been to at Alison's house, where disparate generations somehow muddled together in a happy enough way. In this case, the generational mix was nudged forward at least twenty years in time, so that the 'young people' comprised me, Gideon, Zak, Flora, Jackie, Sebastian and Kieran, and the 'grown-ups' were represented by Lady Eugenie and Stan (who was lately acquiring a status something akin to Prince Consort if I can mix metaphors for a second), Charlie and the other volunteers, Sheryl the cleaner and some of the trustees.

Kieran was providing the music.

'Harry Connick Junior. Something for everyone,' he said, producing a handful of CDs.

Gideon and I exchanged a look. 'You don't by any chance subscribe to a Harry Connick Junior newsgroup, do you?' Gideon asked him.

Kieran looked flustered. 'How did you know?'

'Just a guess,' he said, and added, 'I just hope you don't have anything *really* personal on that laptop.' We left Kieran looking suitably paranoid.

A couple of local councillors arrived, including June Willis, who after a couple of drinks confided in me that Randall Robertson had been 'moved on'. 'It made me a bit suspicious, the way he was so keen to get this place sold off,' she said. 'It's as if it was his pet project. Occasionally I wondered if he mightn't be in league with the developers or something like that, but of course there was no way of proving it.' If only we'd introduced her to Derek. 'But then, of course,' she continued, 'He had this absolute turnaround, made an excellent case for keeping the museum. It's really thanks to him that we're here today.'

How ironic that was, I thought, and wondered what Gideon's response would be. 'So where's he moved on to?' I asked.

She glanced around as if walls might have ears, which just recently of course, they had. 'Shame, really. There wasn't anywhere to promote him to in his previous department, so he's taken a bit of a sideways move.' Her face cracked into a smile. 'He's gone to Waste Disposal and Sanitation,' she said. 'We thought his talents would be put to *much* better use there.' We drank a toast to that.

Jackie had provided the refreshments, and she also provided a surprise guest. 'Cass, I hope you don't mind,' she said to me as she passed by with a plate of sandwiches (crusts off, in deference to Lady Eugenie whose teeth were sadly no longer up to the test of Jackie's special crusty cob).

'Don't mind what?'

'I've asked Greg to come.'

My first thought was that she was trying to matchmake between us; my second thought was to wonder how wide of the mark the first thought had been. And suddenly there he was, looking exactly the same as the last time I'd seen him, except perhaps a tad happier.

'Congratulations, Cass,' he said to me. 'You've done really well.' I felt Jackie fidget a little beside me. Greg glanced at her. 'Jack,' he greeted her. We stood there for a couple of seconds, blinking at each other, then, as if it wasn't awkward enough already, we were joined by Gideon.

'Catherine, you must come and meet this little man from the local paper. He's so funny. He asked me if I was a surfer against sewage—' He stopped and looked at Greg. I introduced them, by name only, but each of them knew who the other was in relation to me.

'You'd be the sports reporter, then?'

'And you'd be the childhood sweetheart,' Greg responded.

'Not exactly,' Gideon said. 'I spent my childhood diligently in my bedroom doing equations. I was practically fully grown by the time I went off the rails and started wearing nail varnish and hanging around with strange women.'

Greg gawped at him. It was fairly clear they weren't going to hit it off and have a man-to-man bonding discussion about the pressing footballing issues of the moment.

'Come and help me in the kitchen, Greg.' Jackie tugged at his sleeve. 'I've done your favourite.'

He had a *favourite*? I thought, watching them go off together.

'He's still holding a torch for you,' Gideon said.

I made one of those disbelieving sounds. 'He's here with Jackie. I didn't even know he was coming. Anyway, you wanted me to meet the little man from the paper . . .'

*

It seems to be a tendency with me that at least once during any party I have to take myself off for a bit of solitary contemplation. Maybe it's just that I can't handle too much excitement – after all, my idea of an adrenaline rush is getting a new Argos catalogue.

When everyone seemed to be occupied talking to someone else I wandered away to a small room on the first floor of the house that contained the Childhood through the Ages display. Not my favourite among the exhibits, childhood not being a pet subject of mine, but the window had the same view as the window seat in my flat, looking out across the park.

Of course, it was already nightfall, so there wasn't much to see. I stood in the darkness looking down at the patch of grass illuminated by the light from the party room, inhaling the damp, musty smell of old furniture. I should have been feeling happy: after all, downstairs there was a party going on because the Hall had been rescued. Like Gideon had said, there was still a lot of hard work to do, but that horrible feeling of uncertainty about the future had gone.

I ought to have felt relieved, but what I was really worried about was that there was no longer any real reason for Gideon to stay. I found it hard to work out exactly what he thought of me. When we were together our relationship was very similar to how it had been at school; we were on exactly the same wavelength, perfectly tuned in to each other, sometimes not even needing to speak to understand what we meant, but I couldn't shake the feeling that he was keeping himself distanced from me. The fact that he was there, that he'd put such efforts into helping me save the museum, counted for a lot, but I wasn't at all sure whether he felt the same about me as I did about him: that he was the other part of me and I wouldn't ever be able to be happy without him. I wanted to tell him this, but I held back, because what if I was wrong, and I'd mistaken kindness and concern for an old friend for something more? What I really wanted was for someone to give me the words to ask him not to go.

There was the sound of footsteps behind me crossing the wooden floor. I turned round to see Sebastian standing in the doorway. 'Oh, sorry,' he said. 'I didn't mean to disturb you. I was looking for another loo. The one downstairs has a small queue forming at its door.'

'There isn't one on this floor. You could go up to the flat, if you like.' I held out my key, and he stepped forward to take it.

'Are you all right? Seems a bit gloomy, standing here in the dark.'

'I'm fine. I just needed a bit of quiet.'

'Sorry. I'll go.'

'Sebastian?'

'Yes?'

'Surfing is the most important thing in the world to him, isn't it?'

He paused to think before replying. 'I wouldn't say that exactly. There are some people who have something missing in their lives, and they search for something to fill it, whether it's religion, or sex, or drugs, or their work. If a person like that gave as much time and energy to surfing as he does, then I'd say yes, it was the most important thing in the world.'

'I don't quite follow.'

'What I mean is, Gideon's not like that. All the time I've known him, he's never struck me as a person who needed to fill a void. Surfing is just something he loves to do. I don't think his whole life depends on it.'

'Do you think I would be able to fit in with his life?'

'Shouldn't you be asking him?'

I guessed I should. It was time to go and find him. The new assertive me, and all that.

I spotted him across the room talking to Lady Eugenie. She

was laughing, and her fingers were playing with the pearl necklace at her throat in a way that you would have to describe as flirtatious.

'I'd watch that one, if I were you.' Stan was at my elbow, carrying two plates of food. 'He's a bit of a charmer.'

'I don't think you've got anything to worry about, Stan,' I said. 'He's no competition for you.' I swear that Stan *preened*.

'I'm sure I've no idea what you mean. But that young lad of yours, you want to get him marched down the aisle ASAP, if you want my advice.' He strode forward to reclaim his position at Lady Eugenie's side.

I didn't know about aisles – didn't think there would be much chance of ever getting Gideon Harker inside a church for any reason other than his own funeral and probably not even then – but I did know I wanted to be with him for ever, if he would have me. The trouble was I was so nervous of letting him know how I felt.

When he saw me a smile lit his face. 'There you are!' he said. 'Come outside a minute – I've got something for you.'

I followed him outside. We stood in front of the Hall, in the patch of light cast by the motion-sensor light above the door. There was a distant hum of traffic, and the sound of people talking and laughing, and, ominously, Harry Connick Junior singing 'Let's Call The Whole Thing Off'.

He held out a package to me.

'What's this?'

'Open it.'

I peeled away the tissue paper. Inside was an old book, bound in cream cloth with black writing: *Far From The Madding Crowd*. 'It smells like your old leather coat.' Inside it was dated 24 November 1874.

'It's the first American edition,' he said. 'It's supposed to be older than the English one by eleven days.' I opened it to a page marked by a green silk bookmark. It was the scene almost at the end where Bathsheba thinks Gabriel is going to emigrate: 'And what shall I do without you? Oh, Gabriel, I don't think you ought to go away. You've been with me so long – through bright times and dark times – such old friends as we are – that it seems unkind almost.'

I looked up at him.

'You know how it ends,' he said. 'Of course he doesn't leave her. He loves her too much.' He pulled me gently towards him and kissed me, and after a while the light above the door went out as if the house was giving us some privacy.

Where The Heart Is

Of all of the heroines of my favourite romantic novels, I think the only one who would have readily taken to a wetsuit is Catherine Earnshaw. She was a person who embraced the unconventional, and would have welcomed any garment that promised to keep her snug as she dashed around the wild and windy moors of Wuthering Heights.

It certainly was snug: putting it on was like trying to squeeze my whole body into one leg of a pair of heavily elasticated support tights.

'Don't tug at it: you'll tear it,' Gideon advised, though the fabric seemed so tough that I thought tearing a telephone directory would be fractionally easier. 'Roll it on. There you go.' I was finally encased from my ankles to my neck, and Gideon pulled up the zip at the back. I'd expected to feel slinky and sexy like *The Avengers*' Emma Peel in one of her leather catsuit numbers, but instead I just felt foolish. I imagined my body looked like the face of a burglar with a stocking over his head, all squashed and distorted. Gideon, obviously, looked gorgeous in his.

'We look like the Black Shadow and his little friend the Black Pudding,' I muttered. 'Does this look as stupid as I think it does?'

Gideon kissed my nose. 'You look cute,' he said. 'Don't worry about it. As soon as you get into the water it'll feel okay.'

Actually, from the inside it did feel pretty okay. It was so cosy and warm and all embracing that I felt as wrapped up and protected as I did whenever he hugged me.

I have to say it felt quite cool in a Beach Boys sort of way to be walking along with a surfboard tucked under my arm, and I enjoyed the short journey from the car to the beach, and the feel of the soft, cold sand under my bare feet. The beach was deserted, apart from an old man walking his dog who greeted Gideon by name and nodded at me. I was beginning to enjoy this.

Then we stepped into the sea. I squeaked. 'It's *freezing*! Ugh! The wetsuit's not working! The water's getting in – it's *ooh*! Very weird.'

He laughed. 'The water's *meant* to get in. It's the layer of water that'll keep you warm.' It was the oddest sensation as the water crept up and into the suit, like it was sucking at my skin. Kind of strange and, I have to confess, kind of erotic.

I'd spent the previous hour lying face down on his kitchen floor. Not the scene of passion you might be picturing: I was attempting to learn how to get from a prone to a standing position on a surfboard in one fluid movement. Not easy for someone whose main form of exercise has always been turning the pages of a book.

'You can kneel first, if it's easier, but it's not a good habit to get into.'

'I'm not sure I'll be doing this often enough for any habits to form.'

'You will,' he said. 'Once you've tried it, you'll want to keep going.'

'Kieran didn't.'

'Kieran has no soul. Now – again. Paddle, paddle, paddle then *up*.'

Even after more-or-less mastering the art of getting to my feet without toppling over and smacking my head on the Rayburn, I wasn't very confident with the idea of moving from the seclusion of the kitchen floor to being out in public with only neoprene to control my wobbly bits. In the certain knowledge that I was going to be crap at this, I attempted to distract him with something he already knew I was good at. 'I think I need to try that one more time,' I said, attempting to sound seductive, 'and I'm sure I'd get the hang of it much better if you got down on the floor with me and showed me again.'

'If you think I'm falling for that you can think again, you evil woman,' he said. 'Come on. Time to find a break.'

'Great. I could do with a cup of tea.'

'I said *find* a break, not have one.'

So here we were, dressed for business, him looking like some kind of Greek god, me looking like something that's been clubbed to death on an ice floe, contemplating a ferocious-looking sea.

'I can't go in there! I'll drown!'

'No, you won't, I'm here. I'd describe that as gently rolling, anyway. They're not real surfing waves at all. If it was any bigger Suzanne would be down here, too.' Well, thank heavens for small mercies. I could do without spectators, particularly of the sarcastic ex-girlfriend sort.

The chill of the water was a shock, like plunging into snow only colder but, as he'd said, a second after the initial shock of the cold I started to feel quite warm and tingly.

'Okay, paddle,' he said. 'I'll stay right beside you. If you get scared, just hang on to your board and I'll get you.' With his strong arms he was paddling effortlessly away from the beach, whereas I seemed to get two feet forward and three feet back as the waves kept pushing me back to the shore. It was exhausting, but eventually we were in deeper water. I lay on the board, panting, horribly aware that the beach seemed to be about three miles away. Gideon had swung up into a seated position, his hair and body gleaming wet, looking as ridiculously beautiful as it's possible for a man to be.

No time to rest and contemplate the view. He told me to turn the nose of the board towards the shore and paddle.

'Don't try to stand up unless you really think you can,' he said. Not much chance of that. Then I felt a wave pick me up and propel the board forward. 'Slide back on the board a little bit – not too much,' he shouted, as it threatened to capsize. 'Keep your head up.' The water pushed me smoothly towards the shore, faster than I would have imagined, and I ended up on the sand, laughing and exhilarated, looking for Gideon to appear beside me. He was still sitting on his board, apparently exactly where I'd left him.

'Good job,' he called. 'Now paddle back.'

Again? I didn't have the strength to do it again, but all the same I dutifully picked up my polystyrene board and floated it along beside me until I was waist-deep in the water, then I hauled myself on – not as easy as it sounds and I fell off a couple of times before I managed it – and paddled out to him.

I did the same thing a couple more times, by then my arms felt like I'd lugged bagfuls of heavy shopping for a very long distance. I didn't think I could do it again. A wind had picked up, and I'd noticed that the swells had been pushing me faster and harder towards the shore than they had at the beginning, and it wasn't only my aching arms that made it hard to paddle out. Luckily he agreed. 'Time to get out,' he said. 'After you.'

I let the water push me to the beach one more time and got out, feeling exhausted and curiously elated, as if my chest was full of champagne bubbles. I unfastened the ankle strap that attached me to the surfboard and turned round to see where he was.

In one graceful, fluid movement he was on his feet, poised, cutting along the side of the wave. He was doing it, really doing it like in the movies, skimming across the face of the water. He looked graceful and sleek and totally in his element. I wondered how many times it was possible to fall in love with the same person.

I sat down on the sand, exhausted, and looked around. He wasn't the only gorgeous thing in the landscape: it really was a beautiful, peaceful place, and I was falling in love with it just like I'd fallen in love with him.

It had been a hard decision to leave Coltsfoot Hall, but as soon as I knew that Gideon felt the same about me as I did about him there was only one thing to do. Besides, Coltsfoot Hall could manage without me.

Zak and Flora moved into my flat. They planned to get married soon and hoped that Zak would be able to start legally earning money, at which time he'd officially go on the museum's payroll. I made them swear that they wouldn't throw any of the exhibits at each other during one of their arguments.

'What arguments?' Zak asked, clearly suffering from the selective memory loss of the romantically afflicted.

So, having discharged my obligation to Coltsfoot Hall, I planned a new life with Gideon. Derek's account of Ben Michaelson's Internet embezzling scheme had inspired him to think about getting a computer and doing some (legal) Internet trading, as long as he could get something done about the dodgy phone lines in the area, so he could work and still carry on surfing as much as he liked.

And me? What would I do? That had been the last piece of the puzzle. Despite being such a romantic, almost old-fashioned kind of girl, I couldn't really see myself playing the little housewife, staying at home cooking dinner and waxing my beloved's surfboards. I thought of various things – there were a lot of museums in Devon and surely one of them would benefit from my recently gained expertise at fund-raising and even my passing knowledge of interactivity – but nothing felt exactly right.

The answer came on a visit to a pretty village a couple of miles away. I stopped to look in the window of an antiquarian bookseller's, and saw a card advertising a vacancy for a manager. I pushed open the door, and the church-like smell of old books instantly reminded me of Coltsfoot Hall. The shop was tiny, but with shelves that went all the way up to the high ceiling so it was crammed full of books; the higher shelves could be reached by a ladder attached to a track that ran around the three walls that weren't occupied by the door and window. A woman sat behind a small desk to the right of the door. She smiled a friendly greeting at me.

'I'm interested in the vacancy for a manager,' I said. She smiled again and stood up to shake my hand. She had a warm smile and beautiful brown eyes; I liked her on sight.

'I'm Sally Renshaw,' she said.

'Cass – I mean Catherine Thomson.'

'You like to be called Cass?'

'No,' I said. 'I like to be called Catherine.' I wasn't being stroppy and I hadn't thought about it until I said it, but a new life deserved a new name.

I told Sally a bit about my employment history, and she showed me round the shop. 'I warn you it can get very dull, particularly in the winter months.'

'I really don't mind,' I said. 'I imagine there's always something to read.'

'There is indeed. And there's always the kettle – would you like a coffee?'

While she made coffee in a tiny room at the back I browsed the shelves: hundreds and hundreds of beautiful books on all kinds of subjects. By the time Sally returned with the coffee and a packet of Jaffa cakes my mind was made up, and so, apparently, was hers.

The water was starting to evaporate from the wetsuit and I was getting chilly. Right on cue, Gideon was jogging up the beach towards me with his board under his arm, scattering droplets of water around him as he ran. His face was blissfully happy.

'This is perfect,' he said. 'You being here, this is the most perfect thing in the whole world.' Then he kissed me, his lips and face salty-tasting and icy cold from the water, but warming up with each second, one of those long, wonderful kisses.

Time After Time

Reader, I married him.

Well, what else could you expect? After twenty years of being in love with each other there didn't seem to be any way we would ever stop, so we decided to make it official.

We were married in a register office in a pretty little town in south Devon. My mum and Dwight came over from Memphis, Heather and Sebastian were our witnesses and Zak and Flora closed the museum for the day to attend. Lady Eugenie sent her best wishes and her best china tea service as a wedding present.

We had a wild and raucous reception at a nearby hotel: it seemed as though half the village was there plus a lot of Gideon's surfing friends and, as I was beginning to find out, surfers certainly know how to party.

Eventually we managed to slip away, to return to our cosy little home by the river. The party was still going on, and I'm not sure anyone noticed us leave, apart from Heather, who fluttered her fingers in a little wave before resuming snogging Sebastian senseless.

At the top of the lane I took off my posh wedding shoes and tucked them into my bag, exchanging them for the wellies we'd left at the post-box earlier in the day.

'I must look like a proper prize,' I said.

'You look gorgeous,' he said, kissing me, 'and the wellies go so beautifully with that dress.' The road ahead of us was in pitch darkness: although the sky was clear and starry, the trees on either side didn't permit any light to penetrate.

'I wonder if I'm the only bride to have a torch tucked into her garter?' I said, removing it and switching it on.

'It's an old Devon tradition: something old, something new, something borrowed, something blue, something luminescent.' We walked hand in hand down the lane towards the house, through a darkness as deep and warm as black fur. Moths fluttered like ghosts in front of the torch beam. The trees rustled, somewhere a twig snapped sharply, but I wasn't afraid. The place had become my home and I was getting used to all these nocturnal noises. And, besides, I had the security of having Gideon with me, and I knew that, like Gabriel Oak, he would always be there to look after me. I squeezed his hand.

'I hope you're not feeling spooked, Mrs Harker.'

'Not at all. I was just remembering the first time I walked down this lane. I had no idea where it led and I thought I was going to die and my remains would never be found.'

He put a reassuring arm around me. 'I would have found you.'

'And rescued me in the nick of time?'

'That's what I'm here for. My allotted role on the planet is to come to your aid time after time.'

'As Cyndi Lauper would say.'